The Tara Bones

The Tara Bones

K.T. McCaffrey

ROBERT HALE · LONDON

© K.T. McCaffrey 2012
First published in Great Britain 2012

ISBN 978-0-7090-9898-0

Robert Hale Limited
Clerkenwell House
Clerkenwell Green
London EC1R 0HT

www.halebooks.com

2 4 6 8 10 9 7 5 3 1

Typeset in 11/14pt Sabon
Printed and bound in Great Britain by
the MPG Books Group

For Iseult Healy and Patricia McGuire
who've supported me from day one.

He sits and thinks. And the physical part of him
Disappears, he becomes one with his thoughts,
And with the soft, inner glances. He might well dissolve;
He is looking at the moon, and the moon has infected him.

Julius Meier-Graefe

ANNETTE CAMPBELL WAS in deep shit. She knew it. What she didn't know was that her predicament was about to get a whole lot worse. Within two hours she would vanish from the face of the planet. The barman who'd just served her a double vodka and tonic was busy giving her the once-over, his scrutiny subtle as a punch to the solar plexus. She'd seen that hungry-eyed look all her life. Never varied. She hated it. He would switch to chat-up mode next, smart-arse blarney, veiled sexual overtures, calculating his chances. So bloody predictable. Well, he could go blow smoke up his own orifice; getting laid by a greasy, pimple-faced barman wearing spectacles was something she could do without, tonight, or any night soon, for that matter. Before the gangly youth had had a chance to lay his spiel on her, she gave him the look, practised to perfection, a withering glare guaranteed to stop predators within sniffing distance. It had the desired effect: the barman backed away, mouth open like a Venus flytrap, message received, consoling himself with the thought that the bitch was probably a dyke.

With one elbow balanced on the bar's counter, her dark, shiny hair framing her face and touching her shoulders, Annette sipped her drink, her body poised on a high stool, unconsciously seductive. Men, she thought, they'd been both the joy and the bane of her life ever since she discovered ... well, ever since she discovered they were different. She drew them in like mice to a baited trap. Shouldn't have been a problem ... but it was. She'd been blessed with looks, least that's what her mother always said. Blessed? Annette wasn't so sure. Cursed more like. Came down to the choices she made. Bad choices, mostly. She'd always been attracted to men with a dash of danger, devilish good looks and the allure of unending romantic adventure. Dashing hunks who promised much beneath dimmed lights, mood music and alcoholic haze, but reverted to type when exposed to the cold reality of daylight, becoming run-of-the-mill heels with nothing more on offer than hyperactive dicks.

Of course, not all of her men turned out bad. As in every walk of life, there were exceptions. Yes, she'd had a few nice Mr Average lovers in her time; trouble was, 'nice' didn't stoke her fire. She cast an eye on the small clique of pint-guzzling men in the bar watching Premier League on Sky Sports; they were oblivious to her presence, whooping and jeering every time a score seemed imminent. Nice men, all. However, true to form, a handful of the other species, some with girlfriends, cast hungry looks in her direction, sizing her up, assessing potential prey. A stylish-looking thirty-something male who hadn't bothered to remove his overcoat or hat caught her eye, gave her his best hot-to-trot wink. She replied with an instamatic on-off smile and a one-finger gesture.

Looking into her drink, she reflected on the impossible mess she'd gotten herself into. She'd just made the first move in trying to get her life back on track, a bit late, admittedly, but she'd finally initiated the process of regaining control of her life. Or so she hoped. Walking out on Stephen signalled intent. Three years down the plughole. The line of ketamine she'd inhaled earlier had run its course; alcohol now the only stimulant coursing her bloodstream. She slipped a hand into the pocket of her Pepe jeans, and extracted the keys of Stephen's Volvo XC60, amazed that she'd had the nerve to steal his most prized possession. She put a finger through the ring, abstractedly rotating them before dropping them on the counter top.

She thought about the plans she'd considered, all of them half-baked. Choices hadn't been great. Going back to Mother: never an option. First place Stephen would look. Her two married sisters? Same story. In desperation, she'd rung Holly. Holly had been a close friend before she went and got married and moved to a town in the middle of nowhere. Annette had other friends, of course, women like herself who lived in the city, most of whom would let her crash for a few days. Trouble was, she'd introduced Stephen to all of them; he knew their addresses, even socialized with them from time to time. He would contact all of them. All except Holly.

Another vodka would help steady her nerves, help her string together some sort of plan. She could do with a friend to talk to right about now. Had she been a man, she'd have been able to bend the ear of the barman or the guy sitting on the next stool. Men, she'd learned, had the uncanny ability to converse freely and frankly with random strangers, discuss their troubles and woes in the knowledge that they'd get a sympathetic hearing. Didn't work for women quite like that, well, certainly not for her. She was dependent on her own wits to bring about a semblance of order to her life. She was about to signal for a third drink – or was it a fourth – when she caught sight of an elderly barman at the far end of the counter staring at her, telephone pressed to his ear. Instinct told her that she was the subject under discussion.

Dammit! Stephen's tracked me down.

Annette knew what he was like: he'd probably phoned all their regular haunts – bars, clubs, restaurants – until he'd found her. Glynn's Inn was not one of their regular hangouts but somehow he'd managed to trace her there.

I need to get out of here … and fast.

Almost midnight. The temperature hovered just above the freezing mark and wind gusts played havoc with her hair. The Volvo's interior felt cold as death but at least it cut out the wind. Dublin's streets groaned under the weight of late-night traffic. That was good; less chance of her being stopped by the traffic cops. She switched on the car's radio. Late news. Same old crap; same economic doom and gloom. She pressed one of Stephen's CDs into the slot – *Should I Stay or Should I Go* by The Clash, the lyrics appearing to mock the dilemma she'd grappled with these past few months. She hit the eject button. Everything, it seemed to her, was conspiring to give her a hard time.

Since Stephen lost his job, since their once great relationship imploded, the unending tale of woe besetting the economy only served to highlight how it had shattered her life. Wasn't just the downturn; Stephen's dominating behaviour had reached frightening proportions. He needed to control and possess her, body and soul, yet he liked to cat around with kittens, incapable of keeping his fly zipped up when it came to younger women. Finding condoms in his pockets, at a time when they both knew she was on the pill, provided all the proof she needed of his infidelities.

Exiting the city via the Liffey quays, moving past the Guinness brewery, she managed to extract a cigarette from a pack and light it, needing its calming effect to ease the turmoil in her head. Smoke filled the Volvo's interior, stinging her eyes. She fiddled with the electric controls, cursing under her breath, trying to find the button that activated the driver's window. *Found it.* Smoke disappeared but a blast of night air attacked her face like a shower of naked razor blades. She closed the window, used her free hand to search blindly for the heating control. Darkness and her unfamiliarity with the car's dashboard hampered the simple task but, eventually, she got the hang of it.

More comfortable now, she settled into a steady speed along the M4, her thoughts drawn back to Stephen as though by some invisible magnetic field. They'd met in Ibiza. An all-night beach party. First night there. Handsome devil, charming, had all the right moves, swept her off her feet. Literally. Met all her requirements, and then some. Like two tectonic plates, their lovemaking exploded with enough intensity to register on the Richter scale, joy without boundaries, helped by Ibiza's narcotic of choice: ketamine.

That had been three years ago. He'd been employed as an accounts executive with a top advertising agency, his salary nudging the six-figure bracket. She worked in an estate agency, salary not as good, but not to be sniffed at either. They'd moved into a plush apartment in Castleknock, lived the high life, partying like there was no tomorrow, drinking, shopping, smoking cannabis, snorting cocaine, popping Ecstasy, whatever.

But there was a tomorrow. Arrived with a vengeance. Stephen, along with half the agency's staff had been given the old heave-ho. Lousy redundancy package. She'd fared little better: option – accept a twenty per cent pay cut or take a hike. Like choosing between heart attack or brain tumour. She took the cut. Hard times proved the well-worn adage: when poverty walks in the door, romance legs it out the window. It affected Stephen in ways that added to her growing reservoir of resent-ment. His habit of dressing up and role playing in their love games veered dangerously towards sadomasochism. Not having a constant supply of top-flight drugs didn't help. His non-payment of debts to suppliers reached epic proportions. Their drug habit had, for the most part, been reduced to a dependence on head shops for supplies of less expensive alternatives.

Their partnership hit the buffers.

The lights in the rear-view mirror bothered her. For several miles now the same set of headlights remained doggedly on her tail. Other cars sped past or veered off on exit lanes – not this one. Was her imagina-tion playing tricks? Apart from Holly, no one knew where she was headed so why would someone be following her? She floored the accel-erator, shoved the speed to eighty, released the pedal and slowed to fifty. Didn't make any difference; the headlights remained on her tail.

Is that you, Stephen?

Surely not. Even if the barman had confirmed her whereabouts, Stephen couldn't have made the twenty minute journey from Castleknock in time to see her exit the car park at Glynn's Inn. The cops? In an unmarked car? She was over the drink limit for sure but, apart from speeding, her driving remained in check. Could Stephen have spotted his own Volvo heading along the west city quays as he sped to the pub? A long shot. Had he reported his car stolen, given the cops the registration?

Suddenly, she had her answer. A blue strobe light flashed. *Damn*! Main beams, on-off, on-off. Her worst fears realized. She was about to be breathalyzed, maybe arrested for car theft. Her mother would read about it in the papers. Her friends ... *frig*! And Stephen, He'd turn it into a big drama, go ballistic. How would she explain the packed cases in the boot? A hundred and one thoughts pulsed through her head as she pulled to a halt. In the mirror, she watched the driver emerge, put his cap on and approach. Cursing between gritted teeth, she lowered her window.

Before catching sight of his face, her door was jerked open. A hand reached for the ignition key and killed the engine. In a blur of action, she felt herself being pulled bodily from the car.

CHAPTER 2

Emma Boylan paid scant attention to the babble coming from the sound system, garbled announcements swallowed up in the cavernous concourse of Busaras, Dublin's central bus depot. Mid-morning crowd. Glad to shelter from the biting cold and persistent drizzle. Like her, they would spend as little time as possible in the cheerless building. Intending passengers ignored the tannoy as they bought sweets and newspapers in a tiny shop that some architect had tucked into a corner like an unloved relative at a wedding reception. Some sat on hard benches, read magazines, studied timetables, glanced anxiously at their watches, double checking bus schedules. Queues formed at the exit doors, passengers hauling cases and shopping bags, anxious to board provincial coaches.

Emma Boylan had no interest in the comings and goings of the buses; she was waiting to be taken to Robert Dillon's office. Dillon, a bus inspector had, in the course of an earlier phone call, agreed to talk to her about the feature she was researching for the *Post*, research that involved the mysterious disappearances of three women from the Leinster area. Joan Keating, the first of the trio to go missing had last been sighted in Busarus. That had been eight weeks earlier. Emma's editorial boss, Bob Crosby, had given her the assignment, his directive straightforward: get to the bottom of it. Starting with Joan Keating's last sighting seemed like the logical place to begin. Her disappearance, treated as a standard missing person's case initially, received scant media attention. Only when two other women vanished did alarm bells start to ring.

Emma almost jumped when a voice beside her said, 'Sorry to have kept you waiting, Ms Boylan.' She hadn't noticed the small wiry man sidling up to her. 'Mr Dillon,' she responded, rising to shake his hand, 'Good of you to see me. I just need you to tell me—'

'No problem,' he cut in, ushering her ahead of him with an expansive hand gesture. His office, on the first floor, overlooked the bus station's massive ground-level concourse. Moving like a human cyclone, he emptied a sachet of Lavazzae into a percolator, filled a water container, fetched mugs from a cupboard, sugar from a drawer, milk from a fridge and a stained teaspoon from an empty coffee jar and placed the lot on his desk before finally pouring coffee for both of them. He sat down, smiled at Emma with warm engaging eyes and sighed contentedly. 'My one great addiction,' he intoned in a strong inner-city accent. 'Sustenance for body and soul.'

Sitting across from him Emma thought, *Maybe you should cut down on the coffee, Mr Dillon, switch to Valium.* Fiftyish, balding, hooded eyes, small moustache – more Poirot than Hitler – he put the mug down, opened a laptop and angled it so she could see the screen. 'You'll find all we've got on Joan Keating in this CCTV footage,' he said. 'We pieced it together after the investigating detectives asked for what we'd got.'

First clip showed a wide-angle perspective of the bus station's interior. A night shot, the place at its quietest. The timer at the bottom of the screen showed 22.59. A second shot cut to the building's exterior and showed a number of buses pulling out from their gates.

The timer clicked to 23.00.

Emma sat, transfixed.

A young woman races across the concourse, and pushes through to the departure bays. The bus she wants is on the move; it fails to stop. She chases after it. An object falls from her bag. She halts abruptly in mid-flight, elevates her arms above her head. Frustration personified. Her breath is visible in the cold night air. She shakes her head, leans down, picks up the object.

'Freeze it there,' Emma asked.

Dillon stopped the tape. 'Something you need to study?'

Emma unzipped the slim folder she'd brought with her and removed a photograph. 'The woman's family released this to the media,' she explained. 'I want to compare it with the tape, make sure we've got the right person.'

The postcard-sized head and shoulders shot showed a smiling woman, late twenties, blond hair pulled back in a ponytail. Slender face, even teeth, grey eyes. Emma held the photo up to the screen and looked with half closed lids at both images. Hair was different but there could be no doubting the matching features. The CCTV image had the advantage of showing Joan Keating's full figure: tall, fashionably thin, fur-lined jacket and a skirt short enough to accentuate shapely legs.

'OK, move it on,' Emma said to Dillon. Together, they watched Joan Keating retrieve a broken mobile from the ground. The missing woman shook her head dejectedly and slowly made her way out of the bus station.

'As you can see,' Dillon said, one finger gesticulating as he spoke. 'Joan Keating just missed the last bus to Kells. Typical I'm afraid; people never allow themselves enough time … expect us to wait for them. But we have timetables, a show to keep on the road. But look, look at this, our cameras pick her up again as she leaves the station. Definition's not the best.'

Joan Keating crosses the tramlines on Store Street, pushing forward to Amien Street, heading in the direction of Connolly Railway Station. She walks ten, maybe fifteen, yards when a car pulls towards the kerb beside her. Red brake lights illuminate the screen momentarily before disappearing from shot. Joan Keating hurries after the car but she, too, fades out of shot.

'Did she make contact? Emma asked. 'Did she get into the car?'

'Can't help you there,' Dillon said, closing the laptop with all the flourish of a magician. 'That's all we got. The cops got other CCTV footage from the financial centre building and the railway station. Don't know if they identified the car or its driver but, well, Ms Boylan, that's something you'll have to ask them about yourself.'

'Sure, I'll do that. Tell me, do you have the name of the driver – the one who drove that particular route on the night in question?'

'No problem. The detectives got me to check it out at the time. Driver's name is Billy Doyle.'

'Could I have a word with him?'

Dillon hopped up from his chair, strode quickly to a rota board on the opposite wall. 'It's your lucky day,' he said, as though announcing she'd won the Lotto. 'Doyle is due here any minute. If you hold on, I'll have him pop up to see you; OK?'

Five minutes later, Billy Doyle shook Emma's hand, his grip dry, strong, assured. In full company livery, he was average height, carried a little too much weight, could have done with a shave. He removed his peaked cap and slouched heavily into the chair Dillon had vacated. 'You wanted to see me,' he said, appraising her with mischievous eyes.

'I'm right in thinking you've been driving the late-night bus to Kells for the past three months?'

'For my sins, yes, indeed I have. Same route, same time, same punters, Mondays to Fridays.'

Emma produced the photograph of Joan Keating. 'Has this woman ever been a passenger on your bus?'

'Let's have a gander,' Doyle said, taking it from her. 'Ah, yes, the cops spoke to me about her. I'll tell you what I told them ... and that's not a lot.'

'You remember her, yes?'

'Her, I remember,' he said, placing his index finger on the photograph. 'I don't remember all my passengers – that would be impossible – but this lady, man, she stood out, know what I'm saying? I'd noticed her a few times, always had a friendly word for me when getting on and getting off. Pleasant, you know. Most punters nowadays are pig ignorant, don't give a monkey's about their driver; they sit there yawning, coughing, sneezing, stuffing smelly crisps in their gobs, yapping on mobiles, telling their friends they're on the bus, fogging up the windows, sticking chewing gum on the back of the seats – Jesus! But she was different; a bit special, know what I'm saying?'

'Always on her own, was she?'

'Couldn't say for sure but far as I recall she was mostly on her own.'

'Can you remember which stop she got off at?'

'Well, like I say, she was friendly so, yes, I noticed where she got off.'

'And where was that?'

'Opposite the Ledwidge Apartments in Navan.'

'Ever see anyone waiting for her?'

'Gimme-a-break. We're talking months here; I have difficulty remembering what I did yesterday.'

'That mean you can't tell me—'

'Whoa! As it happens, the cops asked the same question. I'll tell you what I told them. Wouldn't swear on a Bible though, know what I'm saying? Far as I can tell there was never anyone waiting. I seem to remember thinking it was dangerous for a woman to get off at that spot ... so late. The lighting there is poor; just trees and a bloody great wall. I know the area pretty well; I sometimes take my greyhound down that way for a walk. Two of my fellow drivers – different routes than me – share an apartment on the second floor of the Ledwidge building. We meet there sometimes, have a few bevvies before going to the local track, watch those doggies tear around like bleedin' jets, have a few bets between ourselves – nothing too serious.' Doyle handed the photograph back. 'According to what I hear on the radio the cops think her disappearance might have something to do with those other women who've gone missing.... That why you're checking?'

'I'd prefer not to say. I think—'

'Do you think ... would you say ... foul play's involved?'

'God, I hope not.'

'You don't suppose she could've met a bad end?'

'Hard to know. But there's something odd going on. I've talked to her parents, talked to her friends, and they say she'd never go away without letting them know. She hasn't shown up at work. She's made no bank withdrawals, and she's contacted no one since that night.'

'Sounds pretty serious to me.'

'Yeah, it is. If only you'd seen her that night in your rear-view mirror. Might not be having this conversation now ... if only you'd stopped.'

'Bloody hell, don't go laying the blame on me. Passengers often run after a bus. We're not allowed to stop in that area. It's busy, quite dangerous. Buses come and go all the time. I'd get the sack if I stopped. Anyway, thing is, I didn't see her, but *had* I seen her, I would've stopped, job or no job. But I *didn't* see her ... more's the pity.' Doyle sighed and allowed himself a body shiver. 'She's far too nice a woman for something bad to happen to, know what I'm saying?'

CHAPTER 3

MID-AFTERNOON, GLYNN'S Inn at its quietest. The elderly barman's craggy features remained pleasant, agreeable. He recalled the conversation he'd had with Annette Campbell's partner on the night she disappeared. Seated in an alcove towards the back of the lounge, Detective Inspector Jim Connolly listened with minimal interruption, coffee and biscuits untouched on the small, marble-topped table in front of them.

'You see, I'd never met this bloke before,' the barman insisted, voice hoarse from a lifetime of nicotine abuse. 'First time I laid eyes on him was when he breezed into the bar, quarter of an hour, maybe twenty minutes, after his phone call.'

'You'd spoken to him earlier, yes?'

'I did, yes, he rang the bar.'

'What did he want ... what'd he say?'

'Sounded hot and bothered, said his partner had left home without her medication ... that her life was in danger if he didn't get it to her without delay. From the description he gave me I could tell she was the woman drinking at the counter.'

'You told him she was here?'

'Saw no reason to deny it. Noticed her earlier, good-looking woman on her tod. Hard to miss. Respectable though, definitely not a hooker – we get them from time to time – but this one, well, she looked out of place, knocking them back to beat the band.'

'Did you approach her ... I mean, after you'd got the phone call?'

'That's the thing,' he said, making a clucking sound with his tongue. 'She caught me, clocked me looking at her while I was on the phone; must have twigged I was talking about her. She'd skedaddled before I hung up, car keys jingling in her hand. Last I saw of her.'

'And the man who'd phoned, he arrived, what, fifteen minutes later?'

'Yeah, pushed up to the bar like the Devil was on his tail, all hot and bothered, demanded to know where Annette – that's what he called her – was. I told him she'd gone but he was having none of it, decided to look the place over; poked into both the ladies and the gents toilets. Soon as he discovered she wasn't here, he rushed out the door like the proverbial scalded cat.'

Connolly hadn't learned anything he didn't already know. Annette Campbell was the third woman to go missing in the past two months, her case playing big in the media. A witness claimed to have seen her being manhandled out of a car by a uniformed garda on the night she'd disappeared. ROGUE COP SUSPECT, the banner headlines screamed. Captured the public's imagination. Gave the tabloids and conspiracy freaks free reign to concoct lurid theories. Connolly's team of investigators sifted through the force's timetables, work schedules, duty rosters, surveillance and arrest sheets to see if a colleague had been present in the area. To his relief, the search came up with a clean slate. Didn't mean some off-duty officer hadn't been involved though. That possibility existed but he thought it improbable. More likely, he thought, someone impersonating a garda had been the abductor. Wasn't difficult to get hold of a peaked cap like those worn by the force.

One thing, however, was blindingly obvious: Annette Campbell had disappeared. His job was to find her. Connolly thanked the barman for his help and was about to leave when a younger barman approached and asked if he could have a word.

'Of course,' Connolly said, sizing up the youth's greasy hair, pimpled complexion and cheap spectacles. 'What's on your mind?'

'I served the woman … the one you're inquiring about. She drank double vodkas and tonic. I watched her leave. She'd only gone out the door when another customer, a man, followed her.'

'The man who made the phone call?'

'No, wasn't him, he arrived later.'

'Just checking. So, this other customer, might it just be coincidental that he happened to be leaving at the same time as the woman?'

'No, he was definitely following her.'

'How come you're so sure?'

The young man hesitated, a bright blush materializing on his cheeks. Connolly remembered reading somewhere that man is the only animal on earth that blushes. Meant there had to be a reason for the young man's condition. What was it? Guilt? Embarrassment? Shame? Had the scent of an older woman caused him to get hot in his jocks? Why else would he have noticed another person watching her? Why? Because he fancied the woman himself. Connolly kept these thoughts to himself, waiting for the barman to answer.

'There was football on the box,' he said after the hiatus. 'Most customers were watching the game but this one fellow – the one that followed her – he kept his eyes on her the whole time.'

'What did he look like?'

'Average size, mid-thirties I'd say, bit of a peacock. Looked like he'd stepped out of the royal enclosure at Ascot. Drank Jameson ... *neat*. Wore a dark blue overcoat, sharp, expensive, with velvet collar, snazzy like. Had a trendy hat – very Michael Jackson – never took it off.'

'You'd recognize him again if you saw him?'

He looked at the detective uneasily. 'I'd recognize the woman, that's for sure, but yeah, I'd probably recognize the man.'

'Good. I may need you to come down to the station and talk to our sketch artist, but I'll leave that for the moment. Thanks for your help. I'll be in touch.'

The two detectives had taken the same route Annette Campbell used on the night of her disappearance. The missing woman's planned desti-nation had been Holly Flynn's house. Seventy-five minutes' driving had brought Connolly and his sergeant, Bridie McFadden, to the Flynn household, a modern townhouse in the midland town of Tullamore. Connolly had phoned ahead to let Holly know he was on his way. She'd been the one who'd contacted the gardai about her friend's disappearance.

Connolly and McFadden were ushered into a front lounge and invited to sit on a sofa that looked the worse for wear. Holly Flynn's sad expression and dowdy clothes – well-worn Nike trainers, blue jeans, a blue and white striped T-shirt and faded denim jacket – were in keeping with the house's tired furnishing and fittings. Connolly left the talking to McFadden, knowing from past experience that the woman-to-woman approach brought best results. Bridie McFadden, a 32-two-year old, rose-complexioned woman from Tipperary, had perfected her own brand of down-to-earth interviewing. Occasionally she could stray into tactless territory but on a good day she had the ability to make people feel comfortable, uninhibited, relaxed, in her presence.

Holly Flynn needed little prompting to open up about her one-time friend, Annette. 'She's dead, isn't she?' Holly said, her hands locked together and pressed between her knees.

'What makes you think that?' McFadden asked.

Holly's broad face took on a grim expression. 'She phoned me, said she had to see me, claimed I was the only one who could help her, sounded high as a kite. Always liked the booze, she did. I didn't know what to say.'

'So, what *did* you say?' McFadden coaxed.

'It was awkward as hell, I can tell you. I hadn't heard from Annette in ages. We'd been best friends back in Dublin, but when I got married, when I moved down here she dropped me ... too much bother, I suppose. So, I was pretty surprised when, out of the blue, she phoned.'

'When was this?'

'Day before yesterday.'

'She said you were the only one who could help her; what'd she mean by that?'

'Her partner – someone she referred to as Stephen – threatened to sort her out if she left him. She had to get away from him, said I was the only friend that Stephen didn't know. She wanted to crash here for a few days until she got her shit together – her expression not mine.'

'And you agreed to let her ... crash here, I mean?'

'Well no, I mean yes. Oh God, that's why I feel so bad. I hummed and hawed, tried to put her off, said it was inconvenient but then she began to cry, sobbing like all belonged to her were dead and buried.'

'Why didn't you want her here?'

'Pride,' she said, sucking in her breath. 'Back when we were pals I used to slag her off for not being sensible when it came to men friends – Colin Farrell lookalikes on the make, interested in one thing only, if you know what I mean. I was the prudent one; I went for serious, down-to-earth guys, ones with career prospects, didn't matter about the looks or whether I was head-over-heels in love or not. When I decided to marry Charles – an accountant who didn't measure up to Annette's assessment of what was acceptable in the glamour stakes – she laughed in my face, suggested I go to Specsavers, have my eyes tested. We had a blazing row, said awful things to each other. I got on my high horse, told her I'd have a happy marriage, kids and a nice house and that she'd be left on the shelf when her fancy men traded her in for younger models.

'So, when she asked about coming here, I felt ... I don't know what, ashamed really, didn't want her to see that my life hadn't gone to plan.

Charles and I couldn't have kids ... the marriage ended four years ago. He left me for a glamourpuss half my age. I'm now dependent on social welfare. That's why I didn't want Annette to know. I felt such a fool ... but her crying got to me. I told her she could stay until she got things sorted. When she failed to show I blamed myself for trying to put her off. Next morning, I kept thinking about what she'd said, the bit about her life being in danger.' Holly tapped her forehead with her knuckles. 'Couldn't get it out of my head. I kept thinking, he's gone too far, the brute's gone and killed her. I felt guilty as hell, that's why I called. I think you should question this Stephen person, ask him what he knows about Annette's disappearance.'

'We have questioned Stephen,' Connolly said. '*He* came to us as a matter of fact, volunteered to help. Can't say if he's involved but we're ruling nothing in, ruling nothing out. In the meanwhile, I'd like you to contact us again if you hear from Annette.'

'You don't think she's dead then?'

'We've no reason to believe that's the case.'

CHAPTER 4

THE WHIFF OF cooking greeted Emma as she entered the apartment. Connolly was busy in the kitchen; fancied himself as a cook. Of the two of them, Emma conceded that, on a good day, her detective fiancé had the better skills. He greeted her with a hug and kiss, using elbows to embrace her, his hands held high, not wanting to smear her with cooking oil.

'Fried sea bass, spinach, mash and tomato jus,' he announced. 'How does that tickle your taste buds?'

'If it tastes half as good as it smells, you'll get no complaints,' Emma said, extracting herself from the awkward embrace. 'I'm famished. Give me fifteen minutes to change out of these heavy dudes, take a shower and reacquaint myself with civilization.'

'Had a busy day then, have we?'

'Tell me 'bout it! I'll give you the low-down over dinner.'

Her stomach reacted positively to the aroma of sizzling fat and savoury, pan-fried fish as she headed to the bedroom. She hated to bring work home with her but sometimes it was difficult to park it in the newsroom. Today was such a day. Her investigation into the first of the three missing women had taken a somewhat unexpected twist, a factor she intended to discuss with Connolly later. She removed her jacket – a recently purchased Paul Costelloe number – and checked carefully to make sure there were no grease stains on the sleeves. Satisfied, she stripped and enclosed herself in the en-suite shower, her thoughts turning to the odd set of circumstances that brought about her cohabitation with the man she planned to marry in six months' time. With one failed marriage behind each of them, they'd waited until they'd been convinced about the strength of their relationship before agreeing to trip down the aisle again, or the registry office as it would be in their case.

It felt good to stand beneath the hot spray, sponge away the remnants of the day's debris, appreciate her own space and enjoy some irreplaceable quality time. Alone. Watching soap suds slither down her thighs she appraised her figure, pleased that for a woman her age – still eighteen months shy of the dreaded big four-o – the three Bs (boobs, belly and bum) showed only slight indication of travelling south. Her beauty routine didn't come cheap. Twice weekly sessions in the gym and ever-increasing attention to a healthy regime kept the worst that nature could inflict at bay. Above all else, she never neglected to take care of her crowning glory, a luxuriant crop of toffee-coloured hair with natural highlights. Top dollar went on night creams, ones supposed to maximize the skin's ability to repair itself; trouble was, she'd never found a magic potion to alter her retrousse nose or the freckles that adorned its bridge. Time was the enemy. She fought it with all the willpower and cosmetic arsenal at her disposal.

She towelled herself dry and slipped into a comfortable pair of jeans, sweater and loafers before heading to the kitchen. Connolly was ready to serve the food and had produced the remainder of the Sauvignon Blanc they'd opened the previous night. 'This is good,' Emma said, hand poised mid-air, holding a small portion of sea bass aloft on her fork. 'You know, sometimes I think you might have missed your true calling; you should've been a chef. Might've been a more rewarding occupation than chasing low-life on the mean streets of the city.'

'If I had a penny for every time I heard that I'd be a rich, man.'

'So, tell me again, what on earth possessed you to join An Garda Síochána? Our mutual friend Crosby once told me that you and he got enough points under the tutelage of the Jesuits to take your pick of university faculties.'

'That's true, very true. Crosby was the cute one, though; he went on to read English at Trinity, enjoyed a most illustrious career ever since.'

'And you...?'

'Me? I was a bit of an idealist back then ... followed the dictates of my heart, joined the guards. Sounds naïve I know, stupid even, but it was the fulfilment of a dream I'd had from boyhood, bit like having a priesthood vocation. Hey, there's a thought: I could've been a priest.'

Emma looked up from her food. 'God no,' she said, visualizing him in black and wearing a dog collar. 'You'd never have hacked the celibacy ... and the world would have missed out on one of the great lovers.'

'I don't know about that,' Connolly said, clearly amused. 'From what I read about our clergy of late celibacy doesn't feature too highly.'

'You're right on that score,' Emma said as she watched him fork spinach into his mouth. The thought struck her that here was a man in the prime of his life, a man who'd been blessed with natural good looks. Almost a decade older than her, he carried no excess poundage and, thanks to impeccable grooming, looked more like a successful corporate executive than an overworked, underpaid policeman. He had good eyes, a neatly sculpted nose and a high forehead topped with black hair that ran to silver flecks at the temples. 'From what I know of your parents they can't have been too amused when you opted for the guards,' she said.

'Amused? Certainly not. They were aghast; they did not, would not understand. To be honest, I think they were ashamed of me.'

'That's really sad – hey, this fish is delicious. Did they ever come to terms with your choice of career?'

'It's the way I cooked it. My parents? No, they never got used to the idea, thought I was deranged. Give you a laugh: I once overheard someone ask my mother what career her son had chosen. Guess what she said.'

'I've no idea.'

'She stuck out her chin, uttered just one word: "law". Left it at that.'

'Fair play to her. I wonder how she'd have answered that person if you'd decided to be a chef.'

'I shudder to think.'

They ate in silence for a moment. Emma wanted to move on from the chitchat, discuss the events that had dominated their working day. They had an unwritten agreement not to intrude on each other's patch, a compliance that only came into play when aspects of confidentiality were threatened. Unusually, on this occasion Connolly was first to talk about his work day. Emma, wine glass poised in front of her lips, listened to his account of developments in the Annette Campbell investigation.

'We found traces of blood at the location where a witness claimed to have seen her being dragged from her car. We've sent samples to the lab. The witness claims it was a garda doing the dragging.'

'Could be pretty serious … if it's true, that is.'

'Well, it's *not* true,' Connolly said, defiantly. 'No garda, in uniform or otherwise, was in the vicinity at the time of the abduction.'

'You've checked out all the usual suspects, I suppose – friends, jealous boyfriends?'

'A man named Stephen Murray has identified himself as her partner. His car, the one Annette Campbell was driving, was picked up from the spot where the witness saw the altercation. We've taken it into the garda impound, turned it inside out, upside down, lifted fingerprints from the interior and exterior. The lab managed to identify Murray's prints and Annette's – as expected – but they found a smudged thumbprint on the driver's door. It's of no use to us but it indicated the use of surgical gloves.'

'This guy, Stephen Murray – is he a suspect?'

'Not officially, at least not yet. But if a body turns up or it transpires that a crime has taken place, his status will change.'

'Anyone else in your sights?'

'Well, we're trying to trace the whereabouts of a man who appeared overly interested in Annette Campbell while she sipped double vodkas in Glynn's Inn. So far, we've drawn a blank. I've talked to a barman there who has agreed to help us compose an identikit picture of him.'

Emma listened intently, filing away what she heard for future retrieval. To her, Connolly remained inscrutably enigmatic, making him eminently suitable as a detective and an ongoing challenge for her. Right now, she needed his assistance. Asking for it, she'd learned from experience, was like negotiating an obstacle course. 'I've gone back to the first name on the list of missing women,' she told him. 'I'm putting together an in-depth feature that deals with every aspect of the disappearance of Joan Keating.'

Connolly nodded but remained non-committal.

Emma pressed on, determined to elicit a response: 'I believe your team have examined CCTV footage from cameras in the financial centre and Amien Street area.'

'Yes, we looked at some footage.'

'Did you identify the car that stopped for Joan Keating?'

'We did.'

'Did she get in?'

Connolly smiled, said nothing.

'Ah, come on, don't be such a tight-arse. Don't tell me that this is information you can't divulge.'

'No, I don't have a problem on that score,' he said, enjoying Emma's attempts to extract information. 'Can't divulge the driver's name, but I can tell you he was a kerb crawler ... thought Joan Keating was on the game. And she, it appears, mistakenly thought she recognized the car, or the driver. She refused to get in once the driver made his intentions clear. We've since spoken to the man and have ruled him out as a suspect.'

'You do believe there's a connection between the three cases then?'

'Well yes,' Connolly said, pretending to be bored with Emma's attempt to elicit information on the subject. 'The circumstances do suggest a link.'

'What would you say if I told you there might be *more* than three women connected to this case?'

Connolly shrugged. 'People go missing all the time; children, vulnerable adults, those who wish to remain missing, the list goes on. Doesn't mean they're all linked.'

'Yeah, I know, I know, but I think I may have come up with something that suggests a link.'

'Let's have coffee in the lounge,' Connolly said, getting up from the table. 'I know that look on your face ... means you're busting a gut to tell me something. Or trap me into telling you something I shouldn't.'

Emma smiled but didn't answer. She moved to the lounge and sunk into the velvet-cushioned seat by the big picture window. She could hear Connolly rustling up the coffee as she gazed out on to the River Liffey. It was dark outside but city lights reflected like a scattering of jewels on the fast-flowing current. It never ceased to intrigue Emma that this was the same river that Joyce once christened Anna Livia Plurabella, *the lady of the river*, supposedly modelled on his disturbed daughter Lucia – thought by some to be the secret inspiration for his most impenetrable work, *Finnegan's Wake*.

Muted sounds of traffic from the quays penetrated the double glazing. Emma watched night revellers pull their coats tightly around their shoulders to ward off the biting sea wind whipping up from the estuary. Their fifth-floor apartment offered a spectacular panoramic view of the river stretching from Gratton Bridge to Butt Bridge, with the Ha'penny Bridge, the Millennium Bridge and O'Connell Bridge straddling the flow at intervals in between. The night vista, aided by street lights, shop illuminations and floodlit civic buildings remained every bit as dramatic as Joyce once described it.

Bearing two mugs, Connolly settled into the seat beside her. 'Right, Miss Marple,' he said, passing a coffee to her, 'I'm all ears; tell me what my team of professionals have missed that you – amateur sleuth supreme – have managed to uncover.'

'Adopt that supercilious tone with me,' Emma said, feigning annoyance, 'and that truncheon of yours will remain sheathed tonight. I'm being serious.'

'Hmmm, so much for foreplay. What's got you so hot and bothered?'

'Let's start with Joan Keating. She lived alone in Navan's Ledwidge Apartments. On the night she disappeared, she'd missed the last bus home. I've talked to the driver and he remembers her from previous journeys. I visited the apartments today and talked to some people who knew her. I made the trip by bus and got off at the same stop where Joan used to get off.'

'Why'd you do that?'

'Well, helps me paint a more rounded picture for my readers. Not a pretty one, as it turns out. The building's just awful; a great ugly box with nothing in the way of frills apart from a plaque at the entrance with a carving of Francis Ledwidge.'

'Ledwidge? Wasn't he the poet who professed to be a devoted Irish nationalist yet wore the uniform of the British Army in the First World War?'

'Yeah, bit of a dichotomy there. Led to him being shunned for decades. As a monument, the apartment block does little in the way of rehabilitation. In fairness, though, they've chiselled four lines from one of his poems beneath the plaque, I actually remember it from school days. Goes something like:

Oh what a pleasant world 'twould be,
How easy we'd step thro' it
If all the fools who meant no harm
Could manage not to do it

Wonder if the developer who built the complex and commissioned the plaque was aware of the irony.'

'Probably not,' Connolly suggested.

'Anyway, the tenants I talked to all agreed that Joan Keating was a lovely person – had a friendly word for everybody. Nobody could tell if she had a boyfriend or not. But I did find out something which gave me cause to ponder.'

'I'm listening…?'

'One resident told me about an incident that took place exactly a week before Joan Keating went missing. A young woman, same age as

Joan, was grabbed by a man who attempted to drag her into his car. This was at a spot only a few yards from the apartments. If it hadn't been for the arrival of a group of young lads, she would've been abducted. A report of the incident appeared in the local weekly newspaper, the *Navan Dispatch*, and the gardai were informed. Didn't know that, did you?'

'No reason I should. You wouldn't believe the number of missing persons reports we get. Last year alone we had eighteen hundred. Joan Keating's disappearance was treated as a run-of-the-mill inquiry. All three current cases are still, officially at least, being treated as missing persons files. We might suspect foul play, but until something significant turns up, well ... what with the current cutbacks, there's not a lot we can do; you know how the law works. As for the incident you're on about, unfortunately, that kind of thing happens every other day. We can't always give it the kind of attention it deserves. Might surprise you to know that we find ninety-nine per cent of missing people ... usually alive. Finding them is complicated and costly. In quite a few cases we cannot commit to a search at all because, for instance, it's not a crime for a person over the age of eighteen to go missing. Then there are the ones who disappear deliberately, the ones suffering from psychological stress; they don't take time out to consider the feelings of those they leave behind.'

'Yeah, it's the hell of not knowing that destroys those left behind to pick up the pieces. That's part of the tragedy, a bit like suicides. If they knew the devastation they leave behind, they wouldn't do it. But I don't believe for one moment that Joan Keating's disappearance was a deliberate act on her part. I think – no, I *know* – she was taken against her will.'

'You're probably right. I'll do some checking with my colleagues in Navan but more than likely it's probably a coincidence that the attack you're talking about took place outside the apartment block. Truth is, Emma, we don't even know if Joan Keating made it home to base on the night she vanished.'

'Coincidence or not, I think it's significant. I've decided to check it out more thoroughly.'

'Good,' Connolly said, smiling mischievously. 'With you on the case we're bound to discover if there's anything to it.'

'Condescending bastard,' Emma said, throwing a mock punch in his direction. 'Laugh all you like but I'm positive that I might be on to something and all you can do is take the piss.'

Connolly held his hands up in surrender. 'Sorry,' he said. 'You're right, I mustn't mock an investigative reporter who has won Journalist of the Year, not once but twice. Just the same, I think I should tell you I'm not holding my breath.'

'OK, be like that ... oink! oink! You just wait....'

CHAPTER 5

EMMA WAS ON her way out of her work station when Bob Crosby cornered her. Clutching a page from the *Post* as though it were a precious fragment of papyrus from the Dead Sea Scrolls, he asked, 'Where are you off to?'

'Navan. Need to talk to the woman who was attacked before Joan Keating went missing.'

'There's a connection?'

'I think so. Can't say for sure but a few factors appear to tie it in with the disappearances.'

'Such as?'

'Well for starters, the attack took place outside the block of flats where Joan Keating lived. Then there's the timing; the attempted abduction took place round about midnight, same time frame as the others. This woman could have suffered the same fate if the attack hadn't been interrupted.'

Crosby gave Emma his trademark dubious look. 'Hmmm, could mean something, I suppose,' he said, resting his ample posterior on the edge of her work bench. 'However, I don't want you to lose focus on where we're at. Our readers – the ones who keep us in employment – are fixated on the Annette Campbell case right now. If you can't make a clear connection between this attempted abduction and the three known disappearances then we're losing traction, forgetting the gospel according to Simon and Garfunkel: *keeping the customer satisfied.*'

Crosby's instincts were usually on the money. Emma knew better than to ignore his admonishment. For the past decade he'd been her mentor and they'd forged a healthy working relationship. He'd taken her on at a time when her career as a fledgling journalist had hit a rocky patch. Working for a magazine called *Business World* at the time, she'd penned a damning indictment of a wealthy beef baron in which she'd referred to his involvement in a scam to defraud the EU bureaucrats out of millions of pounds in intervention payments. Unfortunately, she'd omitted to include the word 'alleged' in the article. When the publication hit the shops, the beef baron obtained a court injunction compelling the publishers to withdraw the magazine. Almost bankrupted the publishers. Emma was fired. It could have put paid to her career hopes, but being young, stubborn, idealistic and convinced of her own righteousness, she'd refused to let the incident stall her chosen pursuit of employment.

Luckily, Crosby saw potential in her when other would-be employers treated her as something of a pariah. In the intervening years she'd striven to justify the faith he'd put in her. There had been skirmishes along the way – she could be obstinate; he could be impossible – but a trusting friendship evolved. It helped that she liked the man. At fifty-six, early retirement on the horizon, he continued to work assiduously. He would be missed when he vacated the *Post* and none would miss him more than Emma. But, for the sake of his health, she hoped the change would release him from the increasing pressures his job inflicted. Weight gain put considerable strain on his five foot nine frame, his face taking on something of the Churchillian bulldog countenance. His eyes, though, had lost none of their impressive intelligence or innate decency. Those eyes were now trained on her. He patted down a strand of wayward silver hair on the top of his high-domed crown as he spoke. 'Before you go chasing this woman who may or may not be connected to the missing women, I've got something that might have a bearing on the Annette Campbell story.'

Emma raised an eyebrow. Crosby shifted his weight from her desk and on to the one spare chair in her work station. 'You know who Ormsby, Neville & Neylon are?' he said.

'Sure. They're the country's top advertising agency.'

'They are indeed. Over the years I've got to know their sales director pretty well. We've had many a long liquid lunch together – I blame him for my diabetes, my gout, my hepatitis, my cirrhosis of the liver and my heart disease. That aside, the *Post* has benefited from the advertising space the agency pushes our way. In the course of those gastronomic extravagances I got to meet several of the agency's accounts executives. If you discount the food, business lunches can be tedious, but on a few occasions I met one executive in particular – a rising star, a flash-harry fellow by the name of Stephen Murray.'

'You're not serious! You mean the same—?'

'Yep! The selfsame Stephen Murray who was Annette Campbell's live-in partner.'

'You've met him? What did you think of—?'

'I met him, yes. He's fond of himself, likes to play with words, fancies himself as a raconteur. Told me he was a Marxist, then went on to say he was talking Groucho not Karl. Bloody hell, I've met funnier morticians. Thing is, I've found a half-page ad in which he appears, a little gem that Connolly might like to cast his eye upon.'

'Why do you say that?'

'Number of reasons: apparently, Stephen Murray was the accounts executive on an advertising campaign for the Power's Hotel Group. He was present on a photographic shoot to promote the group when, for some reason or other, the male model they'd hired failed to show. They already had female models, costumes, a vintage car and various props in situ and stood to lose serious money if the shoot was scrubbed. So, Stephen Murray stood in for the male model.'

'And you know this because...?'

'Because Murray told me. When his name cropped up in connection with Annette Campbell, I remembered him telling me. So, I did a little chasing and managed to dig up an old copy of the *Post* with the ad in it.' Crosby gave the page he'd been holding to Emma. It featured a photograph taken in front of a castle-like hotel and showed a chauffeur standing by a vintage Rolls Royce as a hotel porter helped two stick-thin ladies with their luggage.

Emma pointed to the person in chauffeur livery. 'Stephen Murray, I presume?'

'The very man,' Crosby confirmed. 'Notice the peaked cap and uniform – what does it say to you?'

'Well, he looks good in it. Seems a bit tight but it suits him.'

'Think about it, Emma: it's the kind of outfit that could be mistaken for a cop's uniform – especially in poor light like, say, at night.'

'You're thinking about the witness who claims to have seen a garda pulling Annette Campbell from her car. Dressed like this could, I suppose, fool someone into thinking he was a cop. Can we publish this picture?'

'My thoughts exactly,' Crosby said. 'Unfortunately, there are prohibiting factors. In the first place, the advertising agency wouldn't agree, and secondly, the Power's Hotel Group would go bloody ballistic.

More importantly, Murray isn't officially a suspect. To publish the ad at this stage would prejudice any future prosecution, should it come to that. We'd be held in contempt of court proceedings and run the risk of suffering a similar fate as that of *The News of the World.*'

Emma smiled. 'Well, we'd better not go down that road then!'

'I think not,' Crosby agreed, laboriously rising from the chair to retrieve the page, the twinkle in his eye unmistakable. 'But we could give it to Connolly; he could show it to the witness – it could help with the investigation – and then, should Murray turn out to be the villain of the peace, the *Post* gets an exclusive scoop and brownie points.'

Seeing the mischievous twinkle, Emma was reluctant to let Crosby leave. She knew the way his mind worked. Crosby and Connolly were buddies, their friendship going all the way back to college days. To this day, they continued to meet each other for lunch and a chat whenever they got the chance. Emma knew that Crosby couldn't wait to show Connolly the half page ad, knew it would give him a kind of giddy pleasure to present it to him before Emma had a chance to discuss it when she got home.

'Could you let me have the ad for a few hours?' she asked as Crosby made his way out from her work station.

'Why? What d'you want with it?'

'I'd like to bring it with me to Navan, show it to the woman I'm meeting.'

'Why? I don't see how that—'

'What if she got a look at her attacker? Wouldn't it just be too fantastic if she recognized the fake chauffeur as her attacker?'

Crosby smiled dismissively. 'Like you say, it'd be just too fantastic.'

Mary Shaw showed Emma into a small, old-fashioned kitchen. 'I live here with Mum and Dad,' she explained, speaking softly. 'They're watching the evening news in the sitting room so I don't want to bother them. They're in their eighties, both suffering from the onset of Alzheimer's. They've lived here in Academy Street all their lives but they get confused when I have visitors.'

'I can understand that,' Emma said sympathetically, taking the chair she'd been offered. 'I won't take up too much of your time. It's good of you to see me.'

Mary Shaw gave Emma a pained smile. She sat across from her at the kitchen table, rarely making eye-to-eye contact. She was small, pert, late-twenties, maybe early thirties, pleasant looking with somewhat boyish features, a woman who appeared to pay scant attention to her appearance. Her hair, simply done, was a sandy brown and could have done with a little maintenance. Her clothes, casual jeans and jumper, looked as though they'd come off the rails in a charity shop. Her attitude seemed intractable; seemed like she'd concluded there was little to be gained in talking to a journalist. 'I've checked you out,' she said, sounding somewhat fatigued, using hands for expression rather than her face. 'I'm hoping that talking to you might help my case. I've given up hope on getting a response from the guards.'

'This is hard for you, I know,' Emma said, struggling to get the measure of the woman and anxious to put her at ease. 'There's no easy way to talk about the ugly event you experienced.' The house was silent except for the muted sound of a television coming from the sitting room. Getting no response, Emma pressed on, 'Can you tell me what happened?'

'It was a nightmare ... a nightmare I'm still trying to escape from. It happened two months ago but it's still happening in my head, over and over … won't go away. I'd gone to meet an old school friend in Dublin. We went to a play in The Abbey Theatre – can't remember the title – something by Sebastian Barry, heavy but enjoyable. I try to get away from the house once a week. Usually Wednesdays. That's the only day my married sister Jane – she's got two children – can look in on Mum and Dad. I got the last bus home – same one I take most weeks – got off at the Ledwidge Apartments; they're about ten yards down on the end of Academy Street. The bus pulled away and I started to walk home. I could hear some young people in the distance; they sounded in good spirits, you know, shouting, singing, play acting, and there were dogs barking. I'd only gone a few steps when I sensed movement behind me. I was about to turn around when two hands grabbed me by the neck. Everything's a bit of a blur after that.'

'Did you get a look at your attacker?'

'Well, it's pretty dark at that spot. The face I saw … I don't know how to describe it … it was like something I was seeing in a trance, you know, real but not real at the same time. I was terrified, I thought, I'm going to die, Jesus, Mary and Joseph, I'm going to die. I felt pressure on my neck, pressing hard. I thought, a gun, maybe a knife … but it was probably the watch on his wrist. I don't remember putting up a fight … maybe I did … can't remember screaming either but I suppose I must have because I attracted the attention of a bunch of young lads. Were it not for them, I might not be talking to you today. I'd be gone, missing, raped, dead, like them poor women.' She shook her head dejectedly, her face ashen, the reliving of the ordeal too much for her. She took time out to loudly inhale and exhale before speaking again. 'I want the bastard caught,' she exclaimed, an unexpected grim resolve now evident in the inflection of her voice.

'Yes, that's what we all want,' Emma said reassuringly. 'D'you think you'd recognize the man if you saw him again?'

'I never want to see him again,' Mary said, holding eye contact with Emma for the first time. She paused, shook her head and then continued, 'No, no, that's wrong, I mustn't say that. I *do* want to see that … that *creature* again. There's nothing I'd like better than to see him in chains and handcuffs, see him locked behind bars. I want to look him in the eye, I want to ask him why he—' She could say no more. She raised her hands to shield the tears rolling down her face. 'I'm sorry … sorry. Oh God, I feel so helpless … so useless….'

Emma handed the woman one of her tissues. She wanted to comfort

Mary Shaw, put her arm around her, but she realized that such a gesture might add to the woman's distress. 'I have a photograph I'd like you to look at,' she said, producing the page with the advertisement. 'This man,' she said, pointing to the chauffer in the photograph, 'could he be the person who attacked you?'

Mary looked at the page, holding it slightly away from her, concentrating on the image. 'No, wasn't him.'

'You're sure?' Emma asked, disappointed at not getting the answer she'd hoped for.

'Yes, I'm sure. The man who attacked me had a receding hairline, you know, a bit like that prince, what's his name, from the royal family.'

Emma ran a quick mental picture of the British royals through her head. 'William? Harry? ... Charles? ... Andrew?'

'No, no, Andrew's brother, Edward. He looked like Edward ... the mugger had hair like Prince Edward.'

Emma was reluctant to upset Mary Shaw any more than was necessary but felt she had to point out the obvious flaw in her observation. 'The man in the advertisement is wearing a chauffeur's cap; you can't see his hairline.'

'Yes, yes, you're right, I see that,' she said, momentarily flustered. 'But, even so, I can tell from the face that he's not the man. It's his eyes; they're nothing like his. I'll never forget his eyes; they were demented, the eyes of a mad man, the eyes of a tortured soul, a person already condemned to hell.'

Emma folded the ad then put it away and produced her business card. 'Please call me if you think there's anything I can help with ... anything at all. You'll find me at that number.'

Mary took the card, looked at it in an unfocused way, nodded without commenting. Emma didn't expect she'd ever hear from her. She desperately wanted to do something for this woman, seeing first-hand how the suffocating domestic arrangement had trapped both her and her ailing parents. The notion that Stephen Murray might have been her attacker made Emma angry but with Mary Shaw's failure to recognize him, it would appear the ad man was in the clear. Didn't necessarily mean he was in the clear as regards the disappearance of the other women, but right now, with nothing to chew on, it seemed to Emma that her investigation was going nowhere fast.

CHAPTER 7

MATTHEW McDONAGH WAS talking about the events that had shaped his life. Like 1,090 other people, he was giving evidence of the abuse he'd experienced as a child in a series of Irish institutions. He had entered the reparation process reluctantly, his participation secured only by the promise of picking up a small fortune in the shape of compensation at the conclusion of the ordeal. The two commissioners assigned to his case had, at every session, assured him of the statutory requirements imposed on them to ensure that evidence would be treated with confidentiality. He didn't trust them, not one little bit. Truth was, he didn't trust anybody, nor did he hold with forelock tugging to exalted personages from any race, rank, social order or walk of life.

'I've never talked about my experiences before,' Matthew was saying to the two commissioners, 'so I'm finding this very difficult.'

Commissioner Collins's smile contained less warmth than the March daylight struggling to penetrate the room's one large window. 'Just tell us what happened ... in your own words,' he said, the tone of condescension barely cloaked. 'Tell us about your family ... your earliest recollections ... your school days.'

One of the skills Matthew had developed in his childhood, as a mechanism to cope with incidents of an extreme nature, involved transporting his mind outside his body. It allowed him to become both spectator and participant at the same time. Right now, he employed this ability to detach himself from the scene he was immersed in. He saw himself as others did, sitting there, unremarkable, thirty-four years of age, slouched shoulders, average build, height and looks, uneasy expression, grey off-the-rack suit, collar and tie, and hair – what was left of it – brushed neatly back. In marked contrast, Collins and McCann, the commissioners, looked altogether more at home, smug, as they occupied two high-backed armchairs in the hotel's plush conference suite.

Matthew had seen images of Collins in the newspapers and on the television news. The judge usually appeared striding to or from the Four Courts, his gowns floating in the breeze, a knowing expression of gravitas fixed on the face he presented to the camera. Matthew suspected that nothing more than naked greed lay behind the judge's agreement to serve on the commission of an inquiry. In his sixties, Collins had a red fleshy face, great jowls, a glistening bald head and shrewd eyes that displayed a practised look of attentiveness. This contrived visage, complemented by bespoke tailoring, failed to cloak a huge belly that bore all the hallmarks of a lavish expense account. Either that or, as Matthew's imagination preferred to visualize, the bulk resulted from a liposuction procedure that operated in reverse.

Fellow commissioner, Senator Maurice McCann, a thin, bespectacled man in his late-fifties, had a long, pinched face, a high forehead and a hairpiece that looked as conspicuous as a caterpillar clinging to an eggshell. Matthew detected a whiff of expensive cologne. The contrasting size of the men struck him as somewhat risible, echoes of Stan Laurel and Oliver Hardy – with the fun taken out. One of the many freakish recesses of his brain theorized that the senator had undergone a real liposuction procedure, his subcutaneous fat being transferred to the judge.

The senator, who he now thought of as Stan, seldom bothered to participate in the interview, content to leave the talking to the judge. On the few occasions when he did ask a question, he leaned forward, placing his elbows on the table, his hands pressed together to form a temple, in the mistaken belief that the pose conveyed a study in heart-felt intimacy. For the most part, though, he appeared content to jot down occasional notes and underscore the odd word.

'Never knew my parents,' Matthew heard himself say, his voice sounding to him as it did to others: slow delivery, slight nasal tone, little if any modulation. 'They, or at least my mother, abandoned me, handed me over to St Joan's orphanage. I've never been able to ascertain how I got there, or who exactly dumped me.' Matthew could have elaborated on this, given a more truthful account of the circumstances of his birth but decided against it, reasoning that there was little to be gained by doing so. He had, in fact, undertaken quite a painstaking amount of research into exactly who his biological parents were.

He'd been in touch with The Adoption Authority of Ireland who'd been polite and willing to help him. But because he didn't possess a birth certificate, their efforts proved inadequate. He'd contacted the Catholic Adoption Society but they, too, were unable to help. He arranged meetings with the General Office Register in Dublin, the Barnardos Adoption Advice Centre in Christchurch Square and the Citizen's Advice Bureau in Andrew Street, all to no avail.

Finally, after a somewhat fraught confrontation with the Christian Brothers' authorities, he was allowed access to the Industrial Schools Admission register. It provided him with multiple lists of pupils' names, endless columns containing the names of parents and guardians, plus dates of admissions, the years involved, and the relevant class grades. Almost magically, it seemed to him, he found what he was looking for: his name in beautiful script. From this one piece of information he was able to chase down a copy of his birth certificate, which in turn provided a key that allowed him access to a trail of documents, historic newspaper clippings, photographs of gravestones, all of which combined to enabled him to piece together a potted version of his genealogy.

His mother, Theresa Dooley, he discovered, came from farming stock in Co Mayo. At the age of fifteen, she'd come to Dublin and had got a job in Finnegan's Shoe Shop in Summerhill. She liked to go dancing on the weekends and struck up a relationship with a ne'er-do-well coal delivery man named Jacky Bradley. He drank too much, gambled what little money he earned and was heavily involved with the IRA. Records show that the police had been called frequently after he'd beaten Theresa. They never married and when she became pregnant by him he disowned her, but not before hospitalizing her as a result of a vicious beating. A warrant for his arrest was issued but he met his death before the warrant could be served. He'd been knifed in a brothel in Little Martin's Lane – later named Beaver Street, surely a planner's little joke. It appears that Bradley received a stab to the heart from a prostitute when he'd failed to produce the money due for services rendered.

Even more tragically, Theresa Dooley died giving birth to Matthew. She'd been fired from her job as soon as her condition became notice-able – the shop's policy didn't allow for unwed mothers – and being destitute, the courts sent her to the Mary Magdalene Laundry in Leeson Street, a prison-like institute run by nuns for what was then called 'wayward girls and fallen women'. The nuns' policy was to work the girls until the time of their delivery, after which, without exception, the babies were sold into adoption or, if there were no takers, passed on to other religious-run homes. Matthew had passed through a number of these homes before ending up in St Joan's orphanage at the age of three.

'I remember St Joan's as being dismal,' he told the commissioners. 'It was grim as death. Would've been better had they drowned me ... like an unwanted kitten ... yes, that would've been preferable.'

Collins shrugged, his eyes displaying no reaction. 'Paint a picture for us, if you will, of what day-to-day life was like for you in St Joan's,' he asked.

Matthew paused, nodded to the two gentlemen, his mind conjuring up dark memories, memories that screamed at him down through the years. He heard himself enunciate his account of the misery and hardships, the sexual abuse and warped religious indoctrination he'd endured in that hellhole. He listened and watched as the inquisitors probed deeper into the conditions. His answers were heartfelt, spoken in a manner that could only come from someone who'd endured the full horror of the systematic torture that had been meted out to him. He told of how he'd being routinely slapped, whipped and beaten in front of the other boys; he described the physical, emotional, verbal, sexual, psychological abuse that represented the everyday norm in the institution.

The veracity of his account worked like a vacuum, sucking his lungs dry. As far as he could ascertain, not a word of what he'd uttered impacted on the consciousness of either commissioner. Their expressions remained unmoved, akin to indifference. No pity. No sympathy. *Nothing has changed*, he thought. Didn't bother them that pupils had been habitually beaten, bullied and buggered by teachers, supervisors and the bigger boys, starved continually, and forced to work in the kitchen and refectory until they'd collapsed from exhaustion.

'And you remained in this institution for how long? Collins asked, tone neutral as a satnav commentator.

'Until I was nine.'

'Why'd you leave?'

'The place burnt down.'

'Oh, yes, of course, so it did,' Collins said, flicking through the notes in front of him. Bound in a thick lever-arch file, the notes were quite extensive. They contained the full account of Matthew's abuse as a child. He had submitted the account in the first instance in order to be considered eligible for compensation.

'What do you remember about the inferno?' Collins asked. 'I believe there were fatalities.'

Matthew remained silent for a moment, taking time to collect his thoughts, knowing it was important that his spoken account should concur with the description he'd written in his submission. In that moment of silence he was acutely conscious of his own breathing, his heartbeat, the sound of the commissioners' antique chairs creaking beneath their weight. The peripheral atmosphere, too, impinged on his subconscious. Sounds from the afternoon traffic in the street below, sounds like the swishing of tyres on the road's wet surface. But uppermost in his mind he could feel the commissioners impatiently waiting for an answer.

'What I remember most were the flames ... and the choking smoke, the screaming, the fire brigades and the deafening noise as the roof caved inwards.' For an instant, Matthew was back in the zone, feeling the heat from the conflagration. 'Seven children and two supervisors burned to death. An inquiry followed but the government officials who'd came to rake through the burned-out site failed to come up with any conclusions.' He didn't know it at the time but on reflection, as an adult, he'd come to believe that the officials were more concerned with deflecting blame from the religious order who'd run the place than looking for the cause behind the tragedy.

After leafing through several pages of notes, Judge Collins glanced at his watch, an expression of irritation on his face. As well as containing Matthew's submission the folder included an account of his adult life 'on the outside'. An extended section included a wad of legal documentation dealing specifically with his conviction for attempted rape and the subsequent prison term he'd served. This blot on his life was due for discussion at a later session. Right now, though, they were obliged to trudge through the early years.

'It says here that you were sent to The Beaumont Industrial School after the fire. Is that right?'

'That's what the submission says,' Matthew snapped. 'It's written there for you in black and white.'

Collins raised his eyebrows, surprised at the belligerence in Matthew's voice but let the rebuff slide, feigned a smile and spoke in the well-practised placating voice he used so effectively when addressing juries. 'Yes, I have it here in front of me – and very well put if I may say so, Mr McDonagh, but I need to hear from you that it's true.'

''Course it's true.'

'Well, yes, but with all due respect it will be the two of us who ultimately decide on the matter. So, my good man, talk to me about the Beaumont. You claim you were subjected to four years of torture and degrading abuse in that institution, am I right?'

'Yes, it's why I'm here,' McDonagh said coldly.

Collins glanced at his watch again. 'I think it might be best if we hold back on that segment of your submission until the next session. How would that suit you, Mr McDonagh?'

'Like, I have a choice?'

'Yes, of course you do, but we're trying to suit everybody—'

'It's of no consequence, I've waited this long to talk about the Beaumont ... waiting another week won't matter a whole lot.'

'Good, good, that's settled then,' the judge said dismissively. 'We'll see you the same time next week.'

D ETECTIVE INSPECTOR JIM Connolly forced himself into the routine of another day: drank his coffee; enjoyed a make-do breakfast of Ritz biscuits with cheddar. He could see and hear the morning traffic through the window of his cramped cubicle. The slow-moving column crawled, bumper-to-bumper, along Pearse Street, on towards the Dame Street junction with College Green, then round by Trinity College and the Bank of Ireland. The daily cacophony of sounds created by the collective input of combustion engines, squealing breaks, impatient horns, bicycle bells, and occasional bleats from bus tour guides represented, for Connolly at least, the very ingredients that made up the city.

The clock on the wall let him know it was half an hour later than his normal starting time. A sign next to the clock read: TEMPUS FUGIT. Unusual for him, he'd slept through the alarm and continued to sleep while Emma showered and breakfasted. Only after hearing her slam the door on her way out did he finally open his eyes, realized the time and made a mad dash for his clothes, annoyed at Emma for letting him lie in. But thinking on it, he accepted that she'd done it with the best intentions, a sign from her that his amorous athleticism of the night merited some slack. In a departure from routine, he'd skipped breakfast and made it across the River Liffey to the station in less than fifteen minutes. Yes, he thought, checking his watch, the *tempus* really does *fugit*.

A week had gone by since Annette Campbell's disappearance. There was little if any progress to report. In charge of the operation to track down her whereabouts, he was pulling out all the stops. With the cooperation of the minister for justice, equality and law reform, he established a dedicated missing persons unit and a response network, similar to the Amber Alert system they have in the United States. He'd contacted Europol, Interpol, the Schengen Information System (SIS) and the Missing in Ireland Support Service (MISS).

Still came up short.

Annette and the other two women had, for all intents and purposes, simply vanished from the face of the earth. The investigation was in danger of sliding into a limbo dimension: no bodies, no hard evidence of a crime. Yet, the probability that the women were dead hovered above his head like Edgar Allan Poe's famous pendulum. His team had concentrated their efforts on trying to establish what, if any, similarities linked the three women.

Joan Keating, civil servant, aged twenty-nine, the first victim – if she could rightly be called a victim – was single. She rented flat no. 22 on the second floor of the Ledwidge Apartments, one of the many large engineering projects in the Navan area that traced its genesis to the halcyon days of the so-called Celtic Tiger. Until her disappearance, Joan Keating had commuted to Dublin City to her place of work in the births, marriage and deaths department – known affectionately as the 'hatch, match, and dispatch' unit – and had originally hailed from County Galway where her parents and a younger brother and sister still lived.

The second woman to slip off the radar, Siobhan O'Neill, aged thirty-four had been deserted by her salesman husband when he'd taken flight to Australia. She'd returned to live with her mother. Her father was dead. Her only sibling, a twin brother, worked as a pilot with a budget airline. She'd become unemployed three weeks prior to her disappearance.

Annette Campbell, aged thirty-five, the third recorded disappearance, worked for an estate agency and had a mother and two older, married sisters. Because Annette had just split from partner, Stephen Murray, he had come under suspicion but to date they'd come up with nothing like enough evidence to bring him in.

Apart from the fact that the three missing persons were female and within a five-year age bracket of each other, no linkage of any consequence had come to light. Connolly's team had clocked up countless hours chasing down the names of boyfriends, current and past, going all the way back to the women's college days. They'd checked night clubs, doctors, dentists, political affiliations, hobbies, and past employers but failed to establish a common denominator. No similarity of shape, size, hair colour or socioeconomic background came to light.

The artist's drawing of the man in the pub – the one wearing the coat and trendy hat – had come to nought. The pimple-faced barman's recall

46

of the coat and hat was impressive but when it came to the face, his description might well have been that of a shop window mannequin. Could be anybody or everybody. In the course of his description, the barman had used the word 'peacock' when attempting to characterize the mystery man's demeanour. The use of the quaint adjective surprised Connolly. He wondered if it was something the barman had picked up from his parents, a throwback to O'Casey's play *Juno and the Paycock* in which the character, Captain Boyle, is described at one point as 'strutting about like a paycock'. Connolly's mention of this to the team was enough to confer the e-fit image with the name 'Peacock' or, using the old Dublin vernacular – 'Paycock'.

The ad featuring Stephen Murray had been shown to the witness who'd claimed to have seen a garda officer manhandling Annette Campbell. Result: a great big zilch. Frustration all round. The press too, was getting hot under the collar, going nowhere with the ongoing investigations, seeking desperately to breathe new life into the story, keep it current. By now, everyone in the country had become familiar with the pictures of Joan Keating, Siobhan O'Neill and Annette Campbell. The media had begun making sideswipes at the forces of law and order, suggesting that not enough was being done to solve the mystery.

Getting a roasting from the media was nothing new, went with the job, wasn't a whole lot Connolly could do about it, but the pressure coming from his superiors couldn't be ignored. The top brass were feeling the heat from the justice minister and his department heads. Everyone wanted the same thing: find the missing women, preferably alive. Discover what, or who, was responsible. While these thoughts ricocheted like a stray bullet around Connolly's brain, Detective Sergeant Mike Dorsett, a tall, raw-boned 45-year-old, ambled into his office. His long chiselled face, with as many peaks, hollows, plains and hard lines as his native Donegal topography, made it hard to decipher his mood.

'I think we may have something,' Dorsett said, ignoring the empty chair Connolly offered. 'Could be we've hit pay dirt, got ourselves a bona fide suspect, enough circumstantial evidence to go to the director of public prosecutions.'

'Ye gods be praised,' Connolly said, smashing a closed fist into an open palm. This was what he needed to hear. That Dorsett was the one bringing the good tidings made it all the more significant. The Donegal man had worked with him for longer than anyone else and had, in the process, become his most trusted wingman. An untidy man, he embodied an air of constant distraction and gave the impression of carrying the weight of the world on his shoulders. His private life was just that – *private*. It was said he had a girlfriend, a teacher in an all Irish-speaking school. Word had it that they shared a flat in Rathmines. Although they'd cohabited, on and off, for over a decade the girlfriend wore neither a wedding ring nor an engagement ring. Squad room rumours put it about that their shared hobby involved taking rubbings from ancient monuments and bird watching. This may or may not have been true but one thing was certain, left to Dorsett to confirm or deny it, those waiting for an answer would have a long wait.

Connolly was the one person who, apart from the elusive girlfriend, if she really existed, knew him as well as it was possible to know the man. He'd forged a genuine friendship, although paradoxically they seldom if ever met socially. This was down to a set of personalities that couldn't be more different from each other. Dorsett lacked Connolly's social graces but this aspect of the relationship was compensated for by his sense of loyalty and his canny insights into the criminal mindset.

'The search in Stephen Murray's house turned up a uniform and a cap,' Dorsett said, his accent a hybrid of Scots/Ulster dialects. 'We've also looked at his neighbour's car – the one Murray used to drive to Glynn's Inn. The model fits the description of the vehicle our witness saw Annette Campbell being bundled into.'

'You think the DPP will go for it?'

'He should, when we show that Murray borrowed it from the neighbour and, wait for this, we found blood stains in the car's boot.'

'Let's bring him in here … before we go to the DPP. I want to look him in the eye, see what he has to say for himself before we commit ourselves.'

'THIS IS ALL a bit surreal,' Stephen Murray repeated, his voice less assertive than it had been when he'd first entered interview room no. 2, his know-it-all demeanour a tad less smug. 'What could make you imagine I had anything to do with Annette's disappearance?'

He sat on a straight-backed, steel-framed chair, one leg stretched out to its full extent, the other remaining angled beneath the chair, the contrived pose of nonchalance failing to achieve its objective. Directly across from Connolly and Detective Sergeant Mike Dorsett, Murray was having a hard time, annoyed at being packed into a squad car and hauled into custody like some common criminal, but determined not to let them see how much it ruffled his feathers.

A well-built man of thirty-seven, Murray had a longish face that might, at a push, be described as handsome, his cheeks and chin stubble giving him that fashionable five o'clock shadow appearance. His raven-black hair, which Connolly suspected came from a bottle, was sleeked down and cut longer at the back than suited his age. The eyes had an unhealthy red-rimmed appearance, the pupils noticeably dilated. His clothes, unsuitable for the inclement weather, consisted of a crumpled straw-coloured linen suit, white open-necked, button-down shirt, no socks and a pair of Italian loafers with elaborate tassels.

Dorsett flicked through the pages of the folder in front of him, even though he'd no need to do so. 'We have a witness who saw you on the night Annette Campbell went missing,' he said, as though reading from notes.

Murray responded with a sidelong glance. 'You have a witness? Well of course you have,' he sneered, 'I went to her pub. *Everybody* saw me, the punters, the barmen, the whole crew. I mean, come on, guys, I practically put on a performance, told them who I was looking for, searched the place, even poked my nose into the toilets. No mystery.'

'What I mean is,' Dorsett said, his eyes on his notebook, 'we have someone who saw you pushing your partner into a car.'

'You know,' Murray said with a smirk, 'Hitler said it was easier to fall victim to the big lie than to the small one. Your witness, if he or she exists, which I doubt, is a falsifier, a fabricator, or to put it more plainly, a liar. Fact is, no one saw me push anyone into a car, because it didn't happen. *If* some witness saw Annette being pushed into a car, I can assure you I was not the one doing the pushing. Besides, if what I read in the press is true, your witness says it was a garda in uniform. Sounds to me like you're covering up for the actions of a colleague.'

Connolly showed Murray the page from the *Post* that Crosby had passed on to him. 'Here's an ad you were involved in during your time with Ormsby, Neville & Neylon,' he said. 'Recognize the person in the chauffeur's livery?'

Murray looked at the ad, the smirk on his face taking root. 'And to think I never got my fee for that shoot. Right now, though, I don't see what it's got to do with anything.'

'That *is* you posing as a chauffeur?'

'Yeah, yeah, I just said so. Didn't get paid for the gig. I still don't understand why my one-day stint as a stand-in model has got you so hot and bothered.'

'You see the uniform you're wearing?' Connolly asked.

'Yeah, yeah, looks a bit like the one Michael Caine wore in Alfie back in the swinging sixties. Great movie! Bet Caine got paid for his work. Much better than the re-make with Jude Law. Sorry, I digress—'

'The chauffeur's outfit ... could be mistaken for a garda's, if the light was poor ... like at night, for instance.'

Murray laughed out loud. 'Yes, I suppose it could at that. Mind you, it would help if you were partially blind and wearing bottle-bottomed glasses. In the country of the blind the one-eyed man is king.'

The two detectives swapped glances, their expressions conveying mock incomprehension at Murray's facile commentary. Getting no response, Murray continued, 'Let's get real here, OK? You're suggesting I posed as a cop. That's what you're implying, yeah? But that's plum crazy. Look, look, look, putting the silly Michael Caine costume aside for the moment, why would I want to grab Annette? I've been living with her for the past three years. *Why?* Makes no sense.'

'We found the chauffeur's uniform in your house, yes?' Dorsett said, finally pushing the folder aside and looking directly at Murray.

'So what? I forgot to give it back to the agency ... big deal.'

'Would you be willing to wear it in a line-up?'

'Ah, come on, you've got to be kidding. You want me to pose in a line-up so that some one-eyed witness can pick out the person he or she saw in the dark while he or she drove past?'

'Will you do it?' Dorsett pressed.

Murray glanced at his watch, a serious piece of bling that resembled a small clock. 'Sorry, gentlemen,' he said, 'I wasted time, and now doth time waste me.'

'For now hath time made you his numbering clock,' Connolly replied, quoting the follow-on line from *Richard II*, letting Murray know the use of quotations had become tiresome.

'OK, the joke's gone far enough,' Murray said, acknowledging the put-down. He pushed the page with the ad back across the desk. 'Take a good look at the ad,' he said. 'The costume had to be stretched to breaking point to allow me to squeeze into it. Jesus! I could hardly move and my wedding tackle stood out like it was on display. The art department in the agency had quite a job air-brushing my dodrantal down to a respectable proportion.'

Dorsett shot a quizzical glance to Connolly: *dodrantal?*

Connolly smiled in spite of himself. He remembered coming across the word back when he was part of a student group searching for vulgar words no longer in common usage. He would let Dorsett in on the joke at a later stage.

Murray caught the smile on Connolly's face. 'That outfit was tight as tuppence in a miser's clenched fist,' he said. 'I was speaking like a boy soprano. Since then I've gained half a stone, maybe more. I couldn't get into it even if I wanted to.'

'Sounds a bit like OJ's defence,' Dorsett said, looking at his superior, 'the bit where he insisted the gloves were too small. And we all know he was guilty as hell.'

'The quality of mercy is not strained,' Murray said with a mocking smile. 'Actually, OJ was found innocent.'

'We did find something else in your house,' Dorset said. 'We got to meet the young woman who's moved in. Didn't waste much time finding a replacement for Annette, did you?'

'Who I have as a guest in my house is my own business,' Murray said, rattled at last. 'But since you brought it up, I can tell you she's a long-time friend – goes back to my days in the ad game. She's staying with me because she had to leave her flat, and because I was going mental on my own, not knowing what's happened to Annette. No law against that, is there?'

'Maybe not, but there are plenty of laws concerning drugs. The young lady in question appeared to be under the influence of some narcotic substance when we saw her; she was totally zonked, barely able to speak.'

Murray shrugged. 'She's an adult.'

Connolly was about to press on when Detective Sergeant Bridie McFadden entered the room. She nodded to Connolly, using her eyes to indicate that he should follow her out to the corridor. For the benefit of the recording, Dorsett announced that Detective Inspector Connolly was leaving and the interview was being temporarily suspended.

Outside, Connolly turned on McFadden, looking none too pleased. 'What's so important that couldn't wait till—?'

'Got word back from toxicology,' McFadden cut in. 'Thought you'd want to see it before continuing with Murray.'

'What have they got to say?'

'Well, for starters, the blood found at the spot where Annette Campbell was abducted does not match the blood found in the car used by Murray.'

'I see,' Connolly said, grimacing. 'What else did they tell us?'

'The blood traces found in the boot of the car are not even human … they belong to an animal, could be a dog, a calf, anything.'

'Great! That's bloody great; we've pulled in Murray, ready to go to the DPP and all of a sudden we've got what? Diddly squat. Shacking up with a young junkie as soon as Annette is out of the way is hardly sufficient cause to hold him. The chauffeur's uniform doesn't fit him and the blood belongs to some animal … just what we need.'

'There's more, I'm afraid,' McFadden offered. 'I've just talked to Mary Shaw, the woman in the Ledwidge Apartments. I was surprised to find that Emma Boylan had already been to see the woman. Like me, Emma showed her the chauffeur's picture. It rang no bells.'

'What? you're saying Emma had the ad? Damn!' Connolly shook his head, annoyed and looking somewhat embarrassed. He turned to McFadden. 'Sorry about that … shouldn't have happened. I try to keep my domestic life separate from the job here, but sometimes … well, it's something I'll have to sort out.' He sighed, trying to refrain from an unseemly outburst. 'In the meantime we've drawn a great big blank here; back to square one with Murray. I think he's not telling us the whole story but we'll have to let him go.'

'Sure, I'll tell Dorsett.'

Connolly's phone was ringing as he entered his office. *Ignore it*, he told himself, his mind still coping with the disappointment of having to set Murray free, annoyed at how Emma had managed to muscle in on his investigation, annoyed too with Crosby for having passed the ad to her without informing him. But the continued ringing overrode his thoughts. Always did.

It was Emma.

'Had a call from Mother,' she told him. 'She reminded me that we've promised to spend St Patrick's Day with her and Dad. That's just five days away so you'd better make sure you're not tied up at work.'

Connolly moved uneasily in his chair, not feeling in the right frame of mind to talk to her. 'Totally forgot,' he said, his face a grimace of pain. 'Look Emma, I *really* could do without this right about now. I've got the commissioner, the minister and you lot from the press on my case looking for results and you want me to what? Traipse down to Slane, yeah? Make polite conversation with your parents and run through the plans for the wedding while we're at it – that's what you're asking?'

'Well, if that's how you feel, forget it. At least now I know where I stand, where your priorities lie. I'll ring Mum and Dad, tell them you can't be bothered, tell them that you have more important—'

'Emma! Stop it, OK. Look, I'll go, I'll go with you.' He took a deep breath, determined not to allow this develop into a full blown row. 'I'm sorry Emma, it's just, well, the timing's bad. I'm up to my proverbial but I'll find a way; I know ... I know you promised them.'

'I wouldn't ask if it wasn't important. Mum and Dad are giving me a hard time. I need you to put their minds at ease, let them know that we're sure ... I mean, comfortable with the marriage.'

'Ah, Jesus!'

'Dad's OK with our situation – wants whatever I want, but Mum, well, she's upset... dead set against a registry office. She'd like the Papal blessing, the whole nine yards. Me? The church thing is no big deal; I'm a night time Catholic, like Brendan Behan – I pray when it's dark and

I'm afraid – but Mum holds with tradition. So, I'm depending on you to work the old charm offensive on her.'

'Might not be the best time to try out my charm offensive,' Connolly said wearily. 'I'll do my best.' He'd met Emma's parents several times since the engagement; palpable sense of unease always evident. His relationship with Arthur and Hazel Boylan went back to the time when Emma had been married to Vinny Bailey. During that period, he had co-operated with Emma on a number of cases. One case in particular proved pivotal in cementing their relationship. She'd been pregnant at the time with her first – and only – baby. In a move to gain front-page banner headlines, she'd exposed herself to a totally unnecessary risk. The consequences were catastrophic. The criminals she'd been attempting to expose turned vicious, pushed her head-over-heels down an escalator.

Because it had been his case and he'd felt partially responsible for what happened he'd gone to her parents' home to see her. It was, he remembered, a heavenly bright summer's day. A herd of Friesian cows grazed the lush pasture that bordered the Boyne, unconcerned by the lone figure of Emma Boylan, clad in white jumpsuit and trainers, sitting by the river bank. It had been three days since she'd left hospital, since she'd lost the baby.

'How are you?' he asked, sitting down beside her.

'Feeling better, thanks,' she said without conviction.

'Your mother told me you were here. Hope you don't mind me coming?'

'No, not at all, you're welcome.' Emma had spoken to him briefly in the aftermath of the accident – a jumbled conversation, abstract questions, fragmented answers, incoherent words. But now, though, he sensed that she couldn't make up her mind whether she resented or welcomed his intrusion.

'Have you come to tell me you've discovered who pushed me?'

'No, not yet, I'm afraid. I wanted to see if you were strong enough to discuss what happened. I'd like to hear it from you, first hand, find out why you met with an accident that could've proved fatal.'

'It was fatal – my baby is dead.'

Silence followed. Emma wiped away a tear from her cheek. He moved closer, put his hands on her shoulders in what he hoped she took as a reassuring gesture.

'It's all right,' she said. 'I need to talk about it. I'm suffocating here, everyone tiptoeing around like they're walking on eggshells. Don't get me wrong; my parents are doing what they think is best. They're at pains to avoid using any expressions that might remind me of my loss and Vinny, poor Vinny, he has never once hinted at attribution of blame or responsibility for the obvious danger I brought upon myself. Doesn't lessen the weight of guilt I feel though.'

They discussed the events that had led up to the loss of the baby, Emma temporarily caught up in the complexity of detail, willing to give a full account of the case she'd been pursuing. She'd got to the moment in St Stephen's Green Shopping Centre where she'd been about to step on the escalator, but couldn't go on. Tears fell again. He reached out, took her hands in his, allowed for the silence. A docile cow poked its head between their feet to scoop a mouthful of grass, oblivious of the powerful emotions being experienced by both of them. He remained silent, not wanting to intrude on her grief, thinking he might have been wrong to make her relive the dreadful ordeal. Only the soothing echo of running water and the barely audible sounds of grass being scooped into the cow's mouth drifted on the air. Emma dried her eyes and looked into his, as though sensing what was going through his head. 'I'm glad you came,' she said. 'It's time I took responsibility for what's happened … time I got off my backside and did something useful instead of moping around.'

For him, a spark had ignited. That spark blossomed into a romance in double quick time.

Arthur and Hazel were delighted that he'd succeeded in restoring their daughter's wellbeing but, even then, they'd been suspicious of his motives. Observing the cordial body language evident between daughter and cop made them fear for the fragility that clearly existed in Emma's marriage to Vinny Bailey.

The inevitable happened.

Emma and Vinny separated. Everyone suffered in the aftermath but Connolly came in for the harshest treatment. It had taken Emma hours of argument over many months to persuade her parents that the split from Bailey was down to her, not Connolly.

Connolly dismissed the memory. 'I'll get someone to cover for me,' he said, resignedly. 'Pray to God there are no major developments.'

'You're not expecting any, are you?' Emma asked tentatively. 'I mean, it's unlikely there'll be a breakthrough on the missing women during the few days we're down at home.'

'Half an hour ago I thought we *had* a breakthrough but right now I'm back at square one. Can't be easy for you to write about the case – I mean with nothing happening.'

'You're right, but I'm pretty resourceful, I've come up with a few angles that might generate a column or two.'

'Good, I'm glad someone's making progress.'

'Ah, you poor darling,' Emma teased, 'come home to Mamma this evening and I'll think of something to perk your ... ah ... spirits up.'

'Yeah, right,' Connolly replied, Emma's innuendo failing to excite any trace of passion in him. His mind had gone into one of those déjà vu moments that can be so disconcerting. Except it wasn't really a déjà vu moment; he was remembering an episode that contained parallels similar to Emma's proposed visit to her parent's house. In the earlier episode he'd shown up on his own parent's doorstep with his bride-to-be, Iseult, daughter of the wealthy and well-connected Smyth-O'Briens. His parents described the proposed nuptials as being heaven sent. Later, he would come to think of the union as being concocted in hell. He'd likened her beauty to that of fine porcelain, only to discover later that she was every bit as cold and unyielding.

What frightened him most about this recollection was the feeling that on St Patrick's Day he would, once again, be travelling down a not dissimilar path, just a different location.

CHAPTER 10

B REAKING NEWS. BOTH heard it simultaneously. Different places. Connolly was deep in discussion with DS Dorsett and DS McFadden when the flash came through. Across the city, in the newsroom of the *Post*, Emma Boylan was in discussion with Bob Crosby, debating the strategy she proposed to adopt in pursuit of the investigation when the news broke.

Human bones had been discovered.

Crosby motioned Emma to pick up the extension. Quick to oblige, Emma swivelled her seat, reached for the phone, listened. Human remains unearthed near the Hill of Tara. Details sketchy. Workers on the Tara section of the M3 motorway had accidentally unearthed bones while digging on a portion of slip road that branched off the motorway. State pathologist, Dr Mary McElree, had been called to the site. The National Roads Authority (NRA) planned a news conference the following day.

'I can just imagine,' Emma said, replacing the phone, 'what this will do to the relatives and friends of the three women when they hear it.'

'Yeah, their darkest fears realized,' Crosby agreed.

'*If* it's one of them, at least we'll know for sure. Doesn't make it easier to accept though.'

'Where they found the bones,' Crosby said, eyebrows raised, 'isn't that near your neck of the woods?'

'Not exactly, but it's not too far from my home village of Slane.'

'The Hill of Tara, what is it, a few miles, three or four at most from Navan? That's pretty close to where Joan Keating lived. Might be her.'

Emma nodded. 'Dear God, it could be … probably is, but we need to tread carefully. That whole area … well, it could be significant for a variety of different reasons.'

'Such as?'

'Well, according to our historians Tara is, archaeologically speaking, the most important site in this country. Up there with Egypt's Valley of the Kings, if we're to believe the eco warriors.'

'Eco warriors my arse. More like Nazi warriors if you ask me; I mean, look at the methods they employ—'

'True, their strategy is questionable; they're determined to derail the whole motorway project, stop the bulldozers cutting a swathe through what they call, "the soul of Tara".'

'They do have a point, even if I don't agree with how they go about it.'

'A moot point,' Emma offered. 'They've certainly managed to add to the cost of the project.'

'Something the government could well do without.'

'Yeah, to keep things moving, they brought in a bunch of archaeologists, got them to start a dig, undertake geophysical scans. They unearthed a few monuments and passage graves, ancient stuff, some of it going back to the year dot. Shouldn't be surprised if these bones belong to some high king from back when Moses was floating down the river in his basket.'

'Hmmm, I don't think so,' Crosby said, 'but there's always the possibility that they could belong to one of "the disappeared", you know, the poor souls murdered by the IRA during the troubles.'

'You think that's a possibility?' Emma asked, scepticism in her voice.

'Nah, not really but according to what I'm hearing, the state pathologist has been brought in. I'd say that's speaks volumes.'

'In what way?'

'Well, like you say, they've already got a bunch of archaeologists on site. They normally deal with a situation like this, I mean, if the bones were thought to be ancient. No, Emma, I think this might just be what we've all been dreading.'

Connolly, accompanied by DS Bridie McFadden, trudged down the bank's slope, his feet sinking in the sodden earth. It was only mid-afternoon but March's early dusk had already begun its slow creeping descent, casting long shadows over the roadside terrain. It had rained earlier and the clouds overhead still looked dark and threatening. The whiff of diesel from the nearby machinery hung on the air.

Connolly had opted for garda issue heavy padded jacket, trousers and moss green wellingtons. McFadden, with an eye to contemporary fashion, refused the standard issue wellingtons, deciding instead to wear white rubber boots featuring a scattering of large graphic daisies. Not that fashion was her sole concern; she berated herself for not having had the good sense to have put on an extra layer of woollens. The biting chill had transformed her rosy cheeks to an angry beetroot red but she indulged her habit of chewing gum in a determined effort to ignore her discomfort.

The white-clad technical bureau personnel had already erected a prefab tent and were busy cordoning off the area with yards of crime scene tape. Ark lamps had been strategically erected on the perimeter, the technicians preparing to work into the night. To one side of the tent, three well-dressed men – chalk stripe suits, ties, spick 'n' span welling-tons – were deep in conversation, nodding in unison from time to time. Connolly guessed they had to be either board members from the NRA or government representatives.

On the crest of the bank, a batch of uniformed gardai endeavoured to hold back a rabble of protesters. They'd charged from their position alongside the main motorway, their intention to barge their way into the restricted area. Behind them, on the motorway itself, activity was temporarily halted as the workers who'd been erecting the median strip cast curious glances towards the embankment.

On the brow of the bank, a fat, distressed uniformed officer yelled into his phone, demanding immediate backup, his words drowned out by the demonstrators. These hardened protesters, blow-ins from outside the Tara area, had, on previous occasions, attacked workers, smashed equipment and thrown rotten eggs at local politicians – their very own personalized contribution to protecting the tranquillity and peace of Tara's national heritage.

Connolly lifted the tape to allow himself and McFadden into the restricted area. Crouching to pass through, McFadden's left foot came free from its fancy boot, the graphic daisies remaining stubbornly bogged down in the earth. To prevent herself from falling she reached for the support of Connolly's shoulder. 'Ah, shite,' she said, attempting to balance on the one foot while the other hovered inches above the wet muck. Connolly, finding her predicament amusing, hunkered down to extract the embedded wellington. His attempts to guide McFadden's foot back into the boot was greeted with jeers from the protestors, temporarily distracted from their *raison d'être*.

'Sorry 'bout that,' she said to Connolly, finding the presence of mind

to give her detractors the finger. She was annoyed, thinking she probably looked silly in front of her boss. She'd had a crush on him when
she first worked under his command. Connolly was fond of her,
comfortable with how they worked together as a team, but he had
never, not for a moment, thought of her in anything like romantic
terms. Bridie had soon realized and had accepted that a mingling of
hearts was never going to happen. Being sensible, she didn't mope or
bemoan her unrequited passion; instead she put her relationship with
him on a sound professional footing and contented herself by looking
for love elsewhere.

Connolly was about to say something when he saw state pathologist,
Dr Mary McElree, approach. 'Well, if it isn't Detective Inspector
Connolly,' she said, her smile just this side of flirtatious. 'Is this your
case?'

'I'm hoping you can tell me,' he replied. 'Tell us first, who are the
dudes in the Armani suits?'

'Oh, them,' she said glancing to where the three men stood. 'They
were dropped in by helicopter, would you believe. Got here before me.
They're here to make sure that this discovery doesn't delay work. The
tall one in the middle is Dr James Kerrigan, chief archaeologist, and the
other two are from the road authority.'

'I recall a time,' Connolly said with a wry smile, 'when archaeologists had beards, wore tweeds and sandals and used high-frame bicycles
to get from site to site.'

'Ah, yes,' McElree agreed, 'but that was before the Celtic Tiger came
and gave them notions of grandiosity.'

'Isn't that the truth,' Connolly replied. 'You know, I think we lost the
run of ourselves there for a while.' He returned his gaze to the activity
of the pathologist's team. 'So tell me, what've we got here?'

'Come with me,' McElree, beckoning him and McFadden to follow.
'See for yourselves.' Wearing white protective overalls and footwear
sheathed in polythene covers, the pathologist moved through the damp
clay with an ease that defied the detectives. Connolly had worked with
McElree previously and liked her no-nonsense approach to procedures.
Walking behind her now he found it hard to ignore the lithe movement
of her body and the sensual curves delineating her derriere, attributes
undiminished by her shapeless overalls. From experience he knew that,
quite apart from her good looks and shapely figure, McElree was one
of the best forensic scientist he'd ever worked with.

Three white-suits moved out of the way to allow McElree and the detectives through. McElree dropped to a crouch and pointed to a hollow in the earth. 'What we found,' she said, 'are the remains of a sack, a pile of bones – human bones – and a piece of rope … the kind kids skip with; it was used to tie the neck of the sack.'

'You're positive the bones are—'

'Human? Absolutely, no question about it,' McElree said, answering Connolly before he'd asked the question. 'You'll recognize the clavicle, scapula, spine and lilac crest and of course the skull. We're still sorting out what else we've got but it's evident there are ribs, vertebrae, humerus, femur, fibula … everything you'd expect apart from metacarpus, metatarsals and phalanges.'

'Male or female?'

McElree turned her head to look up at Connolly. 'My guess is female.'

'Your guess? You can't say for certain?'

'Well, no, not with certainty, but there are indicators: the shoulders on a female skeleton are usually narrower than the male; a shorter ribcage and a bigger pelvic opening. We'll know better when we get this into the lab.'

'What about age? I mean, how long do you think this person has been dead?'

'Again, a bit early to say but my guess is—'

Her words were drowned by the increased hubbub coming from the protesters. A melee had broken out between the mob and the police, placards and truncheons being used as weapons. 'Looks like our eco warriors have found their true vocation,' McElree said, raising her voice to be heard.

The disturbance, Connolly could see, had to do with the arrival of the media, in the shape of reporters, press and television cameras, all of them anxious to secure pictures and cover the story. In the middle of the scramble, he spotted Emma, notebook in hand, hungry as the rest to capture the moment. McFadden waved to Emma but failed to get a response. 'Can you believe it?' she said to Connolly. 'Emma didn't see me.'

'Doesn't see any of us,' Connolly added with an almost imperceptible shake of the head.

'It's like she's blinkered when she's on a story.' McFadden observed.

'Blinkered,' Connolly said, nodding profoundly this time. '*Blinkered*,' he repeated. 'Now, there's a word to conjure with.'

After much pushing, shoving, whooping and hollering, the protesters, encouraged by the press attention, managed to smash through the police cordon and scramble down the side of the embankment.

CHAPTER 11

NXIOUS TO EXAMINE the final edition of the morning paper Emma leant across her desk to read the front page lead:

WOMAN'S BONES FOUND

Editor's choice of words, not hers. It was, she thought, a somewhat disingenuous headline. Held out the promise of something it couldn't deliver. Beneath the 92pt. Times Bold typeface, the narrative read:

Yesterday, near the Hill of Tara, workers unearthed human bones while working on a slipway exit road attached to the M3 motorway. Work was halted to allow experts to examine the find. Garda officers were called to the scene when protesters attempted to push their way into the restricted area. After heated hand-to-hand scuffles in which the garda had to resort to their batons, the rioters were pushed back and the examination of the site resumed. The area in question, ten minutes from the town of Navan, forms part of the Tara-Skryne Valley and has been the subject of ongoing protest against the motorway. The most recent rally involved 1,500 people who'd formed a human sculpture in the shape of a harp on the Hill of Tara, which spelled out the words 'SAVE TARA VALLEY'.

It's not possible to confirm at this stage whether or not the bones belong to one of the three women who have gone missing in recent months. Relatives of Joan Keating, Siobhan O'Neill and Annette Campbell have been informed and plans are in train to bring them to the location should it turn out that identification of any one of the missing women is confirmed. Dr James Kerrigan, archaeologist, who arrived on the site by helicopter, cautioned people against jumping to conclusions before a more thorough examination of the bones could be undertaken. The initial inspection, he said, inclined him to believe the find did not belong to the distant past, and didn't, therefore, fit within his terms of reference.

Mr Tom Reilly, NRA, said everything possible was being done to let the relatives of the women know who the human remains belonged to. 'It's important,' he said, 'that disruption to work on the motorway is kept to a minimum.' State pathologist, Dr Mary McElree refused to speculate on who the bones might have belonged to, saying she needed time to organize a more detailed examination under proper lab conditions.

Emma, less than happy with how her report had turned out, sat down and booted her computer. She had hoped to get something more substantial from Dr McElree but the state pathologist had failed to deliver. What she'd said had been measured, as though holding back on some important aspect, afraid to speculate on the true implication of what the body parts represented. *Must do better*, Emma admonished. Later in the day, she would attend a joint press briefing organized by the NRA and the Garda Information Office. Hopefully, by then, forensics would have established the status of the bones. Meanwhile, she would attempt to open up her own line of inquiry. Ever since she'd visited the house Mary Shaw shared with her parents, a half-baked idea gnawed at her brain. Mary Shaw's attacker had been thwarted but he had reduced the poor woman to a nervous wreck. Mary Shaw would spend the foreseeable future hiding behind a locked door, attending to her elderly parents. This prospect, and the action that had precipitated it, posed a series of questions in Emma's mind.

What if the failed abductor and possible would-be rapist had been responsible for similar attempts on other women? Who's to say he didn't succeeded on other occasions? And if he did, had the crime been reported? What if Mary Shaw's attacker was responsible for the disappearance of the three women? What if he already had a criminal record? She was clutching at straws, sure, but these questions, she decided, would form the basis of an article. She would surf the *Post*'s database, bring up previous records of sexual attacks on women; they could be significant. Her fingers danced above her keypad for a second, not actually touching the keys, a little idiosyncratic ritual she indulged in before commencing work. She had just double-clicked on the database icon when her phone purred.

Moira, front desk receptionist. 'Gentleman to see you, Ms Boylan,' she said. 'Name's Vinny. Says you'll want to see him.'

Emma took a sharp intake of breath. 'Show him into reception. Tell him ... *oh, damn* ... tell him I'll be down in a few minutes.' She replaced the phone, sighing out loud. *I don't need this.* They'd been legally separated for the best part of two years. Last time she'd seen him had been at his father's funeral. That had been a year ago. Bidding a final goodbye to Ciarán Bailey had been a harrowing experience. Vinny had attempted to lay a guilt trip on her, saying, 'It broke Dad's heart when you ... when we ... separated.' She'd felt like bolting from the graveyard to get away from Vinny, get away from death. But Vinny had seen to it that her agony was protracted, insisting she meet all his and Ciarán's friends, neighbours, aunts, uncles, cousins, their children, most of whom she hadn't seen since the day she'd married him. After an eternity, she'd escaped and made it back to the apartment, back to Connolly. A lot of water had gushed beneath the bridge since the break-up with Vinny. Pain and baggage remained. Guilty feelings lingered. Dark memories that refused to dissipate.

Why does he want to see me now?

She rested her chin in the cusp of her hand, unconsciously tilting her head forward, the tip of her index finger tracing the contour of her nose from bridge down to her lips, a habit she involuntarily employed when in deep contemplation. *The escalator, yes, I'm back there, parking the car on the shopping centre's top-level, walking to the escalator ... there's a push, I'm propelled forward, sent tumbling downwards, hitting against the edge of the steel-teethed flight of steps, falling, hurting, bouncing into shoppers. Blood everywhere, blood on my face, blood in my eyes, a sea of blood. Stopping abruptly, the world funnelling into a black vortex, shoppers surrounding me, a forest of legs, elongated arms, distorted hands reaching down to me. And then a face, a familiar face ... Vinny's face. His face swims out of focus, the world swims out of focus. There is nothing: a void, no sounds, nothing, just blackness.*

She withdrew from the reverie, knowing she had to face Vinny. Checking her face in her compact mirror, she freshened her lipstick and tucked a few loose tresses of hair into place.

Vinny Bailey looked happier than she'd seen him in a long time, a self-satisfied grin lighting up his face. He still dressed in the somewhat idiosyncratic manner she remembered, unfettered by any serious consideration for current trends. But there had been a subtle change; for once his ensemble – tan shoes, straw-coloured cavalry twill trousers, reddish-brown tweed jacket and chequered open-neck shirt – looked as though a modicum of deliberation had gone into the selection.

'Emma, good to see you,' he said, embracing her, kissing her lightly on the cheek. 'Sorry to barge in unannounced, but, well, I just happened to be passing, thought I'd—'

'Good to see you,' Emma said, easing herself from his clasp. 'You're looking great ... I mean it ... really good.' She wasn't lying, it was easy to see why she'd been attracted to him all those years ago. They'd met at a time when she'd been investigating the death of a powerful businessman. He had just turned his back on his involvement with the Irish Republican movement. Unwittingly, he had become immersed in her assignment. Their relationship, initially hostile, moved unexpectedly onto a romantic plain ... and all the way to the altar.

The man who'd played such a major part in her life now stood in front of her. Smiling. He still retained his looks, straight nose, pronounced dimples and generous lips that revealed strong, even teeth when he smiled. But his looks, she had discovered, counted for little when their marriage hit the buffer zone. 'Let's sit down over here,' she said, gesturing towards seats in the corner of the reception area.

'No, no, not at all, I'm fine, honest, I was just passing, wanted to say a quick hello ... let you know I've taken your advice – the advice you gave me last time we talked.'

Emma cocked an eyebrow. 'Advice? Sorry, what advice was that?'

'As I recall,' he said, smiling with warmth that had little conviction. 'The words you used were, "Get a life".'

'I don't remember ...' she started to say, but she *did* remember, and it increased her unease. She was aware that while Vinny continued to smile, a degree of edge had entered his voice.

'Of course you remember – "Get a life" – your very words. What you were really saying was, "get the hell *out*" of yours. So, I did just that. I've found myself a partner, a nice girl – an air hostess. Name's Gina. Didn't think it would ever happen again – love and all that fluffy stuff – but, *c'est la vie*. She's the best thing to happen to me since, well....'

'Vinny, I'm so pleased for you. That's great news.' Emma had hoped for just such a development. For too long she'd felt guilty about the manner of their parting. The separation had been unpleasant. Upset everyone. Her parents, gutted. Vinny's father, shattered. She hadn't set out to hurt anybody but events had charted a course that led to the

marital upheaval. After she'd lost their baby, self-loathing and recrimi-
nation reigned supreme. Vinny put on a show of magnanimity, avoided
apportioning blame for what happened. She hated him for that, hated
the look in his eyes that failed to cloak censure.

Seeds of resentment took root. Veiled hostility. She'd begun to hide
things from him like, for instance, the fact that she'd decided to go on
the pill. He'd wanted her to get pregnant straight away. She'd had no
such desire. Her deception, when discovered, reverberated to the very
end. After obtaining the separation, Vinny went into a state of denial,
begged her to reconsider. And yes, at one point, in total exasperation,
she'd told him to 'get a life'.

'Sure I can't get you a coffee?' she asked, feeling uncomfortable,
perplexed by the fixed smile on Vinny's face.

'Sorry, haven't got a minute, Emma, have to dash. Truth is, I wanted
you to be the first to hear the news. I'm actually on my way to the
hospital to visit Gina … and our newborn son.'

Emma stiffened, the old animosity and suppressed memories igniting
afresh; her thoughts yoked to a guilt that refused to go away; the loss
of her baby returning with all the force of the experience itself. She
struggled to find her voice, her mouth suddenly dry. 'That's great, really
… what can I say. Congratulations.'

'I'm one lucky sucker,' Vinny said, studying the shocked expression
on her face, liking what he saw. 'I've been blessed with the most
precious gift a man can receive from a woman. I knew that you, more
than anyone, would understand what being a father means to me.'

Emma hesitated, feeling ashamed, confused, wanting to argue, give
him a piece of her mind, but she did nothing, just nodded wearily. The
words *newborn son* reverberated round her head like a recurring echo
from a dark place.

'I'm off,' Vinny said, much to her relief. Emma remained static as he
embraced her and kissed her cheek. She stood there, trance-like until
he'd left the building. 'Bastard,' she hissed, through clenched teeth, her
body surrendering to an involuntarily shudder. Instead of taking the lift
to the newsroom, she found herself on the stairs, something she rarely
did. Step by step, with a plummeting feeling, she replayed every word,
every expression, every gesture that had just transpired. Vinny had said
he'd been on his way to see the baby but Emma knew that the *Post*
building was nowhere near the route to the hospital. He had deliberately gone out of his way to bring her the news, to twist the knife

already deep in her guts, let her know he'd found a woman who could give him a replacement for what she'd taken from him.

Once more, she found herself being pulled back in time, back to the hell she was destined never to escape from:

Dr Rose Pattison gave her hand a little comforting squeeze. 'Losing your baby must seem like the end of the world right now,' Dr Rose said, 'but no permanent damage has been done.' Emma pushed her head back into the pillows, emotionally exhausted, a pain, more mental than physical, rocking her body. She wanted to scream but couldn't summon enough energy to give vent to her feelings.

The doctor's kind eyes looked into hers as she mouthed words, technical jargon that, to her, represented little more than abstract sounds; explanations about uterus haemorrhage, pneumothorax, feotoplacental perfusion, severe trauma and suspected perineal weakness – just meaningless utterances. No matter how the words were reshuffled only one truth remained: her baby was dead. Dead. The ultrasound scan had established the absence of any heartbeat in the foetus.

Vinny had seen the danger, had warned her, begged her to be careful. Her parents had voiced concern, as had Bob Crosby and Connolly. The whole goddamned world, it seemed to her, had screamed its warning but she'd remained deaf to it all, believing she knew better than all of them. In spite of this advice and warnings, she'd persisted in believing that she was above the weaknesses of others ... that she was wiser, more intelligent, less susceptible to such adversities. Christ, what grand conceit.

Back in front of her computer, her fingers mimed an erratic tattoo above the keyboard, her soul in turmoil, the unappeasable fury slow to uncoil. She brought up the files but her concentration was shot, her heart no longer in it. Her mind strayed to thoughts of her forthcoming marriage to Connolly but, unbidden, a mental image of Vinny swamped her thoughts. What if her second marriage ended like the first? Did she want to run that risk?

The vision of Bob Crosby approaching her desk brought the disturbing musings to a halt. He leaned his rear end on the side of her desk and glanced at the monitor. 'Why are you digging in the database?' he asked.

'I'm compiling a list of rapists who've been convicted over the past half dozen years, and those who've been released after serving time.'

'I imagine the investigation team have already done that.'

'I'm sure they have.' Emma said.

'So, what's the point of you—'

'I think,' Emma snapped, 'it might be a good idea to let our readers see the extent of the problem.'

'You could be right but I think you should hold off for the moment.'

'Why?' she asked, glaring at him.

'I've heard a whisper that we're about to get something on the bones that will change the course of the investigation.'

'Oh, one of your famous whispers,' Emma said with more edge than she'd intended. 'What precisely did this whisper tell you?'

'I have this friend who has a contact in pathology. The contact says we'll soon have information that's going to play big, real big ... if it's true.'

'What? What is it, tell me?' Emma had long experience of Bob Crosby's network of contacts. His thirty-five-year career in the newspaper business had gained him connections in just about every branch of the country's activities, many stretching back to college days.

'We'll be told officially later today,' Crosby said, removing his weight off the desk, 'but I'm reliably informed that three femurs have been identified among the bones found at Tara.'

Emma swivelled in her chair. 'Femurs? Wait a minute, the femur – that's the thigh bone, yes? Each of us have two of them ... and you're telling me – what – that three have been found? That means—'

'It means that the remains of more than one body have been found.'

WITH A SNORT of derision Matthew McDonagh looked the commissioner in the eye. 'Yes,' he snapped, 'the scars are still visible, but no, I've no intention of showing them to you.' His earlier transposition of Laurel and Hardy's physiques to the men in front of him still prevailed but he no longer derived any merriment from the linkage. Apart from the shared set of body proportions he couldn't imagine two more disparate sets of personalities.

Ensconced in the same conference room they'd occupied previously, Senator McCann ferreted three eight-by-ten black and white photographs from a folder and passed them to Judge Collins. 'We don't ask out of voyeuristic desire,' McCann said, 'it's just that—'

'Just that ... *what?*' McDonagh snapped. 'You get off on this, take pleasure in humiliating me, have me jump through hoops—'

'No, no, Matthew, of course not,' the senator insisted. 'We only ask because we think it will bolster your case.' To accentuate the sincerity he sought to espouse he leaned further forward than usual, his hands pressed together in a steeple that would do credit to the Archbishop of Canterbury. 'We have photographic evidence of the injury inflicted on your person during your detention in the Beaumont Industrial School but, Matthew, you know as well as I do that it's a fallacy to claim the camera never lies. Of course it does. Photographs can be faked, don't you agree? They can be altered, interfered with, doctored in darkrooms, digitally manipulated. It's only reasonable that we should wish to put the question of your injuries beyond all doubt.'

Matthew sought refuge by transporting his mind to a state of benign existence outside his body. The psychologist who'd examined him after his release from industrial school and subsequent breakdown had explained this abnormality as being a way to leave or absent himself from a situation of overwhelming conflict or pain; an escape mechanism to deflect the horrors being visited upon him.

'I'm here to talk about the abuse meted out to me,' he heard himself say. 'I'm *not* on trial. I won't allow you to degrade and humiliate me. I'm here to report on the cruelty I witnessed, to lift the lid off the state-run institutions – what were really concentration camps for kids – where child rape was perceived as a perk for those in charge; for nuns, monks and priests, all of them sexually dysfunctional adults, monsters who in their day held privileged positions like the two of you enjoy today.'

Judge Collins' fleshy face reddened as his great bulk shifted uncomfortably in the chair, as though some hidden restraint held him back from attacking Matthew. Perspiration appeared on his forehead. The senator's reaction was no less pronounced; he flinched as though struck across the face, his elbows lifting from their position on the table, his body sinking back into his chair, every muscle and nerve in his face and body a-quiver, only his spectacles and hairpiece remaining inanimate.

Judge Collins, first to recover his composure, leafed through the file in front of him, one page at a time. 'My function, Mr. McDonagh,' he said with pronounced deliberation, 'is to inquire into child abuse that took place in institutions of the state. To probe such issues, I depend on people like you to provide evidence by way of testimony and the procurement of relevant documentation. To be specific, I – that is, we, the commissioners – need you to furnish incontrovertible evidence of wilful, reckless or negligent infliction of physical injury. We need affirmation that failure to care and protect you has resulted in serious impairment of your physical or mental wellbeing.'

Collins paused for a response. When it was clear that a response wasn't forthcoming, he continued. 'May I add, Matthew, that we are impressed by the dignity, courage and fortitude with which you have thus far endeavoured to recall the painful events from your past. As you rightly state, you are not on trial, nor should you be. I do not act in my official capacity as a judge. I want you to think of me as someone who will champion your cause, seek to assert your rights. Talking to us allows you to avoid protracted litigation and provides an opportunity for you to process the case in a less adversarial manner than would be the case were you to pursue your cause in a court of law.' The judge paused again, hoping for a response. Getting none, he continued. 'So, Matthew,' he said, in what he supposed was a conciliatory tone, 'would you talk to us about the abuse you experienced at the Beaumont?'

Matthew nodded his willingness to continue. He told how, in that climate of fear, their lives were regulated and too disciplined to allow for differences in their physical and emotional development, how, in particular, those children with intellectual disabilities were brutalized and sexually assaulted by their supervisors, and by some of the older residents as a matter of course.

Removed, yet present, Matthew saw himself as the two commissioners saw him. Tense. Pathetic. Defeated. His waxen face, down-turned mouth and uncertain chin, slumped shoulders, closed chest and overall effete figure, might well have been that of a corpse were it not for the flexing of his fingers and the involuntary jig of his left leg. His voice sounded disembodied, his deep-set eyes lost to the world, his consciousness detached from his physical being.

'One of my duties,' he heard himself say, 'as an altar boy, was to help Father Troy prepare the gifts to be offered at Mass. I had to make sure the prayer books, the censer and candles were ready for the service. To do so I had to get to the sacristy before either Troy or the other altar boys. I liked this task, liked wearing the surplice and soutane, was glad to get away from the drudgery and discipline of the school, if only for an hour and a half. I can tell you about one specific occasion, an event that stands out in my mind.'

The version he was about to relate would not include a certain detail that he felt would not enhance his case: *he'd arrived in the sacristy with the intention of indulging in a spot of devilment that involved playing a favourite trick of his on Father Troy. He'd filled a little bottle with pee before going to the chapel, something he'd done a few times before. Alone in the sacristy, he'd poured it into the carafe of altar wine.*

Leaving this information out, he proceeded to relate the incident.

'I arrived earlier than usual – I needed to get away from a gang of lads who wanted to beat the crap out of me – and I'd just assembled the various items in order when I heard a strange moaning noise. I couldn't tell where the sounds came from but after a few seconds I realized it was coming from the music room – that's a small room next to the organ gallery at the back of the chapel. I listened as the moans continued and decided to investigate.

'I made my way up the chapel's central aisle and climbed the steps to the organ gallery. I heard several low groans as I tiptoed to the music room door. Sounded like someone was hurt, in pain. I was nervous, afraid, but I turned the handle, pushed open the door. I couldn't believe my eyes. Two men, partly undressed, lay together on the floor, their hands groping each other. I recognized Father Troy straight away; the other man's face was turned away from me but I later discovered he was our maths teacher, Brother Bernard. As soon as Father Troy saw me he tried to cover up what he was doing and yelled at me ... told me to get the hell out. I backed out as quickly as I could, banged the door shut and dashed back to the sacristy.

'Sister Marie-Theresa was there when I burst into the room.'

'Who was this Sister Marie-Theresa?' the judge asked.

'She was the sacristan. She made the Communion wafers and laundered and starched the cambric napkins for the chalice. She was also choir mistress and she taught us the hymns.'

'OK, I see. Carry on, tell us what happened.'

'Well, when she saw me, she said, "Oh, it's you, Master Matthew. What has you running in the house of God like the Devil himself is after you?"'

'I could hardly speak, and anyway, I couldn't tell her what I'd just seen. But she knew something was wrong. She ruffled my hair the way she liked to do and kept asking me what happened. Sister Marie-Theresa was much younger than the other adults at the Beaumont; she didn't pick on me like the rest of them. She was still trying to coax an answer from me when Father Troy and three servers entered the sacristy. Sister Marie-Theresa bid the priest good day before getting on with the job of filling the chalice with the Communion and pouring wine into a cruet. As the lads slipped into their altar gear Father Troy gave me a look that I knew meant trouble. When we got to the altar I found it hard to concentrate. I forgot to ring the bell during the consecration of the Host.'

Here, Matthew decided to omit the real reason for having neglected to ring the bell: *he'd been so excited by the thought of Father Troy drinking the contaminated wine that he'd lost track of what he was supposed to be doing.*

'I watched Father Troy take the wafers from the chalice with his fingers and place them on people's tongues, aware of what those same fingers had been up to in the music room earlier. I was glad when the Mass ended, anxious to get out of my vestments and away from the chapel as quickly as possible. But, as I was leaving, Father Troy clamped a hand on my shoulder, said, "You, hold on! There's a little matter I wish to discuss with you."

'The lads glanced at me as they left. They'd heard rumours about Father Troy's weakness for *hand-jive* sessions – our euphemism for masturbation – and assumed that was why I'd been held back.

'Of course, I knew the real reason. I waited in silence, fearing the worst, watching from the corner of my eye as he changed into his daywear. When he was ready, he leaned down to speak to me, his face inches from mine. I can see him still, the hairs sprouting from his nostrils, the nicotine-stained teeth, the smell of eggs and cigarettes on his breath. Ghastly. He said, "What you think you saw today didn't happen. Do you understand?"

'I nodded, mumbled that I understood. Just then Brother Bernard strode into the sacristy. He was about thirty, half Father Troy's age. He was fully dressed now, dog collar and all, clasping an open fan belt in his hand, the one he used it in class to tear strips off us.

'He glanced at me, gave me the benefit of his superior smile, but he let Father Troy do the talking. "We need to impress upon you the kind of thing that's likely to happen should you ever talk about what you thought you saw."

'He pushed me across a chair and yanked my trousers down past my knees and said to Brother Bernard, "I want you to teach this little retard a lesson he can bring with him to the grave."

'The beating began. At first I bit my tongue, tried not to cry. I was thirteen, hated to give them the satisfaction of seeing me bawl. But as the ferocity of each stroke increased, as the belt cut into my flesh, I screamed ... continued to scream.

'I was still screaming when I heard someone shout, "STOP!"

'Sister Marie-Theresa had come back to the sacristy. She saw what they were doing. The onslaught stopped. She demanded to know why they were beating me. They called her some terrible name – I can't remember what – and told her to get out, telling her it was none of her business. She stood her ground, demanded answers, threatening to tell the bishop what she'd seen. After a heated argument, Father Troy told her I had deliber-ately neglected to ring the bell during the elevation of the Host and that I needed to be taught a lesson. The nun refused to accept this explanation and insisted she be allowed to take me into her care. They were opposed to this but when she threatened to make a report to the bishop – and Rome itself, if necessary – they allowed her to take me to her quarters to attend the injury they'd inflicted. They agreed that she would be responsible for my wellbeing for the remainder of my time in the Beaumont.'

Matthew stopped talking. He appeared dazed and perhaps a little relieved.

'Did this young woman, this nun, protect you from further hardship in the Beaumont?' Judge Collins asked.

Matthew exhaled noisily. 'She tried her best, yes, but nothing and no one could offer total protection against the evils and cruelty that permeated every aspect of the regime in the Beaumont.'

Collins nodded, looked at his watch. 'We'll leave it at that for today,' he said. 'I think one more session, two at the most, should suffice to put this to bed, tie up the loose ends.'

'Loose ends?' Matthew said, not bothering to hide his irritation. 'What else is there to talk about?'

Senator McCann flicked through his notes and cleared his throat. 'Well, Matthew, there's the little matter of your conviction for assault and attempted rape. I'm afraid we have to take that into consideration before awarding you a settlement. Questions will be asked if we're seen to hand money to a person on the sex offenders' register. So, we have to satisfy ourselves and the taxpayers that your conviction can be attributed to the treatment you received in the state's institutions. Should be little more than a formality.'

'So why bother?'

'We must adhere to the rules,' Judge Collins said, opening his briefcase to insert his papers.

Matthew continued to sit as the two commissioners made their way out of the room. He was thinking: one trial over, another ongoing. Earlier, before setting out for his meeting with Laurel and Hardy, he'd had a call from the Garda Síochána. They wanted to interview him about the women who'd gone missing. Being on the sex offenders' register meant they came knocking on his door every time a woman or child went missing or was attacked.

He'd read about the three women who had gone missing, hard to miss it; saturation coverage on radio, television and newspapers. Two months earlier, he'd been questioned about Joan Keating, the first of the trio to disappear. Two detectives beat a path to his door, accusing him of abducting the woman, demanding to search his premises, examine his mode of transport – which in his case was a ten-year-old Land Rover. He'd been polite, cooperated freely, answered their questions, provided an alibi for the period during which the woman had vanished. Sometime later Siobhan O'Neill went missing. Same two detectives on his doorstep again. 'What have you done with her?' they wanted to know.

He'd found it difficult to hide his irritation but allowed them to go through their usual routine.

And now, they wanted to ask about Annette Campbell. They'd called a week earlier, gone through the same old dance. He thought his answers had satisfied them but apparently not; why else would they want to talk to him again? He knew he could answer their questions, back them up with proof if necessary. Wasn't a problem.

CHAPTER 13

S EATED IN THE front row, Olympus recorder to hand, Emma eaves-
dropped on her fellow journalists as, together, they waited for the
speakers to appear behind the baize-covered table. Like the other
media personnel present she'd heard the rumours. Always rumours;
lifeblood of the newspaper industry. Some plainly daft. Hard-won experience had taught Emma to refrain from rushing into print without first
establishing source references and proof. Besides, what had she picked
up? Nothing she hadn't already gleaned from Crosby.

The press conference was running late. Convened in Tara's newly
built High Kings Hotel and jointly organized by the NRA and the
Garda Missing Persons Bureau, it should have started fifteen minutes
earlier. The older hacks looked to the top table, decidedly unimpressed.
The young Turks appeared content to sip mineral water, shoot the
breeze. None paid the slightest attention to the room's decorative walls,
all of them blissfully ignorant of the colourful tapestries depicting
ancient Irish high kings, scholarly monks, Vikings, Normans, castles,
high crosses and the local spectacular Neolithic passage grave at
Newgrange.

Suddenly, the room went quiet. Chief Superintendent Smith made an
appearance. He was followed by state pathologist, Dr Mary McElree;
chief archaeologist, Dr James Kerrigan; Edward Black, CEO of the
NRA and Detective Inspector Connolly. No fanfares. The chief super, in
full braided uniform, welcomed the media, and introduced his companions. Approaching retirement, Smith retained a strong, open face, his
once handsome features only slightly diminished by time, his assertive
voice as authoritative as ever. He swept the audience with eyes that
missed little, his granite expression lingering for a moment on Emma
before moving on. He liked to keep the fourth Estate at arm's length,
providing them with the bare minimum of information at his disposal,

and only then when its content contained the possibility of provoking a positive feedback from the public. Having one of his top officers 'sleeping with the enemy', as he termed Connolly's liaison with Emma, was an irritant he would prefer to do without.

After welcoming the media, he did what he usually did when facing an audience; he launched into a criticism of their role in crime reporting.

'As yet,' he said, measuring his words, 'there are no proven links between the missing women and the discovery of bones in the Tara location. However, because of ill-informed media speculation the time has come for us to dwell on the facts, clear the air, so to speak. To that end, may I suggest that you journalists gathered here today take more time to reflect on your profession and strive to perform your obligations to society in a more qualified way. Let me make one thing abundantly clear: it is the function of the police and the courts to protect the public against criminality; that's what we're paid to do. This function should never be usurped by the media or considered part of the media brief.'

Audible groans came from the floor.

'I am perturbed,' he continued, 'by the lowering of standards and tabloid mentality I've seen in Irish journalism in recent times. How do we – I mean *you*, the media – measure up when compared with your colleagues in the rest of Europe? Not good, it pains me to say, not good at all. In places like Sweden and Holland, the press voluntarily refrains from publishing personal information about people involved in police investigations yet, I'm sorry to say, that kind of restraint is all too frequently absent in your reportage.'

Longer groans this time.

The chief super pretended not to notice. 'To help you achieve a proper and balanced account of the pertinent facts with regard to the discovery of the bones in the Tara area, I've invited representatives from the relevant bodies to address you.'

Dr James Kerrigan, the chief archaeologist was the first of these representatives to speak. He imparted information of an academic nature, historical data of little interest to the press corps. He went on at length about Tara's pre-Celtic monuments and buildings, some dating back to the Neolithic period around five thousand years ago. He talked about the stone pillar known as the Lia Fáil – Stone of Destiny – that stood atop the hill, and its significance as the place where the High

Kings of Ireland were crowned in ancient times. He droned on about the rebellion of 1798 when the United Irishmen formed a camp on the hillside and were subsequently attacked and defeated by British troops. The Stone of Destiny had to be moved to mark the graves of the four hundred rebels who died in the battle. Only after he'd delivered his long and tedious discourse did he get to the one point relevant to his audience. He assured them that the buried bones did not belong to ancient royalty or any of the long since buried rebels.

Edward Black, CEO of the NRA, spoke next, raising the boredom threshold to a whole new level, his delivery meeting with barely concealed apathy. He appeared to take credit for the fact that the Hill of Tara had been included in the World Monument's Fund, the watch list of the one hundred Most Endangered Sites in the World, and Tara's inclusion in the Smithsonian Institution's fifteen Must-see Endangered Cultural Treasures in the World. When a voice from the floor asked him if he was not the one responsible for the endangerment of Tara's cultural treasures, he became flustered, waffling on about the infrastructure the NRA were providing, how their endeavours were serving the needs of tourists who wished to visit the site, how the NRA deserved credit for allowing commuters get to their places of work without being held up in traffic bottlenecks.

Only when Detective Inspector Connolly spoke did the reporters find reason to go for their notebooks.

In chronological order, Connolly listed the actions undertaken since the time of Joan Keating and Siobhan O'Neill's disappearances, through to the current position with Annette Campbell. Aided by a PowerPoint presentation, he produced images of the three women on a large monitor, positioned on the wall behind him so as to provide uninterrupted sightlines for everyone. He talked over a series of graphics, providing background information on each of the women, outlining the measures taken in the investigation – actions that sounded positive – while cloaking the fact that, in reality, they had gained little in the way of a breakthrough.

Several hands shot up in unison. Emma remained silent, impressed by Connolly's ability to trot out answers to one tedious question after another, as though finding them insightful. After enduring ten minutes of this mind-numbing discourse, she decided it was time to put her oar in, ask a few thought-provoking questions, give him something worthwhile to work with, cut to the chase. She stood up, looked Connolly in the eye, determined to come across as a neutral observer, the cool, detached professional. 'I'm Emma Boylan from the *Post*,' she began in what she hoped was her most authoritative voice. 'Can you tell us, Detective Inspector, with any degree of certainty, if the bones discovered do, in fact, belong to any of the three women at the centre of your investigation, and if they do, can you provide us with a name?'

'No, Ms Boylan,' he replied, deciding, like her, to strike a professional note. 'To answer your question, we have invited the state pathologist here today. She will talk to you presently.'

'But surely it's up to you,' Emma pressed on, determined to get him to commit himself to providing the answer. 'You represent the forces of law and order here today; that's why you're up there, is it not? You've talked about Joan Keating, Siobhan O'Neill and Annette Campbell; surely it's up to you now to let us know whether or not one of these women has been found.'

Connolly smiled, attempting to hide his irritation. Chief Superintendent Smith failed to suppress a smirk, intrigued by the spectacle of Connolly being taken to task by his lover.

'Yes, Ms Boylan,' Connolly said after careful consideration, 'I do have the information you seek, but I have decided to allow Dr McElree to address you regarding that very point because she can provide the kind of forensic explanation that, coming from a pathologist rather than me, will be more readily understood. And, I think now might be a good time to hand over to her.'

'Thank you, Detective Inspector,' Emma said, sitting down, mortified that by trying to be clever she'd unintentionally pissed off Connolly.

The state pathologist thanked Connolly with a beaming smile that Emma thought looked genuine. McElree asked in a soft, attractive Munster lilt for the lights to be dimmed, explaining that she wanted everyone to see more clearly what she wished to show. Wearing a knee-length tailored pale blue skirt, a demure white silk blouse and navy blue jacket, the subdued light cast her profile into sharp relief: short chestnut-brown hair, prominent cheekbones and flawless skin. All in all, a fetching portrait.

'The first picture,' she said, adjusting the image on the monitor, 'shows the bones as they were when we arrived. It shows the sack that contained the bones and the length of rope used to tie the neck of the sack.' As each image appeared, she worked the cursor with nimble dexterity to highlight the various bones, giving them their proper anatomical names. When an image of three femurs materialized on screen, a murmur arose from the assembly. This was the image they'd been waiting for, the image that would dominate all television news bulletins and front-page reports the next day. McElree confirmed the obvious: the bones had to have come from more than one person.

'Unless we're dealing with *Jake the Peg ... with the extra leg*,' an elderly reporter joked, a reference to an old Rolf Harris tune, a reference that meant nothing to most people in the room. Nobody laughed.

Another reporter asked the pathologist if she could confirm that the Tara Bones had once belonged to two of the missing women. The question brought a hush to the room. McElree held the silence for a second, then nodded, acknowledging the seriousness of the question.

'I can tell you with an *absolute* degree of certainty that the bones do not, I repeat, *do not*, belong to Joan Keating, Siobhan O'Neill or Annette Campbell.' The pronouncement brought an avalanche of questions from the floor. McElree indulged the hubbub for several seconds before holding up a hand for silence. 'Let me show you what we've found,' she said, sounding like a teacher bringing order to a bunch of kindergarten children. 'Firstly, I'd like you to look at this picture of the sack and the rope. Our examination of the sack material and its state of deterioration tells us that it has been buried for two years at the very least but definitely not more than six. Likewise, the rope shows signs of having been buried for a similar period.'

McElree zoomed into a close-up detail on the bones. 'We have tested the bones under the most exacting lab conditions and have discovered one particular aspect that could be quite significant. We have identified a series of discoloured indentations on the surface of the bones, cuts that could have been made by a knife, a big knife, a butcher's knife perhaps. Also, we have found indications that some animals might have stripped the bones ... for the flesh they may have contained.'

There was an audible gasp from the press corps.

'You don't mean rats?' a prominent television reporter asked.

'No, not rats, the teeth marks – if they are teeth marks – are way too large to belong to any variety of field vermin. Besides, I believe the marks were made somewhere other than the site where the bones were found.'

Emma's hand shot up.

'You mean, wherever the victims met their deaths?'

McElree nodded. 'Yes, I'd say that's a safe assumption.'

'Anything else you can tell us about the bones?' Emma pressed.

'Well, yes, there is one other factor ... something that the public may find distressing,' she said, enlarging part of the image on the screen. 'It's evident that the joints are more distressed, more discoloured than the main bone surface in general. This indicates that they've been exposed to a greater degree of wear and tear.'

The elderly journalist who'd cracked the joke earlier found his voice again. 'Any idea why, or what would account for this?' he asked.

'A good question,' McElree acknowledged. 'I've only come across one example of this before; it could be that we're looking at something similar.' She paused for a second and made a slight twitch of the mouth before continuing. 'I think these bones, and the bodies they once supported, were subjected to fire.'

'Fire – *subject* to fire...?' Emma questioned. 'Do you mean...?'

'I mean ... they were probably roasted,' the pathologist answered.

CHAPTER 14

TWO DAYS TO go before the big St Patrick's Day bash, 17 March, Ireland's national holiday. The *Post*, like most of the other daily papers would operate a skeleton staff. This year, Emma was one of the lucky ones to have the day off. So, for her this Paddy's Day (the irreverent term that had, for the most part, replaced the full respectful designation due to the country's Patron Saint's feast day) offered a well-deserved break, a chance to leave the city and drive to the village of Slane to be with her parents.

This visit home would be different. Unlike previous breaks, Connolly would accompany her. She would use the opportunity to ease the strain her parents were having in accepting Connolly into the bosom of the family. The cause of tension had to do with the forthcoming marriage. She had two whole days to think about how best to handle the situation, maybe face down a few uninvited rogue thoughts that had invaded her consciousness since Vinny's unexpected visit to the *Post*; his announcement that he'd become a father and his implied criticism of her culpability in the miscarriage – *you killed our baby* – and his unspoken condemnation of her part in their failed marriage – *you wrecked what we had*. She found it hard to rid herself of negative introspection and had begun to question her own suitability to embrace marriage again.

She wanted to believe that this time it would be different. This time she'd found true love. This time she'd met her true soulmate. But a vague disquiet, lodged somewhere in the nether regions of her brain, reminded her that she'd once harboured the selfsame convictions in regard to Vinny. Love and hate, she'd come to realize, were different sides of the same coin. She shuddered, remembering the Road to Damascus moment of revelation – less lofty than St Paul's, admittedly – when she'd realized she no longer loved Vinny, felt no pleasure in his company and felt no desire whatsoever to remain with him. Towards the end, making love had become a passionless predictable ritual. She'd no longer felt the need to fake orgasms, a factor Vinny seemed not to have noticed. She often wondered what went through his head during those times. Didn't bear thinking about. He'd probably been contemplating procreation as he huffed and puffed his way to ejaculation. Even now, as the shudder subsided, she was unable to banish that awful moment when the realization hit her: her marriage to Vinny was a sham.

Newborn doubts assailed her. Did such doubts bother Connolly? she wondered. *Surely not.* His unlined face and policeman's eyes created a mask she was aware even she could not penetrate. He'd been annoyed with how she'd behaved at the news conference, telling her afterwards what a pain in the arse she could be without even trying. They'd verbally sparred, each giving as good as they got until, as usually happened, they ended up in a clinch with the inevitable consequences: they made love. So very different from anything she'd ever experienced with Vinny. With Connolly, making love was always a roller-coaster ride, exposing every nerve ending in her body to the most exquisite torture and delight. With him, she'd discovered the earth-shattering experience of multiple orgasms, an explosive convulsion that brought animal-like utterances of unbearable pleasure from deep down in her soul. Bound together, hearts thumped as one. Sublime ecstasy. They'd touched, teased, kissed, devoured and explored each other, gasping for breath, their naked sweating bodies rising and falling in perfect rhythm.

She smiled dismissively, realizing that she'd been comparing two lovers, realizing too, that it was a pointless exercise, one that only added to, rather than cleared up, the domestic chaos doing the rounds of her head. She parked it in a holding area within the nervous system, knowing she would have to get her head straight on the subject of her forthcoming marriage to Connolly sooner rather than later. But meanwhile she had less than an hour to work on an article for the next edition of the *Post*.

Her front-page piece on the *Post*'s current issue revealed that the Tara Bones did not belong to Joan Keating, Siobhan O'Neill or Annette Campbell. Of course the internet, as well as every radio and television station had already run the story well before the *Post* hit the streets, a point Connolly enjoyed telling her at every opportunity. The fact that he was right just added salt to the wound. Delayed time-lags represented a major downside in printed media, something she found frustrating and difficult to get around. Competing with the more immediate forms of communication limited her ability to be first off the blocks with breaking news, not to mention exclusive scoops. On this occasion, she could live with it. Disclosure about the bones, irrespective of how the message had been conveyed, brought a degree of comfort to those who needed to cling to the idea that an outside possibility existed that the missing women could still be alive. It was probably a forlorn hope, but better than no hope at all. Emma focused on the more immediate questions: if the Tara Bones didn't belong to any of the three women, and weren't part of long forgotten ancient burials, who did they belong to? She'd discussed the quandary with Connolly the previous night but he was unwilling to speculate, saying it was a fruitless exercise at this point, telling her that his energies were concentrated on finding out what had happened to the current list of missing women.

She'd done little else but think about this perplexity since the state pathologist revealed her findings. Who had put the bones in a bag and hidden them? Who? If the bones were female – as the pathologist suggested – what had happened to those females? Had they been reported missing? Were they murdered? The pathologist mentioned fire, intimating that the bones might have been subjected to a roasting process. Jesus! Emma didn't want to think too deeply on that but it gave her a bad feeling in the pit of her stomach.

Initially, before the so-called Tara Bones had come to light, Emma had been about to examine the mysterious circumstances surrounding Siobhan O'Neill's disappearance. This was the area Crosby had instructed her to concentrate on. But before she got to that, she decided to explore a strand of investigation she hoped would provide more worthwhile material for her article.

Her brainwave was born out of the interview she'd conducted with Mary Shaw, the woman who'd been assaulted at the bus stop. What if circumstances had been different, what if the youths who'd saved her hadn't arrived? What might Mary Shaw's fate have been? Raped? Missing? Injured? Disfigured? Murdered? Emma trawled the computer's archived *Post* files, needing to find if any other similar incidents had been reported.

It amazed her to discover just how many sexual predators were out there, criminals who'd come to the attention of the courts. It brought to mind something she'd once read in a James Ellroy book, a crime story where the author talked about perverts, peepers, panty-sniffers and pimps when referring to low life in America. His description struck Emma as being relevant to the Ireland of today, a place that had long since shed its image as the island of saints and scholars.

She read the names on the sex offenders' register, made a note of those who'd been linked to assaults with intent to rape. Creeps, all of them. She brought up files with headings like – Abductions, Paedophiles, Psychotic, Convicted Rapists, Released Rapists. Every imaginable deviation was there: child abuse, pederasty clerics, parents' incestuous relations with sons and daughters, sports coaches interfering with children, the list seemed endless. The files contained more than enough information to incorporate into her article. Hard to believe that only one in every four rape cases reported to the police ended up being prosecuted. This was an area where the newspaper came into its own; here at least, the press could provide in-depth analysis, a distinct advantage it held over its radio, television and online competitors. In an age that elevated the sound bite to king status, the printed media still retained the capacity to accommodate comprehensive detail in their reportage. Even so, Emma realized that readers, conditioned by this faster and more immediate age of Twitter and Facebook, had come to expect a certain degree of brevity.

It was important to infuse a human dimension into what she'd distilled from the files, give readers a handle, a hook, to come to grips with what was, essentially, a list of ugly statistics. Easier said than done. Employing her self-edit discipline, she selected a number of items to reflect the overall tone of corruption, brutality, vice and depravity.

The missing persons file was exactly what its title proclaimed. She looked at the records for the past six years. People, young and old, male and female, had gone missing. Some had been found, others hadn't wanted to be found; sad stories all of them. A child of six, who'd been on a holiday with her parents in a caravan park in Tramore, had vanished in broad daylight. A schoolboy, aged ten, who'd set out for his home during lunch break, never arrived there. The abandoned car of an elderly television producer was all that was found after the man had been reported missing. A young farmer's body had been found in a freezer four years after his disappearance. So many stories to choose from. Most without happy endings. Some with no endings at all. But for the article she was putting together she would concentrate on women who'd gone missing during a specific time frame.

With this decision made, she honed in on cases that had a chilling similarity to the current case of missing women, women who'd disappeared in the Leinster area and hadn't reappeared. Mindful that the state pathologist had stated that the Tara Bones had been buried in the ground for at least two years but not more than six, Emma focused on reports filed within those time limits. In the older cases, the women, like the current missing trio, had been going about their everyday business one minute, then had vanished into the ether the next. Emma printed off their files with a view to selecting the pertinent factors. It was old news, sure, but publishing it might jog someone's memory, shed light on the cases. When she'd discussed this angle with Connolly the previous night, he'd poured cold water on the notion, saying that the cases she referred to had been investigated to an exhaustive degree and that regurgitating them at such a highly emotionally charged time would only serve to upset relatives and reignite the hurt they'd experienced at the time. He had a point, Emma conceded, but it hadn't deflected her from pursuing that line of inquiry.

Searching for correlative points of interest, Emma read through past articles that dealt with physical and sexual abuse. Gross, stomach-turning stuff. The cruelty and violence that people inflicted on each other made her feel nauseous. Apart from everyday drug induced carnage, there were the familiar alcohol-fuelled domestic rows, break-downs between couples who'd walked up the aisle a few years earlier, swearing to love, honour, and obey, only to go at each other's throats as soon as the honeymoon ended. Some didn't even make it through the honeymoon. Sad, sad reading. She decided not to incorporate this material into her article, thinking there was no good reason to depress her readers any more than they, perhaps, already were.

After much consideration she decided to concentrate on two rapists who'd served time for their crimes and were now enjoying their freedom, at large in the community. She needed to contact the two men. The files she'd printed off identified the ex-cons and gave details of their physical data and their addresses. The only thing missing was their telephone numbers. Within a matter of minutes, telephone inquiries provided Emma with both numbers. Emma dialled the first.

'May I speak to Cathal Watson, please?'

'Cathal no longer lives here,' a woman answered. 'He's gone to live in Australia. I'm his ex-wife. What did you want him for?'

'Oh, it's nothing, nothing important,' Emma said. 'Sorry to have bothered you.' She hung up without further explanation and dialled the second number. 'May I speak to Matthew McDonagh?'

'Speaking,' a guarded voice answered. 'Who is this?'

'Name's Emma Boylan. Can you spare a few minutes to talk to me?'

'Depends on what you want to talk about.'

Emma was prepared for this question. 'I'm doing research into how the state helps people re-engage in everyday society after they've been released from detention.'

'You're a reporter?'

'I'm an investigative journalist, yes. I'm with the *Post* and I've been looking into—'

Click!

'Damn you,' Emma said through clenched teeth. She'd drawn blanks with both calls and was about to return to the files when Crosby approached, his breathing laboured as though he'd just climbed the Twelve Pins in Connemara – all twelve of them. He wanted to know if her feature was complete, reminding her of the public's insatiable appetite for more on the story. 'The thing about the bones being burned has got their imaginations in a spin,' he said, easing his large posterior against her work bench. 'The red tops are in their element, suggesting cannibalism, human sacrifices and the devil knows what. That's the kind of dumbed-down crap we're competing with. That's why I've asked you to look into the Siobhan O'Neill case – it's recent, still fresh in everyone's mind. Please tell me you've come up with something solid, something for the readers to latch on to?'

Emma deftly sidestepped her inactivity on the Siobhan O'Neill case, describing instead the feature she'd spent the best part of a day putting together. Crosby's nod of approval helped. When she talked about the unsuccessful calls she'd made to the two rapists who'd served time, he expressed the opinion that she was on the right track. 'If we're to connect with our readers; we need to understand the impulses that drive the predators to do what they do, we need to get down 'n' dirty in the gutter, crawl inside their heads, poke around the cesspools of their minds, however warped and sick that may prove; we need to look at the despicable acts they perform ... from their perspective.'

'Couldn't agree with you more,' Emma said. 'Unfortunately, one of the two ex-rapists I wanted to talk to has buggered off to Australia; the other hung up when I admitted I was a journalist.'

'Why'd you want those two in particular?'

'The crimes they committed happened within the same time frame as the disappearances of the earlier missing women.'

'Well in that case, Emma, the choice is clear: we'll cite both cases.'

'Even though I didn't speak to either of the perpetrators?'

'In a funny way, that works to our advantage.'

'How do you make that out?'

'Had you succeeded in getting them to talk, they would've insisted on certain restrictions. They would probably seek an injunction against publication. They've served their time ... won't want the past raked up. This way, you can quote from the records, use what's already in the public domain.'

'What happens when they claim we didn't allow them put their side of the story?'

'But we did, I mean *you* did. Don't you see? Our telephone records will show that you made every effort to offer them an opportunity to talk.'

Emma looked dubious. 'That's not quite accurate. I didn't manage to contact Cathal Watson so, in essence, he wasn't afforded the opportunity to put his side of the story.'

'You're splitting hairs, Emma. Didn't you say that he'd gone to Australia? And, didn't you also say that you made an effort to track him down? So where's the problem? Never let an awkward unknowable factor get in the way of a good story. You with me?'

'Sure, if that's how you want to play it, Bob. Give me half an hour and I'll pop the article up on your monitor.'

Crosby was all smiles as he moved his bottom off Emma's work space. 'Tomorrow, Emma, is the day before St Patrick's Day. Our readers will be able to hold the edition over for the big day itself ... they'll have oodles of time to watch the parades on television and read your *oeuvre*.'

Emma nodded, her fingers poised above her keyboard, ready to complete the feature. She felt better having discussed it with Crosby. But his mention of St Patrick's Day reminded her again that the holiday break she intended to share with Connolly and her parents was less than twenty-four hours away.

CHAPTER 15

HOW MANY MISSING WOMEN?

EMMA BOYLAN Crime Correspondent

The level of fear among women caused by the recent disappearances of Joan Keating (29), Siobhan O'Neill (34), and Annette Campbell (35), remains at an all time high. Women now look at strangers in a different light. Who can they trust? Illustrative of this new climate of fear, one woman in the Swords area claims that she now keeps her runners on instead of her heels when going to work. This reflects the measures some women are prepared to take to ward off what they perceive as an ever-present threat.

Is their fear justified? Certainly, crime rates in the country have increased dramatically in recent years. In the past decade the number of women murdered in Ireland averaged out at ten per annum. In eighty-eight per cent of these cases the women were killed by their partner, their ex-partner or someone known to them. In the remaining twelve per cent of cases, the killers remained elusive, unconnected to the victim and consequently more difficult to bring to justice. But the cases that present most difficulties are those where the victims have disappeared. Many of these investigations remain unresolved, leaving unanswered questions like: Was the victim dragged away kicking and screaming, to be exposed to who knows what, or did the missing person wish to leave their family and friends behind? Both scenarios are equally intolerable. Those left behind must deal with what is, essentially, a bereavement, even though no body and no killer has been found. They may contact Operation TRACE (Tracing, Reviewing and Collecting Evidence), the Garda's task force set up specifically to investigate the disappearance of women, but, unless someone comes forward with information that heralds a breakthrough, they can provide little, if any, help. That's what the families and friends find so agonizing: not just the

absence of their loved one, but the absence of any plausible explanation.

The revelation that human bones have been unearthed in the Hill
of Tara area is the kind of outcome most feared by those who've
experienced this kind of trauma. This development must have been
particularly distressing for the families of Joan Keating, Siobhan
O'Neill and Annette Campbell. Initially it was feared the bones did
belong to one of the three missing women but state pathologist Dr
Mary McElree has ruled that possibility out, stating that the bones
uncovered had been in the ground for more than two years but less
than six. So, the question remains, whose bones are they? Records
show that during the three-year time frame identified by Dr McElree,
many cases of missing women were reported in the Leinster area but
of these only four were never seen again. Police who investigated
their disappearances remain baffled by the mysterious circumstances surrounding the four cases. Is it possible that a link exists
between these missing women and the current cases? Looking at
the older set of disappearances, the parallels between them and the
current cases are compelling.

Shannon Hughes (27) Harolds Cross, Dublin.
Shannon lived with her parents, Joe and Maura Hughes and her
younger sister Claire. She left her home at 9.30 p.m. on a Friday night,
her intention to meet up with friends in The White Goat public
house, and then to attend a disco later. Shannon was seen getting
onto a bus a short distance down the street from her home. She was
also seen getting off the bus some fifty yards from The White Goat.
But she never met up with the friends waiting for her in the pub. One
of those friends, Margaret Moran, rang her mobile at 10.45 p.m. to
find out what was delaying her. When she got no answer she rang
Shannon's parents. That was the start of the nightmare. No trace of
Shannon has been found in the three years since.

Melanie Sweeney (31) Newbridge, Co Kildare.
Melanie shared a flat with a friend, Trish McKinney, in the town of
Newbridge and worked in Ryan's Bookmaker shop. On Thursday 24
Sept she left the flat at 8 p.m., telling her flatmate that she needed to
collect her laptop from her workplace. She never returned and there
is no evidence to show whether or not she made it to Ryan's

Bookmakers. She'd left all her possessions, including money, credit cards, passport and some mild medication, behind in the flat. Melanie's friend Trish and her family – who live in Sligo – found it difficult to get the Gardai to treat the disappearance with the urgency they felt it merited. Three years later, no sightings of Melanie have been reported.

Rachel Fagan (24) Sycamore Drive, Longford.

Student nurse, Rachel Fagan, was returning from her evening shift at St Joseph's Hospital, Longford, when she went missing. Rachel shared an apartment with three other student nurses and was not missed until the following morning when they returned from their shifts. Thinking that Rachel might have gone to stay with a friend, they remained unconcerned until the following day when she failed to turn up for her shift in St Joseph's. The police set up the usual procedures to trace her movements and interview everyone who knew the student nurse, but, to date, no trace of Rachel Fagan has been found.

Alison Hogan, (30) Ballinderry, Mullingar, Co Westmeath.

Alison Hogan, a single mother with a 3-year-old baby boy, worked in the County Buildings, Mount Street, Mullingar in the planning department. Alison went missing on the evening of the 12 Nov, on her way to pick up son Darrel from the Little Chiselers crèche. When she failed to turn up at 5.45 p.m., the crèche immediately contacted the local Gardai. A nationwide search began with television, radio, internet and press appeals. The media's inclusion of photographs of Alison's baby ensured that the case built up the kind of human interest that Madeleine McCann's kidnapping received in 2007 when Madeleine went missing in Portugal's Algarve region. Like Madeleine, Alison Hogan's whereabouts remains a mystery to this day.

All four cases fall neatly within the three-year time period that Dr Mary McElree specified when referring to the Tara Bones. Is it possible that what was unearthed could be the remains of one or more of those four women? And if it is, how did it come about? Who was responsible? Are the police following up on this line of inquiry?

The possibility that the four cases referred to above were incidents of sexual violence that went wrong must surely be given some consideration. Records of successful prosecutions brought against persons accused of aggravated sexual assaults and rapes during the period that Dr McElree singled out are worth closer examination. Seven of those who received custodial sentences are still behind bars. Three others have since died and five have been released. Details of the five who have been freed are contained in the sex offenders' register. These offenders were obliged to notify the gardai of their place of residence within seven days of being released. One of these five, John Grennan, with an address in Lucan, Co Dublin, has since been arrested and imprisoned on a charge of armed robbery in which the owner of a post office was severely wounded. Another of the five released men, Joseph Flanagan, is currently attending a sexual behavioural clinic in Britain for counselling and psychiatric evaluation to deal with his deviant and compulsive sexual obsessions.

Peter Casey, another of the prisoners has found religion. He has joined the third order of the Brothers of the Sacred Heart of Jesus, a division that consists of laypeople who wish to spend their days in contemplative prayer, making amends for past occasions of sin.

Cathal Watson, who served his time for two cases of aggravated rape, walked free from Arbour Hill Prison in Dublin's inner city three months ago, the event illuminated by rapid-fire flash photography from within the large media scrum camped outside the prison's gate. He fled to Australia within days of release, failing to provide the gardai with the address he intended to reside at in Australia. The authorities in Australia have been informed of this development but to date, they have not been able to apprehend Watson.

Matthew McDonagh is perhaps the best known of those who've been released. Three years ago, he gained a certain degree of notoriety on account of the huge publicity his court case and subsequent imprisonment attracted. Judge Rory McCall found him guilty on a count of attempted rape. His victim, Kathy English, lived with her partner in a flat in Beggar's Bush. Evidence had been produced to show that Ms English had been beaten, punched, slapped, and kicked by McDonagh when she tried to resist him. He was in the act of forcibly dragging her into his car when people from the area, who'd heard the shouting and screams, hurried to her rescue. Outnumbered, the attacker fled the scene but not before several witnesses made a note of the registration number on the departing car.

Contacted by the *Post*, Mr McDonagh refused to comment on the case or talk about the recent disappearance of women.

CHAPTER 16

HABITUAL MORNING GROUCH DS Bridie McFadden usually found something to moan about before her 11 a.m. cuppa. But not this morning. Approaching Connolly's desk she appeared bright and bushy-tailed, more cheerful than she'd been for a long time. The next day being Paddy's Day might have accounted for the change, that, and the fact that she was due the day off.

'Could have a breakthrough on the missing women,' she announced. 'We've got Jenny Higgins in interview room 2.'

Connolly eased his copy of the *Post* down from his face and looked up. He'd been about to read Emma's article for a second time.

'Sorry, Bridie, remind me, who exactly is Jenny Higgins?'

McFadden had never known Connolly to forget a name in one of his investigations no matter how insignificant or peripheral. She looked at him with a quizzical tilt of the head. 'She's the young one who's moved in with Stephen Murray.'

'Oh, yes of course, they got together after Annette Campbell disappeared. What's she doing here?'

'You're going to love this: she's filed a complaint against Murray. Claims he assaulted her.'

'Now that is interesting,' Connolly said, pushing his chair back from his desk. He glanced at his watch before folding the copy of the *Post* and placing it in the top drawer of his desk. The newspaper, which he suspected had been left by Superintendent Smith, had caught his eye as soon as he'd entered his cubicle earlier that morning. Conveniently, it lay open at the feature with the headline that read *HOW MANY MISSING WOMEN?* Connolly had glanced through the article, surprised to see that Emma had concentrated on a list of previous missing persons, going against the advice he'd given her when she'd asked him about the wisdom of pursuing such a course. It never ceased to amuse, and annoy him in equal measure, how Emma so often asked for his advice and then, pig-headedly, ignored his views and went out of her way to take the opposite direction. *Why am I not surprised?* He readily acknowledged his failings when it came to his relationships with women and took little solace from the old Samuel Beckett admonition: *Ever Failed – try again. Fail again, Fail Better.*

Emma's article, for him, represented yet another failure – he'd failed to prevent its publication, and in all honesty he could hardly claim to have *Failed Better.* She'd been diligent with her research, though, he couldn't fault her on that count, but it irritated the hell out of him that she'd included such specific details on the list of convicted rapists who'd served their time and been released.

Not clever, Emma.

In the half-hour since his cursory perusal of the article, he'd answered e-mails, made several calls and settled down to re-read Emma's feature more carefully. He was still considering the ramifications that could follow on from what she'd written when McFadden appeared with the news about Jenny Higgins.

'Why've you put her in interview room 2?' he asked.

'Well, it's freezing outside and the radiator in room 1 has packed up; it's like Siberia in there. So, I thought—'

'Yeah, OK, Bridie, you're right, it is cold today. You've talked to her; has she really been assaulted, d'you think?'

'I think … I think you'd better come see for yourself.'

Two minutes later Connolly, accompanied by McFadden, entered the interview room. Sitting on a metal-framed chair at a small table, a sultry woman acknowledged their presence with a barely perceptible blink. Picked out in sharp relief against the room's institutional green walls, she looked stylishly thin, her face framed by a mass of dark, shiny hair that swept onto her shoulders. She had a short body, long limbs, rouged face with prominent cheekbones, painted lips and big vivid green eyes. Her clothes were quality-casual: red bomber jacket zipped up high, designer jeans and soft leather pumps.

The first thing Connolly noticed, though, was the dark bruises on her neck and the swelling beneath her eyes. Unlike Dorsett and McFadden, he hadn't visited Murray's house so this was his first contact with Jenny Higgins. He quickly established her identity and ran through the required initial formalities. McFadden had a junior organize coffee and chocolate digestives for three and the interview proper got underway.

'Why are you here, Jenny?' Connolly began.

'Why?' she repeated, her accent akin to that of a female Bob Geldof. 'I've already told your sergeant. She knows why I'm here.'

'I'm sure she does but I'd like you to tell me ... for the record.'

'Stephen Murray tried to kill me,' she said, indicating her neck and eyes. 'Would've succeeded if he hadn't been stoned.'

'How long have you known Murray?'

Jenny ignored the biscuits but took a tentative sip of coffee, eyes fixed on Connolly. 'Worked with him in the ad agency.'

'What were your respective positions?'

'He was an accounts executive. I was his PA.'

'His PA? Your relationship was a bit more intimate, was it not?'

'Excuse me!' she snapped, staring defiantly at him. 'I don't see that that's got anything do with you or, for that matter, with why I'm here.'

'OK,' Connolly said, knowing he could revert to Jenny's relationship with Murray later, establish whether or not the affair had begun when Annette Campbell was living with him. 'Is this the first time he attacked you?'

Jenny cradled her coffee cup and thought for a second. 'Stephen can be a rough bastard,' she said, eyes downcast. 'He likes to ... to inflict pain when we ... when we, like, get it on. He's into games, likes dressing up in ridiculous costumes, pretends to be Don Juan or Marquis de Sade, crazy shit like that. He tries to turn the sessions into theatrical productions; uses drugs and erotic music to heighten the high. At first it was, like, different, exciting, you know, passion, pain and pleasure, but I called a halt when it got out of hand.'

'Out of hand ... in what way?

'He's a pervert; he likes to hurt me, wants to insert objects ... gets off on inflicting pain.'

'So, what went wrong? Why are you here?'

She took a deep breath, put her coffee down and exhaled slowly. 'Because ... because ... well, because he was being particularly nasty ... and when I mentioned Annette Campbell he threw the head altogether.'

Connolly glanced at McFadden, registering his surprise at the turn the interview had taken. Looking back to Jenny he saw that her eyes remained downcast, her long slender fingers intertwined, her palms pressed together tight as a sealed oyster shell. Were it not for her injuries, he would've considered her attractive, a bit skinny, for sure, but not bad looking. 'Jenny, look at me, please,' he said. 'I want you to take your time; just tell me what happened.'

Jenny lifted her head, tossed her hair, allowed her eyes to settle on Connolly. 'He ordered me out of his place, which would've been fine except I'd, like, done a runner from my flat ... months behind on rent. So, I pretended to change my mind, agreed to his demands for a kinky encounter. He was beside himself, panting like a dog with two dicks. We shared a fat joint, got a little high before getting down to, like, what he wanted. He persuaded me to put on the chauffeur's uniform.'

'Ever done that before?'

'No, I was surprised when he asked.'

'Surprised? Why would that be?'

Jenny waited a beat before answering. 'I knew the chauffeur's outfit had been taken away by the detectives who came to search the house. They only returned it yesterday.'

'Did Murray dress up?'

'Sure did. Wore a big frilly shirt, big wig, period costume, shiny shoes. I remembered seeing an old clip of Elton John in a get-up like that – thought that's who he was supposed to be, but turns out he was Lord Byron.'

'Ever see *him* wear a chauffeur's uniform?'

'Never.'

'So, you're both wearing fancy dress; what happened next?'

'I asked him why the detectives were interested in the chauffeur's outfit. He flew into a rage, blew a fuse, ranted on about how he would do to me what he'd done to Annette if I didn't mind my own business.'

'You've met Annette?'

'Yes, she called to the agency a few times. I knew – everyone knew theirs was, like, a stormy relationship.'

'OK, so, what did you do when Murray threatened you?'

'Told him I wanted to quit the game.'

'And, did you ... quit, I mean?'

'Never got the chance; he jabbed his fingers into my eyes, grabbed me by the neck, began shaking me.' A bead of sweat appeared on Jenny's upper lip as she spoke. 'I rammed my knee into his balls, knocked him backwards. In the tussle his big fancy watch fell to the floor. When he bent to pick it up I broke free, dashed to the bathroom, locked the door. He chased after me like someone possessed. It was like the scene in *The Shining* where Jack Nicholson breaks through the door with his hatchet. I was shitting myself.'

'Right place for it,' McFadden blurted out, before she could stop herself.

Connolly gave his sergeant a withering glance but Jenny continued as though unaware of the interruption. 'The door didn't budge so he gave up after a few minutes. I was, like, totally traumatized. I could hear him making a noise in different parts of the house.' Jenny rubbed her eyes, leaned her elbows on the table, her breathing laboured.

'We can take a break if you—' Connolly began to say but Jenny wanted to continue.

'Twenty minutes or so later I heard Stephen back at the door again. He begged me to forgive him, said he was sorry, promised it wouldn't happen again. He asked me to come out, said he wanted to give me back my own clothes. I was petrified, didn't know what to do. Eventually, I opened the door a fraction, peeped out. He'd changed out of the fancy dress and seemed to be back to his normal self – if you could ever call his behaviour normal. I took my clothes, changed into them, went to the kitchen. He wasn't there but I could hear him some-where else in the house. I noticed two suitcases on the floor. His passport and an airline reservation sat on the counter top. I was looking at them when Stephen snuck up behind me. "What the fuck are you doing, snooping in my things?" he shouted, pushing me back and slap-ping me on the face. "You've blown it this time, you filthy little trollop," he said. "Should never have taken a dope-head like you into my house." He just went on and on and on, ranting and raving, effing and blinding, making all sorts of threats as he pushed me out the front door.'

'What kind of threats?' Connolly asked.

Jenny swallowed hard, her larynx bobbing up and down her black-ened throat. 'His threats … frightened the life out of me. He warned me not to open my mouth to anybody, swore he'd make me disappear if I talked.'

'You've done the right thing by coming to us,' McFadden said.

'I hope you're right,' Jenny said, sounding perilously close to breaking point, her eyes darting erratically from McFadden to Connolly.

'We can offer you protection,' Connolly assured her. 'We'll bring him in and we'll—'

In a move that threw both detectives, Jenny kicked off her pumps, drew both legs up to her chest, using her heels on the edge of the chair's seat to contort her long-limbed body into a gawkily misshapen ball.

Looked like a circus acrobat preparing to commence some sort of anatomically impossible contortionist act. She ducked her face behind her knees and began to whimper and rock back and forth. Just as suddenly, she lifted her head up again, replaced her feet on the floor but made no attempt to put her pumps back on. She looked at Connolly and McFadden, her expression conferring the status of simpleton on both of them. 'Just how do you propose protecting anybody?' she asked, desperation in her voice.

'We can—' McFadden began to say.

Jenny cut across her, holding her hands out in an imploring gesture. 'You haven't been listening; I *told* you I saw his airline reservation. According to the times on it, Stephen should have touched down in Toronto about an hour ago.'

Finally, Emma made time to visit Siobhan O'Neill's mother. Didn't have much choice; Crosby had hounded her for days, insisting she write a 'human interest' article based on the second woman who'd vanished. The salient facts in Siobhan O'Neill's case had been well documented. At thirty-four, her husband Darren, a salesman, had walked out of her life and moved to Perth, Australia. Her father was dead, her twin brother a pilot and she'd moved back in with her mother. Information already out there. Crosby wanted more. No surprise there. He always wanted more, wanted what he liked to term, 'the story behind the story'.

After taking several wrong turns in and around the Ballsbridge area, Emma eventually found the O'Neill residence, a well cared for red-brick townhouse just off Havelock Square, in the shadow of the magnificent new Lansdowne rugby stadium. Mrs O'Neill invited Emma in as soon as she discovered it concerned her missing daughter. Tea and scones were prepared before the talking began. Three photo albums were produced; each page, each photograph accompanied by a poignant anecdote. The images showed a small, fair-haired athletic-looking woman with a wide mouth and a small, straight nose. She looked smart. Tough. Triumphant.

Mrs O'Neill insisted Emma call her Rosalene, drying her eyes from time to time during her harrowing recital. A petite woman, small like her daughter, she had a pale face, ash-blonde hair and tragic grey-green eyes, underscored with dark circles.

Siobhan's past, captured in the album, would help Emma's article and satisfy Crosby but Emma felt it necessary to get the woman to return to the day Siobhan disappeared, create a picture of the events as they'd happened.

'It was a Thursday night,' Rosalene said with an intake of breath and a deep sigh. 'Never forget it for as long as I live. Siobhan took Scotty – that's our terrier – for his walk. Same route all the time – down Bath Avenue, on to Lotts Road, then Ringsend and back the same way. She always left it late on Wednesdays, Thursdays and Saturdays because of the races at the Shelbourne Park greyhound stadium.'

'Why?' Emma asked. 'What difference would that make?'

'Siobhan liked to wait until the dogs and their owners had left the area after the races. You see, the problem is, if the greyhounds were still around, Scotty would kick up a racket – the little rascal thought he could take them on.' Rosalene smiled at this thought but, almost instantly, her expression reverted to its sad countenance. 'Anyway,' she continued, 'on the night we're talking about, I wondered what was taking Siobhan so long. I figured she'd probably bumped into a friend or something like that but when midnight came and went I got seriously concerned. Then, at about a quarter past twelve, I heard this thump on the front door. Needless to say I rushed to see what was wrong.'

Emma, watching her choke with emotion, handed the distraught woman a paper tissue and waited while she dried her eyes, thinking it best to say nothing.

'Sorry about that,' Rosalene said, regaining control of her emotions. 'When I opened the door, there was poor little Scotty – on his own, lead dragging on the ground – no sign of Siobhan. I knew something awful must've happened. I thought she might have been hit by a car, something like that. I called the gardai straight away, thinking they'd get to the bottom of it, let me know if she'd been carted off to a hospital or whatever. The not knowing was the hardest part, still is. It's a nightmare, a living nightmare. I'm a realist though, I fear the worst – what mother wouldn't – but I pray to God she's out there somewhere. All I want is for her to come home.'

Emma tried to comfort the woman as best as she could, trying to ease her fears while inwardly doubting her own words. Before leaving, she borrowed half a dozen photographs from the album. Mrs O'Neill had given her permission to use them in the article she intended to write.

CHAPTER 17

RICHARD J BRADBURY stood to one side of the crowd outside the Kylemore Café. Like the gathering, he was watching a troupe of American musicians and their cheerleaders as they rehearsed their performance for the next day's celebrations. A scattering of indifferent snowflakes fluttered in the mid-March breeze, the chill factor near enough to skin a whippet. The unseasonal conditions didn't appear to bother the visiting band who, like sixteen other bands from the States, had come to participate in the parade. Wearing decorative military-style uniforms, they performed a rousing rendition of *The Wearing of the Green*, while the high-stepping cheerleaders, pompoms and tutus to the fore, marched on the spot in time with the beat, tossing batons in the air with great gusto.

Wearing his favourite double button Italian cashmere overcoat and fedora, Richard J. Bradbury still felt the chill. So how come, he wondered, the American girls had the ability to keep smiling under such conditions. Exposed faces, midriffs and bare legs remained smooth, impervious to the biting east wind, not a goosebump in sight. As the band struck up Sousa's *Stars and Stripes Forever*, two boisterous young lads clambered onto the statue of James Joyce, a life-size sculpture situated in the centre of North Earl Street, directly across from the Kylemore. The bronze depiction had Joyce cloaked in a long coat, head cocked at a slight angle and covered with a broad-brimmed hat, cane in hand; the landmark was affectionately known by the Dublin populace as, *The Prick with the Stick*. (Statues in Dublin invariably acquire nicknames from the locals, e.g. Molly Malone's statue at the bottom of Grafton Street is variously called, *The Tart with the Cart, The Dolly with the Trolley* or *The Dish with the Fish* while poor old Oscar Wilde's statue opposite his boyhood home on Merrion Square suffers the indignity of being called, *The Queer with the Leer*.)

The two ruffians, perched precariously on the statue's shoulders, used the brim of the bronze hat to secure their grip as they directed a tirade of abusive language and obscene gestures to the high-stepping American girls. 'Look!' the bigger of the lads cried out. 'One o'them Yankee tarts has no knickers.'

'And she's had a Brazilian,' the other one piped up.

A few onlookers guffawed, their eyes busily scanning the cheer-leaders' apparel to see if the girls really had gone commando. The crude banter continued unabated until one of the foul-mouths lost balance and slipped. The crowd gasped. On his way down the lad glanced off a woman, knocking her to the ground.

Richard J. Bradbury, seeing the youth fall, dashed to the stricken woman and helped her back to her feet. The two offenders scarpered, pushing aside those attempting to block their way. Bradbury ignored the shemozzle, his full attention focused on the fallen woman.

'Are you OK?' he asked. 'Did those little shits hurt you?'

The woman nodded, too dazed to speak, her eyes letting him know she was grateful for his assistance. He acknowledged her gratitude with a smile and a reassuring arm around her shoulder. 'Let me get you a coffee,' he offered. 'You need to sit down for a minute, get your breath back. The Kylemore is beside us; it'll do you good.'

'I'm fine, thanks,' the woman said, finding her voice. 'It's the shock … didn't know what happened, that was all. I'm fine now, thanks all the same.'

'That's great. No harm done then; no broken bones. You're a lucky lady.' Bradbury blocked out the chatter of the crowd, the street noises and the rousing beat of the marching band, his total attention fixed on the woman, all the while giving her his full-wattage smile. She was striking, he could see: pretty face, expressive eyes, good bone structure, flawless complexion, understated make-up. Mid to late twenties, he guessed, tidy figure clad in denims and dark blue fleece; a head of auburn hair adorned with a white floppy woollen affair. 'I'd still like us to have that coffee, if you wouldn't mind, that is,' he said silkily, feeling he'd made a connection.

'Sorry, I can't,' she said, sounding as though she meant it. 'I'm working today; just stopped for a minute to listen to the band. I didn't expect someone to crash down on top of me … and I didn't expect to be rescued by a gallant knight in a cool hat. But look, sorry, I have to get back by two o'clock.'

'Where do you work?'

'The bank,' she said, pointing to a building past the 398 foot high pin-like Spire monument in the O'Connell Street junction with Henry Street and North Earl Street (built to commemorate the millennium and nicknamed *The Erection in the Intersection*). 'I work in the building you see on the corner.'

'How about tomorrow? They let you off for Paddy's Day?'

'What! You want to meet me *tomorrow*?'

'Why not! We're talking serendipity here ... fate even. Can't be sure which. What do you say? Tomorrow?'

'This is mad,' the woman said, a giddy smile on her face, 'You do this kind of thing on a regular basis? I mean ... rescue damsels in distress, chat them up? I don't even know your name. You don't know mine.'

'Well now, that's easily rectified; tell me what your name is.'

'This is mad,' she repeated. 'Name's Gemma Moore. What's yours?'

'Pleased to meet you, Ms Gemma Moore,' Bradbury said, taking her hand and kissing it in a playful parody of period manners. 'I'll make a deal with you, OK? I'll tell you my name when we meet tomorrow.'

Smiling, Gemma leaned towards him and gave him a quick peck on the cheek, then turned to walk away. 'Who do you think you are?' she asked, looking over her shoulder. 'The last playboy of the western world, huh? Give me one good reason why I should meet you?'

'Because you want to,' he said. 'And because I have to see you again. I'll be waiting for you in the lobby of the Gresham Hotel at three o'clock. The parade will be over by then. It'll give us a chance to get to know each other a whole lot better, yes?'

Gemma didn't answer. She strode away, giving him a coquettish toss of her head, her back towards him, one hand waving light-heartedly above her head. Richard J. Bradbury's smile broadened as he watched her hips sway with an exaggerated balletic swagger.

You're mine.

Five minutes later he was in the multi-level car park in Marlborough Street. He sat behind the wheel of his Mazda MX-5 feeling elated, pleased with the outcome of his unplanned encounter. Maybe there really was such a thing as serendipity. He'd been spoofing when he'd said it to the woman but it was kind of spooky how sometimes things fell right into your lap, as though preordained. He didn't bother to engage the ignition as he sat contemplating the moves he would make when they met. He angled the central rear-view mirror in order to look at the face that had so easily beguiled the woman. He liked what he saw. The rim of his fedora cast a mysterious shadow on his forehead and eyes; the velvet-collared coat sat proud around his neck, the combination projecting an unequivocal masculinity, masking the face's more prosaic features. He readjusted the mirror to its normal position and picked up the copy of the *Post* he'd left sitting on the passenger's seat. He'd bought it on his way into the city centre earlier, and had glanced through it before stopping to listen to the band. Like most people in the country he'd followed developments in the missing women's story.

His interest was deeper than most. With good reason. He'd been shocked the first time his e-fit image appeared in the media. But after studying the drawing he realized it looked more like a comic book caricature than anything that might resemble him. The identikit, he saw, was reproduced again as a side-bar piece to complement the main feature – *HOW MANY MISSING WOMEN?* – written by Emma Boylan. The *Post* crime correspondent had gone into great detail, referring to cold cases of a similar nature, providing full details of offenders and victims. He had read her earlier reports on the subject of the missing women and had been surprised that she'd made only fleeting references to the man who'd been seen to follow Annette Campbell out from Glynn's Inn. He found it curious that someone who came across as a clued-in crime correspondent should have made no serious attempt to link that occurrence with the missing woman.

Richard J. Bradbury finished reading Emma Boylan's latest article, put it back on the passenger's seat and switched on the ignition. Anyone seeing him drive out of the car park would surely have found the enigmatic smile on his face puzzling.

BREAKFAST TURNED OUT to be a pleasant occasion. Emma's parents, Arthur and Hazel Boylan, went out of their way to make the couple feel comfortable. Connolly, under Emma's watchful eye, was at his most genial. Kept the conversation light. Avoided mention of contentious issues that included any reference to his and Emma's past marriages, and equally importantly, any references to the forthcoming nuptials. That particular topic represented the elephant in the room that no one dared mention. It would come centre stage later – after all, that was the main purpose of the visit – but first they had to observe the expected civilized niceties, and that included taking the time to digest breakfast and let the obligatory chitchat run its course.

On the drive down there had been coolness between them, more an Arctic breeze, really. Connolly was at his grumpiest, a barracuda with toothache. His resentment at having to abandon his pressing caseload in order to attend a tedious parents-in-law get-together had grown to epic proportions since Emma's first reminder some days earlier. On top of this unspoken resentment he remained highly perturbed over Emma's recent piece in the *Post*. His wrath, like a lanced boil, spewed out its venom, given free rein to the acrimony he'd allowed to build up in recent days.

'Your article, Emma,' he said, not bothering to look at her. 'What in the name of Christ did you think you were doing? I mean, what was it supposed to achieve? I'm mystified ... so tell me, tell me how does it benefit anyone? How can it help your readers to be told about ex-prisoners who've served their time?'

'Well, I would've thought that that's pretty obvious!'

'Not to me, it isn't. Enlighten me – tell me what is it I'm missing here.'

'I can't talk to someone who just won't listen.'

'I *am* listening. I'm listening intently. I'm listening to hear some sort of rationale. I'm listening to hear you explain what entitles you to describe crimes of sexual violence that took place in the past. I'm listening to hear you justify the implied insinuation contained in an article that ties in these old cases with the current situation. And, I'm listening to hear you tell me what, apart from titillating your readers with the salacious detail and selling a few extra miserable copies of the *Post*, what your article is supposed to achieve.'

'What the hell's got into you?' Emma asked, taken aback by the outburst. 'How dare you question my integrity; how bloody dare you? My article focuses attention on depraved men who prey on women, monsters who mug, threaten, attack, terrorize, rape, kidnap and in some cases kill their victims.'

'And how is that supposed to help anyone?'

'By highlighting these crimes, by citing examples from our recent past I can make the public aware of the depravity, prick their conscious- ness, force them to become more vigilant.'

'Oh, I see; this is a crusade.'

'Goddamm it, yes, if you want to put it like that. I have a duty as a responsible journalist to do whatever it takes to highlight these crimes.'

'Very laudable,' Connolly said sarcastically. 'But while you're busy putting the wrongs of the world to right, while you're pursuing your personal crusade to bolster your own self worth and influence, why not stop a minute to consider the collateral damage your self-righteous exposé is having on the innocent parties – the families, children, spouses of those who've paid their debt to society. There are always conse- quences, Emma. Have you stopped to think that your article might impede the prospect of rehabilitation for those former wrongdoers? Have you ever considered the fact that your article could act as a touch- stone for the creation of civil unrest?'

Breathing noisily through her nose, Emma hit back. 'I'd like to know how rarefied the air is up there on that high moral ground you occupy. All of a sudden you've become a smoked-salmon socialist, a pinko liberal. Well, let me tell you what you are, Jim Connolly. I'll tell you *exactly* what you are – you're a two-faced phoney, a moralizing upholder of the law who, when the veneer is stripped away, is nothing more than a hypocrite.'

'Emma, now you're just being silly. Shall I tell you—'

'No!' Emma snapped. 'I'll tell you! You have no hesitation in locking up shoplifters, chasing vagrants off the street, arresting poor buggers on the dole when they're found earning a few bob on the side to feed their families; you side and protect developers who throw families onto the side of the road as they attempt to repossess their properties. You allow blue-collar criminals, crooked politicians, fraudulent bankers and corrupt developers and anyone out there with enough money to afford fancy accountants and solicitors to flout the law and get away scott-free. And now, you want to silence me because I've had the balls to draw attention to the evil deeds perpetrated on defenceless and vulnerable women.'

At this point, Emma stopped. She knew her jibes were way over the top, knew too that Connolly resented the injustices she'd mentioned just as much as she did but her dander had been up and she'd wanted to get back at him. It was, she decided, no less than he deserved, and somewhere deep down it made her feel better. The feeling didn't last long. A palpable silence took over after that.

But now, here in her parents' house, she was determined that they put their best foot forward, put the unpleasantness behind them, present a unified and loving front. As a teenager, living here, she hadn't fully appreciated the comfort and security of the place. Like her pals, anxious for independence, she'd taken her parents' love for granted. When she'd moved to Dublin, the city overwhelmed her and delighted her at first but within a matter of months, returning for weekends became something to look forward to.

It would have been nice if this visit resembled one of those pleasant weekend trips but life had somehow become more complicated in the intervening years. So far, she believed, they were doing fine. Perhaps Connolly was overworking the smile a tad, dispensing the bonhomie a little too liberally, agreeing too readily with everything being said, but her parents appeared delighted to see them. In keeping with the St Patrick's Day tradition, Arthur, recently retired boss of Boylan Solicitors, had gone outside to the lawn first thing after getting up to pick sprigs of shamrock.

Hazel, like her husband, was a stickler for the trappings associated with St Patrick's Day. She divided the three-leafed plants into small, tidy sprays, one for each of them. Connolly couldn't help but notice the grace of Hazel's gestures. At sixty-three, she was, quite simply, an exquisite woman. The creamy texture of her skin retained a soft transparent delicacy; her cheeks, faintly rouged and her lips, still sensual, coloured with discretion. If, as Connolly had once been assured, a man wished to know what the woman he intends marrying will look like when she's older, he need look no further than the prospective bride's mother. Connolly suppressed a smile. He had never, until now, given any thought to such a notion but the idea that some day Emma would come to resemble her mother, well, it wasn't all that distasteful a concept.

Taking the sprig of shamrock from Hazel, Connolly was glad she couldn't read the thoughts flitting through his head. He hadn't worn the iconic national emblem since he'd been a boy but, with an almost imperceptible wink to Emma, he attached the spray to his lapel. Emma reciprocated with a barely perceptible wink of her own, the signal amusing Connolly, knowing that she probably assumed his gesture represented contrition for his earlier quarrelsome behaviour, having no idea what had really prompted the coy interplay.

With innate aplomb, Arthur, balancing a silver tray on one hand, produced four crystal glasses filled with generous measures of vintage sherry. He proposed a toast, his smooth baritone voice inviting them to join him in drowning the shamrock. They clinked glasses, said *sláinte* and drank to the nation's health.

The toast out of the way, Connolly offered to help load the dish-washer, his gesture appreciated, but politely rejected, by Hazel. Emma, less than impressed, responded with a glance that said – *no need to overdo it, Jim*. Being more familiar with family nuances, she gravitated unobtrusively to the kitchen where her mother had gone, purposely leaving Connolly alone with her father. Emma's subtle manoeuvre had not gone unnoticed by Connolly; he cleared his throat in readiness to introduce the son-in-law/father-in-law dialogue he'd rehearsed the previous night. Arthur, sensing the detective's awkwardness, made something of an initiatory pawn's move. 'Weather's not bad outside,' he remarked, gazing out the window, his eyes closed to slits. 'I'm going for a walk down by the river. Maybe you'd like to join me … if you feel like a stroll, that is?'

'Great idea,' Connolly said, glad that his dreaded talk had been granted a stay of execution … at least temporarily. 'I'd love to stretch my legs, fill the ol' lungs with some clean country air.' He wasn't lying. A city boy at heart, he liked to get away every so often from the smog and noxious fumes, the congested traffic and the incessant noise; give his respiratory system a chance to replenish and purify itself. Arthur, who took this healthy invigorating environment for granted, looked every bit the country squire: deerstalker hat, Donegal tweed waistcoat and jacket – complete with leather elbow patches – cavalry twill trousers, sturdy leather brogues and, to complete the picture, a knobbly blackthorn stick.

Connolly cut quite a dash himself but, alas, not in a good way. He wore the only outdoor casuals he'd brought with him: commando denim jacket with fatigue design – more Disney than army – heavy-duty chinos lined with multiple empty pockets, and hiker's laced-up boots, yet to be broken in. The immaculate ensemble, original creases still in place, made him look like the mannequin in the Great Outdoors shop window that displayed the outfit on the day he'd bought it. Self-conscious as any city boy would feel in a rural setting, he caught Arthur attempting to stifle a smile.

Didn't help.

On the positive side, sharing the pristine environment with his future father-in-law would, he hoped, create a more congenial atmosphere in which to talk. He would, in all probability have to answer questions about his plans for the future, questions like: Was he in line for career advancement? Would he eventually get away from the daily rough and tumble of fieldwork? What were the prospects of being promoted to the level of commissioner? Had he plans to move out of the apartment, invest in the kind of house that might befit his social standing? As yet, Arthur hadn't asked any of these questions but Connolly fully expected they would come.

Moving away from the elegant three-storey period residence, they could hear the echoes of running water making its way through the rich pastureland. A shift in the breeze carried the raw countryside fragrance to Connolly's nostrils, the rare experience giving him an overwhelming sense of wellbeing. He had taken this very same walkway before on the occasion when he'd come to talk to Emma in the wake of the loss of her baby. And it had been amid this same verdant scenery that he'd fallen in love with her on that day. He could never have imagined then that one day – today – he would be back again, using the same backdrop, to talk to Arthur Boylan about marrying his daughter.

Chatting more easily now, the two men strolled along the tree-lined pathway that led to the banks of the River Boyne. Arthur, in an expansive mood, shared his vast wealth of knowledge on the various aspects of the local scenery, its inhabitants and its history, his pleasantly malicious tongue deriving great pleasure in recounting salacious scandals that involved exalted personages from the locality. Laughter came easily to the retired solicitor but it was evident to Connolly that the mirth was merely a cover for what was a very astute mind.

As they neared the banks of the Boyne the roar of the river's swell became the dominant sound. An overcast sky imposed a tumultuous reflection on the water's swirling surface as it raced through a stretch of rapids on its way towards the multi-arched stone bridge that allowed access to Slane village.

Using his blackthorn stick, Arthur pointed to the eighteenth-century Slane Castle which stood partially hidden behind dense woodland on the far side of the river. 'That's where the outdoor pop concerts are held,' he said, sounding somewhat ambivalent. 'Never went myself ... didn't have to; could hear the damn noise from my garden. Hell of a racket! Not my kind of music – Rolling Stones, U2, Bob Dylan, artists like that. I'm more a Tony Bennett person myself. I do remember that Emma once brought a bunch of her friends to see ... what's his name? Bruce Springsteen. In fairness to her, she was young at the time.'

Connolly, beginning to feel less outside his comfort zone, talked about his likes and dislikes in music and entertainment, all the time waiting for Arthur to bring up the subject of marriage, but instead Arthur seemed actively to avoid any mention of it at all. As both men gazed across the water, they heard a birdcall that went *qurrack-rack-rack ... qurrack-rack-rack*, a sound unlike any Connolly had heard before. 'What is that?' he asked.

Arthur pointed to a marshy area on the far side of the river. 'Well, I don't believe it. Look, Jim, it's a grouse, a red grouse. D'you know, I haven't seen one of those beauties in these parts since I was a lad.'

'I see it ... looks like a pheasant ... with attitude,' Connolly said, struck by the bird's iridescent plumage 'The colours—'

'Hmmm, they're a bit alike, I suppose, but the sound it makes, it's like a bark, don't you think? Quite unique, unmistakable. Did you know that the red grouse is responsible for *The Guinness Book of Records?*'

'Really?'

'True! Happened back in the fifties when a shooting party that included Hugh Beaver, the then managing director of the Guinness brewery, became involved in a discussion over whether the red grouse or the golden plover was the fastest game bird. They searched every guidebook they could find but couldn't come up with an answer. This got Beaver thinking; it struck him that questions of a similar nature were being asked every night in pubs throughout the country. People had a great interest in questions like, for instance, who was the strongest, the oldest, the tallest, the fastest and so on. That's when the idea hit him to create a book with all the answers. And that's how *The Guinness Book of Records* came into being.'

'Never knew that,' Connolly said, his mind still on other matters, still wondering when the real purpose behind the walk would kick in. Thinking about this, he decided he would bring up the subject. 'Arthur,' he said, 'I would like to talk about—'

'Shhhh!' Arthur said, pressing his index finger to his lips. 'Listen, listen, Jim, there it is again … the red grouse's bark.'

At that moment, Connolly's mobile trilled. The look on Arthur's face contained a mixture of annoyance and incomprehension. 'What the devil—?'

'Sorry about this,' Connolly said, sounding as embarrassed as he looked. 'It's Emma. Something's come up. She wants me to come back to the house. I'm really sorry.'

Arthur nodded, stony-faced, before turning on his heel and heading back to the house, his stick stabbing the ground with renewed vigour.

Hazel Boylan, who could have passed for Emma's older sister, broached the subject of Connolly and the forthcoming marriage as soon as the men set off on their walk. Self-reliant, imperturbable and possessing that kind of watchful reserve most Irish mothers have in abundance, her daughter's marriage break-up did not fit comfortably within Hazel's moral compass. Made it difficult for her to come to terms with the idea of a second marriage. Emma had done her best to bring her mother round to a more favourable view of the situation. Wasn't easy.

Trouble was, Hazel had always had a soft spot for Vinny. She saw him as the one who'd been wronged, blamed Emma and Connolly for the upheaval. Emma found it hard to mount a defence; determined not to bad-mouth Vinny or talk about his contribution to the separation, knowing, if she did, it would make matters worse. She'd decided not to mention Vinny's visit to her place of work or tell her how he'd boasted about the woman who'd given him the child she'd taken from him. To compensate, she decided to talk about the good relationship she enjoyed with Connolly. 'He's a good man, Mum. He loves me and I love him. He's very fond of you and Dad. I don't know why you're so dead set against him. There was a time when you couldn't heap enough praise on him. *He* hasn't changed since that time but *you* have. He's still the same kind-hearted man who took the trouble to come down here back when I lost the baby, when I'd lost the will to go on living. He was the one person who understood what I was going through.'

'Yes, he got to you when you were at your most vulnerable … he took advantage of you. He—'

'No, Mum,' Emma said, cloaking the irritation she felt with a smile. 'That's not true, he wouldn't do that. Connolly is the last person in the world to take advantage of anyone. He is the most thoughtful, generous, person I've ever known. When we're together I feel whole, fulfilled, loved, respected and without feeling any loss of my independence. He respects me, Mum, for what I am and for who I am. He doesn't try to control, change or dominate me like—'

Hazel sighed. 'Why do you call him Connolly all the time? I seldom hear you call him Jim. I wouldn't call that a very friendly way to behave.'

'I call him Connolly,' Emma said, this time with a genuine smile, 'because it's what his closest friends, friends like Bob Crosby, call him. I suppose you could call it a term of affection; goes back all the way to boarding days with the Jesuits in Clongowes Wood College.'

The two women continued in this vein, batting compliments and put-downs back and forth like some verbal tennis match. Emma continued itemizing all the wonderful things Connolly brought to her life, throwing words like fulfilment, happiness, understanding, respect, compatibility and fun, about like confetti. Allowing her tongue full reign, she laid it on a bit thick, gilding the lily, she knew, glad Connolly couldn't hear her eulogy. A mocking voice asked if the exaltation might not represent an effort to convince herself as much as her mother, especially if she took the recent difference of opinion that had caused such unease between them into account. She was still extolling Connolly's virtues when her mobile vibrated. 'Sorry about this,' she said to Hazel, 'must be something important. Damn, it's the office, I told them not to ring.'

'Could have switched it off,' Hazel offered firmly but not unpleasantly.

'Hello,' Emma said into the mobile, shrugging her shoulders for her mother's benefit. 'Oh Bob, it's you. Something wrong?' As Emma listened, a pained expression darkened her face. After several seconds, during which she nodded and mumbled the word *yes* repeatedly, she closed the circuit. 'I'm going to have to interrupt the men's walk,' she said to Hazel. 'I'm really sorry about this but something serious has cropped up.'

CHAPTER 19

EMMA HAD THE mobile to her ear when Connolly and her father returned to the house. Hazel stood next to the open fire, the expression on her face letting them know she was not best pleased. Arthur moved to her side, his face mirroring her displeasure. Connolly confronted Emma.

'What the hell's the matter?'

Emma closed her mobile and pointed to the television in the corner. 'Switch it on,' she said, 'I'm told it's on screen right now.'

Connolly turned to her parents, nodding towards the television, seeking their OK to turn it on. Arthur shrugged, as much as to say, Why bother about us? Do whatever you want.

The screen flickered into life.

Floats and bands in the St Patrick's Day parade make their way past the general post office in O'Connell Street. Crowds cheer from behind barriers at the footpath. A commentator is speaking excitedly about the visiting bands and the creativity that has gone into each colourful float as it passes before the civil dignitaries on the reviewing platform.

'Wrong channel,' Emma snapped. 'Try TV3.'

The picture on TV3 showed a group of people chanting slogans outside an ugly decrepit house. Uniformed garda officers stood with their backs to the house, facing down the group. The camera panned to a close-up on the wall of the house, focusing tight on a series of scrawled words:

SEX OFFENDER OUT.

A voiceover is explaining that the house belongs to Matthew McDonagh. A file shot of McDonagh being taken down to serve his sentence at the time of his trial fills the screen. It cuts quickly to current footage. Wearing a coat with a hood, he is returning from a walk with four greyhounds on leads. He appears surprised by the activity and pulls up the hood. Attempting to avoid the media presence he tugs on the dogs' leads to hurry them towards the house's entrance. He isn't quick enough. In a matter of seconds a microphone is thrust in front of his face.

'*Is it true that you've done time for rape?' a reporter behind a hand-held microphone asks.*

'*Never raped anyone,' McDonagh snaps.*

'*But you were found guilty of that crime, yes?' the reporter presses.*

'*I was wrongly accused.*'

'*What? You're saying you are the victim of a miscarriage of justice?*'

'*Yes, now go away! Leave me alone, you're frightening my dogs.*'

'*Is it true you refused to participate in any of the therapeutic counselling and rehabilitation programmes for sex offenders on offer in Arbour Hill Prison?*'

'*Those programmes are for sex offenders, that doesn't include me.*'

'*Why have you shown no remorse?*

'*Remorse for what? I'm an innocent man.*'

'*Have the police questioned you about the missing women?*'

'*Nothing to do with me. I've said all I'm going to say, now would you please get the hell out of my face.*'

'*The story in yesterday's* Post *links you to the investigation into the missing women. Can you comment on that?*'

'*Gutter press! The hack who wrote that will be hearing from my solicitors. Now, please, get the hell away from my property. I have nothing more to say.*'

The camera pans back to the reporter as he approaches the protesters to seek their views.

Connolly switched the television off, facing Emma with anger in his eyes. 'I knew this was going to happen,' he said, his hands clutching air as though trying to grasp some intangible stupidity. 'I told you there'd be trouble but would you listen? Course not, you never do. What in God's name were you thinking, Emma? This ... this is down to you.'

'Who says it's down to me?' Emma replied dismissively.

'Who says? Are you serious? Of course it's bloody well down to you. That's what I've been trying to tell you. What we've seen on the screen is the inevitable consequences of your actions, I mean, come on, what did you think would happen when you gave out all those details on Matthew McDonagh.'

'I was doing my job; I'm a reporter, damnit,' Emma growled, every word articulated with teeth clenching clarity. 'It's what I do.'

'Oh, I see, so that makes it all right, does it? Jesus! Next you'll say you were just following orders.'

Emma swallowed hard. 'Well, if you must know, my esteemed boss – your great buddy Bob Crosby – did approve.'

'And, what, his imprimatur makes it OK? The bit I don't understand is: how in God's name did he allow what you wrote to get into print. What you've done is just plain stupid, Emma, you hear what I'm saying? Stupid.'

'Stupid? I don't believe this. Who's the stupid one here? Three women have been abducted, probably raped, murdered more likely than not, and a convicted rapist has been released early, set free among ordinary, decent people ... to do what? We depend on our police to protect us but you lot just sit on your fat arses getting nowhere fast. At least I've devised a strategy. I'm not afraid to shake the trees, see what falls out. I'm trying to create a breakthrough. Goddammit, I'm doing your job, I'm doing what needs to be done to achieve results.'

'Well, congratulations, Emma,' Connolly snapped, staring defiantly into her eyes. 'You've got a result all right; your article in yesterday's *Post* outlined McDonagh's past in graphic detail and today a bunch of vigilantes are ready to run the man out of town.'

'I'm not the one who let him out of prison,' Emma said, her voice rising, her hands balling into fists. 'What I wrote is already out there – his trial hogged the press, television and radio at the time; it was big news.'

'Yes it did,' Connolly retorted angrily. 'But that was then; this is now. The man has served his time. There isn't a scintilla of evidence to link him to the current cases of missing persons. But your article has managed, by implication, to create a link in the public's mind. He called it gutter press; I call it irresponsible journalism ... at its worst. I thought, at least I *used* to think, that you were above that kind of sensationalism.'

Arthur and Hazel looked on in astonishment as Emma and Connolly tore strips off each other, amazed that the two people who'd appeared so loving moments earlier could turn on each other with such viciousness. Arthur cleared his throat to gain their attention. His tactic worked. Connolly and Emma, in a moment of stark realization, pulled back. Their eyes transmitted an understanding between them, the silent communiqué saying, *What the hell have we just done?* Sheepishly, they faced Hazel and Arthur. The expressions on the elderly couple's faces demanded explanation.

Connolly spoke first. 'I must apologize for—'

'No,' Emma cut in, 'I'm sorry ... can't think what we thought we were doing. It's just that, well, this case, we both care so passionately about it.' Emma laughed, more a snort of embarrassment than mirth. 'This case is difficult for all of us – the women who've gone missing – and Jim has a point, even though I only used information that's already out there, the fact that I drew attention to this man McDonagh – who served time for attempted rape – at a sensitive time like now is, well....'

Her words weren't getting through. The pained expression on Hazel and Arthur's faces said all that needed to be said.

CHAPTER 20

I T WASN'T THE first time Richard J. Bradbury had been to the pleasure retailers shop on O'Connell Street. This afternoon, he took time to browse the merchandise: saucy lingerie at the front; bondage gear at the rear. Smiling, he visualized the shenanigans people got up to with such intimate toys. Crotchless knickers, PVC bras, edible underpants. Unbelievable! Several of the customers were young women, most of whom, to judge by their gaudy green outfits, had attended the big parade earlier. There were a few middle-aged maiden aunt types who, in Bradbury's opinion, might be better served by checking the miraculous medals, scapulars and holy candles in the nearby Pro Cathedral. Bradbury wore his usual hat and overcoat, knowing it wouldn't look out of place or cause undue attention on account of the inclement weather.

He picked out the item he'd come for and moved to a pay station. Ahead of him an American lady with a voice shrill enough to shatter glass had no qualms in engaging the cashier in a discussion about the Rampant Rabbit she'd bought. Bemoaning men's ineptitude in matters sexual, she sought assurance that the item was the same all-singing, all-dancing toy she'd seen in *Sex and the City*. A smile lingered on the cashier's face as Bradbury approached. He paid in cash, preferring to avoid the use of credit cards, cheques, anything that might leave a paper trail.

He walked from the shop back to the car park in Marlborough Street and deposited the item in the boot of his Mazda. He consulted his watch, nodded with satisfaction; the time had come to find out if his plans for Gemma Moore were about to be realized. With an extra bounce in his step, he strolled back to O'Connell Street and crossed to the old Carlton Cinema site, opposite the Gresham Hotel. He paced up and down, glancing in both directions, scanning both sides of the street, his eyes on the alert to spot his quarry.

Pavements remained thronged in the aftermath of the parade; American tourists and a scattering of indigenous families who'd lingered on in the capital's main thoroughfare, parents striving to keep an eye on the children they'd brought to the celebrations. A young drunk with spiky hair and grunge apparel was busy relieving himself against a building site hoarding, bottle of cider in one hand, dick in the other, untroubled by the trickle of urine spreading across the footpath. Bradbury hated to see this kind of vulgar display and would've rebuked the youth had his mind not been resolutely fixed on more immediate matters.

At ten minutes past three his heart gave a flutter. He spotted her.
Better late than never.

Coming from the direction of the Gate Theatre, he watched her head past the Parnell monument, saw her pause at the pedestrian lights, waiting to be allowed to cross to the east side of O'Connell Street. As she waited, mobile to her ear, he couldn't help but notice that part of the inscription on the statue behind her read: THUS FAR SHALL THOU GO AND NO FURTHER. Just as well, he thought, that Gemma Moore didn't see the engraved words. He was doubtful, in any case, that she would be familiar with the line or understand its significance in the fight Charles Stewart Parnell conducted in the British parliament back in the nineteenth-century to achieve Home Rule for Ireland.

She was wearing a white woollen cap, a three-quarter length blue overcoat with white fur-like collar and knee-length black boots, her appearance it seemed to him, even more striking than on the previous day. Richard J. Bradbury took one last glance at his reflection in a shop window, lowered the brim of his fedora to a more rakish angle, and fixed his tie, before making his way across the street. He needed to hurry to get his timing right; important to come face to face with her on the Cathal Brugha Street junction, just a few yards short of the Gresham Hotel.

Game on, he said to himself.

CHAPTER 21

THE VISIT TO her parents' house had been a bit of a downer. No, worse than that – an unmitigated disaster. Everything that could possibly go wrong had gone wrong, and then some. Emma's parents, sceptical about the relationship to start with felt, with some justification, that they'd been right all along. Attempting to convince Arthur and Hazel that the spat represented nothing more than a display of passion for their work hadn't convinced anyone, least of all Emma. Connolly's OTT reaction to her article was, for him, out of character. It brought the whole notion of a second marriage into question, got her thinking seriously on the subject. What was wrong with continuing to live together – maintaining the status quo? It merited consideration. Only since accepting the engagement ring had tensions crept into the easy affectionate spontaneity they'd got used to.

How had that happened? Unbidden, she was back in the moment, the life-changing occasion when Connolly had popped the question. They'd been getting along just fine, no pressure on either side, living in sin as the craw-thumpers liked to say, but loving it nevertheless. She'd just come back from an assignment in London feeling dog tired. As soon as she opened the door he took her in his arms, swung her about in an arc, kissing her passionately in the process. 'What's brought this on?' she asked when he'd finally set her down.

'Will you marry me?' he asked, the question seeming to trip easily off his tongue. Swept off her feet, in every sense of the word, she was rendered incapable of speaking. Connolly then went into Jane Austen mode, down on one knee, taking hold of her hand. 'You can be the most infuriating woman on the planet,' he said, 'but God, I do love you.' Tears welled as she pulled him to his feet and kissed him. The kiss would have gone on forever except that she needed to breathe.

'Yes, I'll marry you, Jim Connolly; I'd be honoured to be your wife.'

She wiped her eyes and allowed him to slip the ring on her finger, a beautiful eighteen-carat gold and single-stone marquis-cut diamond.

Emma tried to recapture that state of happiness on her return from her parents' house. They'd kissed and made up, tangling in each other's limbs with renewed vigour, promising undying love. Yet, Emma sensed that something different, a feeling of disenchantment, had entered the relationship. They'd *had sex* as opposed to *making love*. She'd like to believe that their recent disagreements had been a temporary blip brought on by work-related stress but she began to doubt herself; her mind all over the place, her thoughts shooting off in a dozen different directions at once. She needed time to think things through. The best way to find a solution, solve a problem, she'd discovered, was to park the issue for a few days, a few weeks even, and channel her mind exclusively to her workload.

Connolly had only just left for work when a call came through on Emma's mobile. It was Mary Shaw. At first she didn't recognize the voice, the caller making no attempt at identification. But a few words in, she remembered. It was the frightened woman who'd had a lucky escape from an attack outside the Ledwidge Apartments. 'I saw the report ... saw my attacker on television,' she said, breathlessly, as though struggling to get each word out. 'It's him ... that man they called McDonagh, I recognize him. I know it's him ... those eyes ... I'll never forget them.'

'Would you be willing to—'

Emma heard the click. Mary Shaw had hung up. That was as much as she was going to get. But it helped Emma decide what her immediate course of action should be.

On her way to Matthew McDonagh's house, she decided that the best approach would be to doorstep the man, brazen her way into his house, get him to talk. Her article had thrown a merciless spotlight on McDonagh, a factor that Connolly had taken grave exception to and something that, with the benefit of hindsight, she might have handled a little better. On the televised news clip, McDonagh referred to her article as 'gutter press journalism', and to her specifically as a 'hack'. That didn't bother her, well no, correction, it did hurt – *if you prick us do we not bleed?* – but worse things had been levelled at her during her time with the *Post*. She was a big girl; she'd get over it.

However, McDonagh's assertion that he'd been the victim of a miscarriage of justice could not be let go unchallenged. His claim, whether true or fanciful, provided her with the perfect opportunity to write a follow-up piece. Mary Shaw's call had provided a fresh impetus. Her identification of McDonagh would have been great as a source for what she needed to write but the woman was way too fragile to depend on. Emma needed something equally compelling to give her article credibility; confronting Matthew McDonagh face to face would, she hoped, provide that important ingredient.

Connolly wished his cubicle had a door, a door he could close. The semi-partitioned interior of the Pearse Street Garda station had about as much privacy as a red light window in Amsterdam. People breezed in and out all the time, non-stop activity, everyone wanting a piece of his time. Not quite *Hill Street Blues*, but getting there. Today, struggling to concentrate on his case load, his mind insisted on reverting to his visit to Emma's parents' home. Every conversation, every gesture and action re-enacted, frame by frame in high definition. He regretted the harsh words he had thrown at Emma, regretted that they should have been voiced in front of her parents, but he remained unrepentant for the views he'd espoused at the time. Trouble was, what he'd said could not be unsaid. Because of the non-stop interruptions in his office, his re-run of the Slane misadventure was denied time for contemplation.

Right now, in the space where Connolly would have liked to see a door, DS McFadden stood, polystyrene cup in hand, waiting to be invited to approach his desk. 'Thought you might like a coffee,' she offered, 'and ... I've got something that could be significant.'

'Come in, Bridie, take a pew,' he said, gesturing to the one guest chair his office possessed. 'Ah good, coffee, just what the doctor ordered. Your bright eyes tell me that you're bursting a gut to get something off your chest ... if that's not being sexist.'

'Sexist? Naw, never! But yeah, I do have some breaking news, as they like to say on *Sky News*. Got something on our prime suspect.'

Connolly took a swig from his coffee, nodding his approval. 'The missing women, yes?' he said. 'Wasn't aware the case had thrown up a prime suspect as yet.'

McFadden shrugged an indifferent shoulder. 'Well, yeah, technically, I suppose, that's true but Stephen Murray is the next best thing ... well, as near as dammit.'

'Oh, him! Please tell me he's been picked up by the Mounties.'

'No such luck. And with good reason: Murray never got to Canada.'

'What? Jenny Higgins lied to us...?'

'No, she didn't. Murray *did* have a reservation to fly to Toronto just like she said. He made it to the check-in desk but never boarded the plane.'

'What happened?'

'The airport authority allowed us to view the CCTV footage recorded around the time that Murray drove into the short-stay car park. A few minutes later he is captured walking into the departure concourse. Interesting viewing! Murray is seen going to check-in and having two cases put on the conveyor. After that, he moves towards the boarding gates but before he passes through he is stopped by two large heavies. With no audio-feed, it's impossible to make out what's being said but it's obvious from the body language that the exchange is far from friendly. Heated arguments continued for several minutes before all three head for the parking area.'

'They forced Murray to leave, right? You sure about that?'

'Yeah, it's all on the footage. The two heavies bunched up real close to Murray, one on either side, forcefully controlling his movements.'

'Do we know where they took him?'

'The CCTV caught them entering the short-stay car park. Another camera captured Murray being forced into a four-wheel drive – silver Mitsubishi Pajero with smoked windows. They drove away without delay. We've run the reg number but the plates were stolen.'

'Is Murray's own car still there?'

'Yes, it's been identified.'

'Wonder why he left it in the short-stay parking area ... I mean, why leave it there if he was going to Canada?'

'Probably because he wouldn't need it again. According to the airport authority, they've had a glut of abandoned cars since the country's economic downturn. People who've lost their jobs and are behind on their mortgages and hire purchase agreements are bailing out in droves, abandoning their cars as they wave goodbye to the ould sod.'

'You searched it?'

'Yes. Clean as a whistle.'

'And the two cases? Have they been searched?'

'Well, as it happens, the airport security people did that for us. You see, Murray's luggage was responsible for a one hour departure delay on the Canadian flight. When security discovered that they had cases belonging to a passenger who hadn't boarded, they got a bit hot and bothered. They unloaded all luggage, singled out Murray's cases and removed them. Explosive experts used a small charge to blow them open, found nothing more offensive than a few dog-eared porn magazines. Gives a whole new slant to the term, blow job.'

Connolly pretended to wince at the poor joke. 'Any sign of Murray since?'

'Nope! No one's seen hide nor hair of him. Hasn't been back to his house, hasn't collected his social welfare. He's gone missing just like the women we thought he might know something about.'

'There has to be a connection but I'm damned if I see it.'

'Me too,' McFadden admitted.

The cul-de-sac that led Emma's car to Matthew McDonagh's house on Rosemount Lane was littered with loose stones and deep pot holes, conditions that made her anxious about the car's shock absorbers. She peered through the windshield, her hands gripping the wheel, attempting to avoid the worst of the craters. She could see a pair of open wrought-iron gates, rusted beyond repair, framing a pebbled pathway that led to the front of the house. A dozen or so people stood outside the gateway holding placards with the words: SEX OFFENDER OUT!

She parked a short distance from where they'd gathered and approached on foot. She was glad to note that the media scrum she'd seen on television the previous day had moved on to their next story. The protesters, now bereft of the oxygen of publicity, glared at her, curious to know what business she might have with McDonagh.

'Wouldn't go in there if I were you,' a hard-featured woman, wearing glasses with thick lenses, shouted, her voice shrill enough to curdle cream. 'You'll probably get raped ... or worse,' she added, looking to her friends for affirmation. These were women of like vintage – forties or fifties – and a token male, a pot-bellied, red-faced man with a bald head who looked as though he'd rather be anywhere else.

Emma asked what they were doing, hoping to get a quotable quote from one of them, something worth inserting into the article she planned to write. The lone man used the back of his hand to wipe snot from his nose and looked at the women surrounding him, an expression of bored fatigue on his florid complexion. 'I wish someone would explain to me what the hell we're doing,' he said, each word ground out as though from a meat mincer. 'We could be indoors right now, feet up, watching telly.'

The woman who'd appointed herself spokesperson pushed her glasses up the bridge of her nose and said, 'We're here because the pervert in that house is a threat to all us women living in Rosemount. And if Sean, my husband here,' she paused to prod him in the stomach, 'doesn't want to support us, he can take a hike ... and he needn't expect me to put out for him when this is over.'

'As I understand it,' Emma said, addressing the women, feeling some-what hypocritical, 'the man who lives here has served his time ... paid for his crime. He is entitled to—'

'He's entitled to sweet Fanny Adams,' the woman retorted. 'He was caught attacking women and served time for it, or at least part of his sentence. Can you believe he had one year suspended for good behav-iour? They get it automatically whether they're good or not ... has nothing to do with him showing remorse for what he did or apologizing to his victim. What I'd like to know is this: How many other women did he attack and get away with? That's what bothers me. Bottom line: he's a rapist. He'll do it again. Can't cure people like him ... always on the lookout for the next victim. Well, he's not wanted in this neigh-bourhood ... him or his greyhounds. We'll not sleep easy in our beds till he's back where he belongs – behind bars in Arbour Hill. Look at them three poor women who've gone missing ... it could be him who's got them. Who's to say? We don't want to end up like them.'

'Is he at home at the moment?' Emma asked.

The man named Sean shrugged his shoulders. 'Yeah, the bugger's in there, probably watching porn on the internet while we—'

'Oh, do shut ya face, Sean,' his wife said before turning to address Emma. 'Yes, he's in there right now. We are monitoring his every move, keeping track of when he goes out and when he returns ... writing the times down. I hope you don't intend going in there alone, God alone knows what he might do to you.'

'I'm sure I'll be safe enough,' Emma said, moving towards the house. 'He's hardly likely to do anything while you people are out here watching his every move.'

The house looked forlorn, picked out against a dishwater sky; a stone built, century-old, two-storey with bay windows on the ground floor, bereft of curtains, and a row of small dog-kennel-shaped windows protruding from a slate roof. The ramshackle building was clearly in need of attention. Red ivy snaked up the walls, gripping cracks and crevices and, in all probability, helped stop the place from falling down. Dark blotchy stains showed signs of recent water seepage. A mature horse chestnut tree that looked even older than the building, pressed against the gable, some of its branches resting on the roof, obliterating one of the dog-kennel protrusions. The houses on either side were, Emma could see, part of a close homogeneous housing estate of more recent vintage – probably 1980s – separated from McDonagh's house by ugly concrete block walls. All houses on the lane appeared to back on to the rear gardens of the more upmarket buildings on the parallel Roseland Road.

There was no bell push so Emma used the old-fashioned brass knocker. The door opened within seconds. Emma recognized Matthew McDonagh from recent television news clips and from the media photographs that had been taken during his court appearances. Even so, seeing him in the flesh, so to speak, made quite an impression. His eyes bore into her, deep-set orbs that were an eerie shade of blue, so dark that the iris merged with the pupil, giving them an inner darkness that she found disturbing. The man holding her in his near-hypnotic gaze wore a brown plaid jacket with frayed cuffs and collar and a tan pair of corduroy trousers. He had a rugged, lived-in appearance: medium height, receding hairline, deadpan face with sharply angled cheekbones and hollow temples.

'Who are you?' he asked in an assertive voice.

'My name is Emma Boylan; I'm an investigative journalist with the *Post*. I'm here because—'

'YOU!' he said, bristling, his voice now an octave higher. 'You have the audacity to call here after the trouble you've caused? That miserable crowd of sanctimonious craw-thumpers out front are there because of you.' He threw a venomous glance at the protesters. 'Miserable sods with nothing better to do. I'm no rapist, Ms Boylan. Fact! You got that? And, as for that lot at my gate, no self-respecting rapist would touch any of them with a forty-foot barge pole.'

'Perhaps we can talk inside—'

McDonagh continued, as though Emma hadn't spoken, his every word laced with withering scorn. 'You know the bit that really bothers me? They scare my greyhounds … and that's something I can't allow. I depend on my dogs for a living, so you see, Ms Boylan, you've caused me great inconvenience by what you've written.' As though on cue, the sound of barking came from the back of the house.

'Do you race your dogs?' Emma asked, trying to sound matter of fact.

'No, they're much faster than me,' he sneered.

'What I mean is, do your dogs participate in races?'

'Of course they do ... it's what greyhounds do. They run.'

Emma remembered Siobhan O'Neill's mother telling her that her daughter had taken her dog for a walk as far as the Shelbourne greyhound track on the night she disappeared. 'Where do they race?' she asked.

'The track. Was there anything else?'

'Well, yes, yes there is. I'd like to ask you about ... about you being wrongfully imprisoned,' Emma said, intrigued to find that McDonagh, in spite of his obvious indignation, was well spoken, eloquent even. 'I think it would help us, Mr McDonagh, if we could go inside. I would like to hear your side of the story so that—'

'No, Ms Boylan,' he interrupted, his face distorting into a chilling smile. 'There's nothing to be gained by crossing my threshold. Shall I tell you why?'

'Please do.'

'You call yourself an investigative journalist, yes? But you are woefully lacking in the attributes, awareness and specialist insight required for such a profession. A proper investigative journalist would have undertaken some homework before rushing into print.'

'That's exactly what I did. I looked up—'

'No, Ms Boylan, you're wrong. What you wrote was sloppy journalism, it was lazy, poorly researched, way too reliant on second-hand source material and, I have to say, amateurish in the extreme.'

'Whoa! Just you hold on a second, I tried to contact you; I phoned—'

'Big deal! You phoned me; I didn't talk to you. Is that what goes for investigative journalism these days, huh? If you took your job seriously you would've looked up the records of my court case. Did you do that? No, of course you didn't. If you'd bothered your backside to examine the trial records, you would've discovered that I didn't rape anybody ... nor indeed was I accused of so doing. I was, as it happens, falsely accused of *attempted* rape, a charge that should have been thrown out by anyone taking the trouble to analyze the defence evidence in a fair and impartial way.'

'So, you're saying the judge and the jury got it wrong?'

'Exactly,' McDonagh replied, the arctic smile back on his face.

'What about your defence counsel? Surely your barrister should have been able to point out the flaws you say existed in the prosecution's case?'

'My barrister had all the facts before him – enough detail to prove my innocence beyond doubt – but he got bogged down in a quagmire of legalistic meanderings. He did something no barrister should do; he lost sight of the salient facts, the ones that really mattered, and in doing so, he mishandled the brief.'

'Who was your barrister?'

'Name's Trevor Shields.'

'Oh! I know Trevor Shields ... well no, what I mean is, my father knows him, he's—'

'He's a top legal eagle according to those who should know but he failed me. So, Ms Boylan, if you really are interested in getting to know my case then I suggest you live up to your job description: go do some investigation.' The arctic smile again. 'And when you've thoroughly exhausted all avenues of inquiry then, and only then, you may come back here, at which time you'll have earned the right to enter my house. When you're in possession of all the facts, then I'll happily provide you with an exclusive story about the machinations of law and how it is that an innocent man can be made to serve time for a crime he didn't commit.'

CHAPTER 22

RETREATING WITHIN HER own bubble Emma strode back to her car, only vaguely aware of the protesters. They yelled at her, demanding a response, their words failing to fully penetrate. Their lips moved, their mouths opened, but the mental barrier she'd erected between her and the outside world held firm. The bald, pot-bellied man followed her, swaying like a drunk on the deck of a ship being tossed in a gale, cursing and waving his hands. Her brain's filter mechanism blanked the man's obscenities as she hurriedly got behind the wheel of her car, keyed the ignition and executed an ill-judged and awkward three-point turn.

Ignoring the potholes now, she sped away from Rosemount Lane, a mental picture of McDonagh engraved on her brain. His deep-set eyes staying with her, an after-image like no other. The intensity of those eyes, their coldness, their arctic indifference burrowed deep into her soul. Her reaction, she realized, was way over the top. Extreme. If pressed, she could give no sane explanation for the feeling of violation she'd experienced. Speeding towards the city, one persistent voice sought amplification: the strangulated voice of Mary Shaw. '*It's his eyes,*' she'd exclaimed when Emma visited her house. '*His eyes ... they were demented, the eyes of a mad man, the eyes of a tortured soul, a person condemned to hell.*' At the time, Emma considered Mary's response an overreaction. Not now. She remembered Mary Shaw's other observations: '*My attacker had a receding hairline ... like that of Prince Edward.*'

'Could it be him?' Emma asked herself out loud, waiting for a set of traffic lights to turn green. The notion that Matthew McDonagh had been Mary Shaw's attacker became less a probability and more a certainty in her mind. *Am I leaping to conclusions?* she asked herself, almost stalling the engine before pulling away from the lights. *I'm not*

... *it has to be him*! McDonagh's criminal record was there for all to see. He'd already served time for attempted rape. In an ideal world she would urge Connolly to haul him in for an identity parade, have Mary Shaw inspect the line-up. But it wasn't going to happen, was it? No, because, for one thing, Connolly didn't share her convictions, and for another, they didn't live in an ideal world. Problem was, Emma had no proof. Just intuition. Connolly and Crosby both made it plain what they thought of women's intuition. Besides, even if an identity line-up could be arranged, Mary Shaw was never going to agree to participate.

And then there was the great leap of faith required to connect McDonagh to the missing women. Emma believed that his greyhounds provided a tenuous link, something that Connolly dismissed as bordering on the fanciful. Media accounts, written at the time of McDonagh's trial, claimed that the woman whose case had landed him in jail had been attacked in an area close to the Shelbourne Park greyhound stadium, the same locality that Siobhan O'Neill had disappeared from. McDonagh took his dogs to the racetracks, he had admitted that to Emma. And Siobhan O'Neill's mother had confirmed that her daughter walked their dog in the Shelbourne Park area on the night she'd gone missing.

Coincidence?

Having come face to face with Matthew McDonagh, Emma didn't think so. She felt she was on to something, something big, and decided on a number of actions: one, she would check to see if McDonagh had attended the track in Shelbourne Park on the night Siobhan O'Neill was abducted; two, she would chase down Trevor Shields, the barrister who'd represented McDonagh and three, she would unearth the trial transcripts in the McDonagh case.

Arriving back at the *Post*, Crosby intercepted her as she made her way to her desk. 'We've got another missing woman,' he said.

'Oh, God no! When, I mean where?'

'City centre. Broad daylight. I've picked up on a few names that I'd like you to talk to. If you're quick, really quick, you'll steal a march on the rest of the media. And this time we've got a proper description of his car.'

CROSBY'S 'CONTACT' FROM the inner-circles of the Garda Síochána had come up trumps. Emma, the beneficiary of this unofficial, if not wholly ethical leak, felt peeved that Connolly, her very own deep throat in the force, had failed to pass the intelligence to her in the first place. She understood his reluctance, understood the rationale for keeping their personal relationship separate from their professional careers, a distinction he'd made all too plain in recent days. But, unlike Connolly, her interpretation of the self-imposed guidelines allowed for a degree of wriggle-room to enter the equation.

Just as well her editorial boss, Crosby, had no such scruples about hitting on his contacts, otherwise Emma would not now be talking to Kathleen Morrison. Ms Morrison worked as a cashier in the Hibernian Trust Bank – HTB – in Henry Street and claimed to be Gemma Moore's closest friend. She'd become worried when Gemma failed to turn up for work that morning. Kathleen had been looking forward to hearing Gemma tell her all about the mysterious date she'd agreed to on St Patrick's Day.

It surprised Kathleen that the press should be interested in talking to her. The novelty of the situation coupled with concern for her friend had made her agree, without protest, to join Emma for a coffee in Nelson's Eye, a landmark public house across the street from the bank. The Eye, as Dubliners called it, established more than a century earlier was the last of the city bars to relinquish its 'men only' policy. One of Emma's favourite watering holes, it retained an old-world charm: yellowed stuccoed ceiling, brass counter rail, polished pump handles, genuine antique mirrors, carved redwood panelling and stone-paved floors. Half an hour before the lunchtime rush, Emma ushered Kathleen to a quiet corner that was out of earshot of other customers. A waiter dressed in retro-style Georgian livery served them the pub's speciality: hot scones, home-made jam and freshly ground coffee.

Emma neglected to warn Kathleen that she would be set upon by reporters from every media organization in the country as soon as wind of the latest disappearance became known. She should have felt guilty about this omission but instead felt a tingle of excitement; not warning Kathleen meant the *Post* would be first with the exclusive scoop and she, Emma Boylan, would be the first to garner an account of the missing woman's activity in the days and hours leading up to the disappearance. If that made her a bad person, well, so be it; her overriding concern was to come up with the scoop, beat her competitors to the punch.

'Oh, God, I just hope I'm making a fuss about nothing,' Kathleen said, her voice quivering, her eyes misting. In her early twenties, she had an attractive innocence about her, not at all as worldly as Emma would have expected for a person in her job. Wearing the bank's standard blue suit and silk blouse, she was tall with better than average looks, her face adorned with a generous application of make-up, her head crowned with shiny black hair, cut short. 'But I know Gemma,' she insisted. 'I *know* my friend ... and what's happened has frightened me. I told the detectives this, I told them—'

'When did you first suspect something was wrong?' Emma asked.

Kathleen looked into her eyes, so trusting, so honest, biting a trembling lip to prevent herself from crying. 'Gemma said she'd call me; we text and call each other all the time when we're not at work. She promised to let me know how her date went.'

'And this date, when was it?'

'Yesterday, yesterday afternoon, after the parade.'

'The man she was meeting, do you have his name?'

'No, that's the crazy thing; Gemma didn't know his name.'

'A blind date?'

'No, no, well, not exactly,' Kathleen said, putting her coffee down and brushing a crumb from the corner of her mouth. 'They'd met the previous day. He came to her rescue when some young blackguards knocked her down. They got talking and, like, one thing led to another. A real charmer according to Gemma, like something from a Mills & Boon novel, that's how she described it. Anyway, she agreed to meet him in the Gresham Hotel yesterday afternoon.'

'Do you know if she met him?'

'Yes, she did. She wasn't sure if he'd turn up. Actually, she wasn't all that sure herself whether to turn up or not but Gemma's a true romantic like myself; curiosity got the better of her. She called me just before meeting him, promised to sneak a picture of him on to her mobile and e-mail it to me when she got the chance. We were chatting away when she stopped in mid-sentence, told me she could see him crossing the street, coming towards her. She had to cut me off there and then. I haven't heard from her since.'

'What time did she make the call?'

'A bit after three, yeah, about ten past three.'

'So, Gemma met this man whose name she didn't know at ten past three. I don't suppose she described him, his looks I mean?'

The question made Kathleen stop to think for a moment. Her eyes expressed apprehension and a frown clouded her face.

'Funny you should ask that,' she said. 'Like I said, I was expecting his picture on my mobile but it didn't happen. Gemma told me about everything he wore, you know, like from head to toe but she never described what he really looked like. She mentioned his overcoat, its style, material, shape and shade of blue; she described his hat, his shirt and tie, his expensive shoes but when it came to his face, well, she couldn't give me a decent description. I trotted out all the usual compar-isons, you know, like, did he resemble Tom Cruise, Robert Pattinson, Johnny Depp, Brad Pitt, Matt Damon, all the heart-throbs we fancy, but she said he didn't look like any of them, that his face was part of the whole package that made up who he was. Made no sense to me and to tell you the truth I'm not sure it made sense to Gemma either.'

'Did she say what age he was?'

'She was a bit vague on that score, too, but of course I pressed; I managed to wheedle out of her that he was in his mid-to-late thirties.'

'What age is Gemma?'

'She's twenty-six, three years older than me. And that's another thing that bothers me; she usually goes for men around her own age; I've never known her to take up with someone older. The way she talked about this guy made him sound like he was, like, ten years older.'

'Do you have a picture of Gemma?'

'Yes, lots. I've got piles of us taken together on my mobile and loads more at home. Gemma has oodles of photos too; they're on the walls of her flat.' As Kathleen spoke, the distress in her eyes showed deep concern. 'The detectives I spoke to said I shouldn't worry; they seemed to think Gemma will show up in the next day or so.' Kathleen stopped, looked earnestly into Emma's eyes, said, 'That's not going to happen, is it.'

Before Emma could answer, Kathleen continued.

'I know Gemma too well; she wouldn't go away without talking to me. She would've been burstin' a gut to tell me how the date went. She'd promised to send me his pic, give me the whole low-down. We always discussed the fellahs we go out with; it's something we do. Apart from that, she'd never miss work without contacting the bank.'

Emma nodded sympathetically, unwilling to give false assurances. The sense of déjà vu was unmistakable. This was the second time in the space of a few days that she had played out the same comforting role in this unfolding tragedy. It was a part she had no wish to repeat. She finished her coffee, handed Kathleen a tissue and accompanied her across the street to the HTB. Hearing the conviction in Kathleen's voice in regard to her friend's mysterious disappearance left Emma in no doubt that Gemma Moore represented number four on the growing list of women to vanish without trace.

CHAPTER 24

MATTHEW McDONAGH RESIGNED himself to the presence of the protesters. The number had reduced to half a dozen diehards. He regarded them as a pathetic narrow-minded clique of busybodies. *Have they nothing better to occupy their miserable lives?* He'd watched them use a tattered, dog-eared school notebook to jot down his comings and goings. Shook his head at the futility of it all.

Then there was the reporter, the one who'd visited him the previous day. She'd identified herself as Emma Boylan, investigative journalist with the *Post*. The exchange they'd had encouraged him to revisit her article. In it she'd tried to tie in a bunch of cold case histories with the current missing women's files. He liked her approach, liked her looks and her manner, but he had no intention of telegraphing those benign observations to her. Instead, he'd sent her away with a flea in her ear, advising her to raise her game, probe deeper into the miscarriage of justice that had condemned him to two years behind bars.

The challenge he'd thrown down to her had encouraged him to revisit the circumstances of his own downfall, to ponder the ramifications of the court's verdict. He was due to meet with the commissioners in two days' time. Clear up what they referred to as 'loose ends'. The prospect of having them probe further into his time at the Beaumont gave him cause for concern. It was just as well, he thought, that Father Troy and Brother Bernard were both dead. Dead men couldn't be called to offer their account of the happenings in that institution. Not that the two clerics were innocent or could be excused their crimes; far from it. They were every bit as evil as he'd painted them but, had they the power to return from whatever hell they currently inhabited, they might be tempted to present a different account of how events transpired in the aftermath of the beating they'd inflicted on him in the sacristy.

They would certainly have a lot to say about the intervention of Sister Marie-Theresa and her role in subsequent developments. One thing was sure: they would do him no favours; they'd lie through their teeth to ensure the reparation board threw out his case. That first day when the nun saved him from the two clerics was an event he'd rather forget, but like all bad memories, it remained lodged inside his head, repeating constantly, as though on some never-ending loop, a recurring nightmare ready to roll at the oddest of times. He forced himself not to go there again, at least not today. It was way too painful. He wished there was a mechanism in his brain that could, on demand, erase some of the dreadful stuff he'd experienced on his painful journey through life.

From the back of the house he could hear the greyhounds barking. He looked at the clock, saw it was feeding time for the animals. Two of his greyhounds, Princess Lulu and Shady Lady were scheduled to race in Shelbourne Stadium the following evening. Princess Lulu was entered in the second race at 8.10 p.m.; Shady Lady would compete in the fifth race at 9.00p.m. One of them, most likely Princess Lulu, he fully expected to win. The dog had performed badly in her last three outings but Matthew knew a few tricks when it came to training greyhounds. He'd worked his charm on the bitch, got her into peak condition, entered her in a few unofficial trials and fully expected her to beat the five pitted against her. Going on form, the other five dogs had all recorded better race times recently and would be expected to come in well ahead of his charge. And that was exactly the way he wanted it; it meant he would get a good price from the on-track bookies, make himself some serious cash.

He put aside the copy of the *Post* with Emma Boylan's article and moved to his front window to check if the protesters were still there. Needn't have bothered; they were still in position. Well, he had given Ms Boylan the opportunity to change all that and put things right. All she had to do was re-examine the details of his incarceration. By doing so she would be able to inform her readers of the miscarriage of justice that had taken place and, in the process, bring the ridiculous protest to an end.

CHAPTER 25

TIME HAD LOST its capacity to be measured. Gemma Moore's existence was now little more than a blur. Her arms and legs, extended and secured by leather bondage cuffs attached to her wrists and ankles, no longer felt as though they belonged to her. The hyperventilation she'd experienced earlier had eased, her mind, her naked body, no longer in touch with reality, floating, falling, spiralling into some vast, dark nothingness. A place beyond panic. And yet, curiously, a measure of primal survival instinct remained intact, enough to make her writhe, fight the bindings, struggle for freedom.

Her tormentor moved in and out of focus like an object viewed through a zoom lens in the hands of a drunk. Gemma heard the thud of a shoe being kicked off, then the thud of a second shoe. Through a haze, she discerned the outlined shape of a person – a man? – a woman? – appearing to discard their clothes. Having been injected, sedated and drugged, she experienced a buzzing in her ears but through it, she heard the sound of buttons being undone, a zip pulled down, discarded clothes falling to the floor, a strap snapping against bare flesh. A large, naked, pink blur now clambered on top of her. Splayed fingers groped and roughly caressed her flesh. No part escaped violation. Eventually, the fingers withdrew, only to be replaced by a probing tongue, its serpent-like tip licking and tracing every curve, tip, valley and orifice of her tethered body.

Exposed.

Vulnerable.

Gemma's mind hit overload, ceased to function. How long she remained in that state, she'd no idea. But, cruelly, a vague state of semi-consciousness returned. Once more, she was aware of the unimaginable horror of her ordeal. The drugs administered earlier retained the power to constrict her throat, incapacitating much of her bodily functions, impairing selected areas of her brain's command system. A segment of that brain still functioned intermittently; it let her know she'd be better off had a total state of shutdown remained imposed. Unaccountably, her sense of smell escaped unimpaired, her olfactory nerves detecting a cocktail of noxious odours: disinfectant, the whiff of urine from the stale mattress and the sour pong of what she supposed were past carnal confrontations.

The person hovering above her had large breasts and gave off the smell of a woman's perfume. Gemma's drugged brain struggled to figure out if she was being molested by a member of her own sex. The mattress sunk beneath the weight of knees on either side of her as a pair of fleshy thighs pressed against her hips. She felt air disperse about her as a heavy navel fell, lifted, and flapped against her own navel. Madness engulfed her, pushing her over the edge. Fighting to retain a vestige of sanity, she caught sight of what her impaired brain informed her was a phallus-like object.

Gemma's confusion was total.

Was the person straddling her male or female? Impaired vision meant that what she saw appeared as though in 3D but without the benefit of 3D glasses. The protrusion was either a penis or, if not, a somewhat enlarged, but realistic imitation of that organ.

The woman, or man, began to gnaw at her, paying special attention to her lips, her chin, her neck and her nipples. Gemma arched her head, screamed, the strangulated sound in her throat unable to break through the wall of saliva. Her eyes, uncoordinated, rolled crazily in their sockets as the monster worked slowly down from her breasts to her stomach and on to her navel, not stopping there. Gemma was only partially aware of this, paralyzed by the activity taking place south of her waist. She struggled defensively but her legs remained splayed and bound. As the depravity continued, her mind finally gave out, blanked completely, which was just as well. It saved her from the rest of the grossly-humiliating defilement being perpetrated.

Only Gemma's unresponsive body remained to bear witness to the on-going debasement.

CHAPTER 26

BAD NEWS PREDOMINATED: Gemma Moore remained missing. The whole world demanded she be found ... and found fast. Connolly, the person charged with the task of finding her, was supposed to snap his fingers, say *Abracadabra* like some magician pulling a rabbit from a hat, conjure her out of thin air.

Like it could be that simple.

There was encouraging news, too. His team had worked round the clock and their diligence had gained some traction. They'd collected CCTV footage from the city traffic authority, the stores on O'Connell Street and, most importantly, the Cathal Brugha/Marlborough Street car park.

Splicing the footage into a sequential timeline made it possible to follow the movements of Gemma Moore, pinpoint the moment of her rendezvous with the Peacock, the moniker Connolly's team now used to identify the man with the fedora and coat. The cameras caught Gemma as she walked past the Gate Theatre, saw her halt for the pedestrian lights beside the Parnell monument, then proceeded towards O'Connell Street, heading in the direction of the Gresham Hotel. Other cameras picked up her intended 'date' on the opposite side of the street. Wearing the trendy hat and coat that had first been observed on his visit to Glynn's Inn, he dallied outside the Carlton Cinema site, anxiously pacing up and down like an expectant father outside a maternity ward. Eventually, with a spurt of energy he dashed across the broad thoroughfare, deftly dodging the moving traffic, and met up with Gemma on the corner of Cathal Brugha Street. The cameras next captured them entering the multi-level car park at the Marlborough Street entrance. It was clear from Gemma Moore's body language that she was uneasy in the man's company. In contrast, his body language was expansive, his gestures persuasive as he appeared to cajole her into following him.

Because the surveillance cameras were mounted high and because the man retained the hat at all times, the uppermost part of his head remained in shadow, making it hard to get sharp focus on the top half of his face, his eyes, at all times, lost in shadow. Connolly had already asked the technical boys at the photographic lab to work on the definition, to enhance the quality and provide a workable likeness of the man.

On the car park's second level, Gemma Moore could be seen to hesitate while the Peacock held the passenger's door open. She appeared to remonstrate, shaking her head, but eventually, with what looked like marked reluctance, she got into the car. Connolly jotted down the car's make: a Mazda MX-5. The cameras lost the car momentarily as it descended the ramps to street level but picked it up again when a barrier delayed it at the pay point exit. A shot of the number plate was clearly visible as the Mazda pulled into the street and merged into the traffic.

'Got the bastard!' Connolly said, sounding a much relieved man and giving McFadden a big thumbs up. She responded in like manner but thought the breakthrough deserved high-fives at the very least, a gesture she knew he'd never countenance. 'All we got to do now,' she said, scribbling the reg number in her notebook, 'is connect the owner to the plate, get his address and bring him in.'

Almost midday, Connolly and McFadden pulled into the driveway of a modest semi-detached house on the Navan Road, a short distance from the junction with Nephin Road. The pounding beat and vibrating bass of heavy metal music could be heard coming from somewhere inside the house. McFadden rang the doorbell. A young man – Connolly put his age at twenty – opened the door after a wait of two minutes. With shaved head, bare feet and a tattered tracksuit that hung from a lanky body, he appeared to have just woken from sleep. 'What d'ya want?' he asked, his manner insolent, his voice drowsy, his eyes blinking as though having difficulty focusing.

'This the home of John Gribben?' Connolly asked.

'Yeah, 'tis. Who are you?'

'I'm Detective Inspector Jim Connolly and this is Detective Sergeant McFadden; we'd like a word with Mr Gribben.'

'Mr Gribben? Ah, you mean me da. He's dead ... died a year and a half ago. Cancer.'

'Oh, I'm sorry to hear that ... we didn't know.'

'What d'ya want him for?'

'Does he, I mean, did he drive a Mazda MX-5?'

'He did, yeah.'

'Where's the car now?'

'Should be here ... should've been mine,' the young man said with an expression of regret. 'My mother, in a rush of shit to the brain, went and sold it.'

'Sold it?' Connolly and McFadden said in unison.

'Yeah! The guy who bought it fooled her, charmed her into selling it for half its worth.'

'Who'd she sell it to?' McFadden asked.

'Better ask her. She handled the transaction all by herself.' It was clear from the youth's demeanour that the deal his mother had done failed to meet with his approval.

'Is she here?' McFadden asked. 'Your mother ... can we talk to her?'

'Yeah, I'll get her for ya.' He turned his back on them, yelled, 'Ma!' and disappeared into the interior of the house. The volume of the music increased while the two detectives stood looking to each other, with raised eyebrows. 'That's *Napalm Death*,' McFadden informed Connolly.

Connolly, surprised by this revelation said, 'Never pegged you as a heavy metal fan.'

'I'm not – can't stand it. I'm more a Daniel O'Donnell fan, but my younger brother is into metal big time, can't get enough of it.'

Connolly, dismayed that anyone should like either type of music, decided to say nothing, wondering what was keeping Mrs Gribben. After involuntarily listening to way too much of the deep guttural vocals on Napalm Death's rant against the United States government, a tall, good-looking woman appeared, cigarette poised between two fingers, 'I'm Stella Gribben,' she said in a strange, toneless voice, blowing a great cloud of smoke from her nostrils as she spoke. 'Who are you? What do you want?'

Connolly introduced himself and his sergeant, explained that they were making inquiries into who now owned her late husband's car. While Connolly spoke, McFadden noticed that the woman's hair had that in-between appearance that results from being dyed and allowed to grow out. Except for a streak of red on her lips she had no make-up on and there was a tired emptiness in her pale grey eyes. She wore a dull, wine-coloured blouse, crumpled and stained, and a calf-length black skirt.

'Your son says you sold the car, is that right?' Connolly said.

'Turn that bloody racket down,' Mrs Gribben shouted, turning her head to address the din coming from behind her. She sighed, took a deep drag from her cigarette and turned back to the detectives, 'Sorry, what were you saying?'

'The car. I was asking—'

'Oh, yes, the car. Had to sell it after John died. I don't drive and I don't want John Junior to kill himself ... or worse, kill someone else. Truth be told, with all this economic doom and gloom I can't afford the petrol, the insurance, the tax and the NCT tests. Goes on and on, no end to it. I had to place an ad in the advertiser. Got shut of it within a week.'

'Who bought it?' Connolly asked.

'Swanky guy. Dressed to the nines, gift of the gab. His name? Sounded sorta posh, a bit West-Brit public school, if you know what I mean. Richard J. Bradbury. Now, there's a name for ya – not the kind I'm likely to forget easily.'

'And this man, this Richard J. Bradbury, he bought the car?'

'Sure did. He didn't part with as much as I wanted but considering the damage that John Junior did to it, I can't really complain.'

Connolly wanted to hear more about the damaged car. 'You say that John Junior – that's your son, yes? – had some mishap with the car? When did this happen?'

'Happened a few weeks after the funeral. Grief, I suppose. He took the car out, drove too fast, ended up colliding with another motorist, nothing too serious but the estimate I got to repair the Mazda was just crazy. That's why I decided to sell. As part of the deal, Bradbury agreed to pay the cost of fixing the other car and, of course, he would have to fork out for the damage done to the Mazda. In the end, I got four and a half thousand euro into my hand ... in cash.'

'Cash?' Connolly repeated.

'Yeah, crisp fifties; that clinched the deal.'

'Do you know where he lives?'

'No, haven't a breeze.'

'Did you notify the appropriate authorities about the sale?'

'Didn't have to; Mr Bradbury took care of all that. Said he'd sort out the changes to the tax and insurance.'

'Well, in that case I've bad news for you. The car is still registered to your late husband; that's how we got this address. You have a legal obligation to notify the motoring authority when you sell a car; I would strongly advise you to get onto it straight away. In the meantime, have you some way of getting in contact with Mr Bradbury?'

'Sorry, 'fraid not. Didn't think I'd have any reason to.'

McFadden produced the photo of Stephen Murray and a print taken from the CCTV footage showing the man who'd met Gemma Moore. Mrs Gibben didn't recognize Murray but thought the man in O'Connell Street had a hat like the person who'd bought the car. Connolly thanked Mrs Gribben and took his leave. Napalm Death was back to full volume as he and his sergeant made their way to the car.

'Back to square one,' McFadden said, as they waited to nose their way onto the traffic on the Navan road.

'Maybe. Maybe not. We can chase down Bradbury's name. If it's his real name it's got to be on some official records somewhere. Everybody in this country has a PPS number; it's impossible to get by without one.'

McFadden looked sceptical. 'What's the betting he didn't give Mrs Gribben his real name?'

'That's a distinct possibility but we've got to hope that that's not what's happened.'

Consciousness of a kind returned, the solid world now distantly graspable. Gemma's brain struggled to instil a sense of order, a sense of sanity. Her first intelligible thought concluded that she'd just woken up from the most horrific nightmare imaginable, worse than those she'd experienced as a child, the ones where she'd been chased by a great hairy bogeyman when her child's legs had refused to propel her forward. A second intelligible thought, more rational than the first, let her know that what she'd just been through, what she was still going through, was not the inexplicable stuff of nightmares but the indisputable logic of reality. She tried to move; found she couldn't. Her arms and legs were secured with plastic stays, her torso trapped in some sort of chain harness. Confirmation, were it needed, of the seriousness of her predicament.

Indefinable fear enveloped her. She had no idea how long she'd been in this state, her mind too zonked to provide answers. A dryness in her mouth and throat made her cough, the simple exertion triggering a thousand spasms of pain throughout her whole body. She couldn't tell whether the harsh blue/white florescent tube fixed to the ceiling above her was responsible for the buzzing sound that persisted in her head or if the noise was a symptom of the substances that had been injected into her.

She could feel hardness beneath her and realized that she was no longer on the stinking, piss, sweat and vomit-saturated mattress on which she'd been raped and brutalized. The floor and walls around her were paved in grimy white tiles, like those she remembered seeing in old public toilets. Some tiles were cracked, some missing, some stained with splashes of a substance she'd prefer not to identify, though she inwardly acknowledged the matter as dried blood. Another truth dawned: the space holding her was some kind of butcher's slaughterhouse or anti-

obligation to notify the motoring authority when you sell a car; I would strongly advise you to get onto it straight away. In the meantime, have you some way of getting in contact with Mr Bradbury?'

'Sorry, 'fraid not. Didn't think I'd have any reason to.'

McFadden produced the photo of Stephen Murray and a print taken from the CCTV footage showing the man who'd met Gemma Moore. Mrs Gibben didn't recognize Murray but thought the man in O'Connell Street had a hat like the person who'd bought the car. Connolly thanked Mrs Gribben and took his leave. Napalm Death was back to full volume as he and his sergeant made their way to the car.

'Back to square one,' McFadden said, as they waited to nose their way onto the traffic on the Navan road.

'Maybe. Maybe not. We can chase down Bradbury's name. If it's his real name it's got to be on some official records somewhere. Everybody in this country has a PPS number; it's impossible to get by without one.'

McFadden looked sceptical. 'What's the betting he didn't give Mrs Gribben his real name?'

'That's a distinct possibility but we've got to hope that that's not what's happened.'

agonizing pain through her body. It didn't stop her. She continued to fight, to buck, twist and writhe, her silent screams tearing at her throat. Stupefied, beyond fear, her eyes blinked in an attempt to see through the sweat, tears and strands of wet hair lodged there. The chains on her ankles were now connected to a second longer chain. The man, after connecting the longer chain to a pulley wheel fixed atop a tall steel-framed apparatus, began turning a handle. It pulled the chain around the pulley, clacking loudly as each link ratcheted a pawl further. The chain continued to *clack, clack, clack* around the wheel. Her feet began to rise slowly off the ground.

Clack, clack, clack.

She was now suspended upside down, head dangling inches above the floor. With her last ounce of strength she tried to right herself, jerking her body even after she knew it was a pointless exercise. The blood, now pooled in her head, throbbed in her veins, adding to her distress. Her upside down world swam to-and-fro before her eyes, appearing more and more out of focus. Her mouth opened and closed, forming the word, *help.*

In a blur, she felt her head being grabbed, felt it being forced back in a harsh grip. Then, like a burn from an ice shard, the knife's blade sliced into her throat. Wasn't painful at all. A feeling of blessed relief coursed through her. The flow of life's blood from her body provided a release. The tiles below her turned bright crimson before darkening to an ever deepening shade of burgundy. Sense of sound and motion ceased and the world she'd known simply blinked out.

CHAPTER 28

THE HOUSE ON Rosemount Lane was the last place Emma expected to revisit. Matthew McDonagh, its owner, represented number one on the list of people she'd rather not confront a second time. The motley group of protesters who'd camped outside his gate came a close second. Such likes and dislikes were, alas, luxuries she could not afford to indulge in. She was a journalist; she had an editor to satisfy, not to mention her readers. On her previous visit to the potholed cul de sac, when she'd doorstepped McDonagh, the protesters told her they kept a record of the owner's comings and goings. If true, and if they were willing to share that information with her, it could confirm a niggling gut-feeling that had begun to bother her in recent days. Such a record could prove pivotal in shaping the future direction of her investigation.

Gemma Moore's abduction had taken place in broad daylight and had been captured on several CCTV cameras. That gave Emma a solid basis of fact to contemplate. The police investigation team, in their trawl for information, had supplied the *Post* and the media in general with a series of black and white stills lifted from the footage. The definition, taken at long distance, was surprisingly good, proof of a kind that the person spotted in Glynn's Inn really did exist. It would be logical to assume that he was also responsible for Annette Campbell's disappearance. But no doubt whatsoever remained that this man had abducted Gemma Moore. On that basis, he must be the prime candidate in the frame for the abduction of Joan Keating and Siobhan O'Neill.

Emma parked the car, walked to where the protesters had grouped. The domineering woman with the time-worn face still headed up the group. 'Oh!' the woman exclaimed, her voice sounding less shrill than Emma remembered. 'Didn't expect we'd see you back here after the way you skedaddled last time. Don't tell me you want to talk to him again?'

'Actually, no,' Emma replied, giving the woman and her dwindling band of supporters an all-embracing smile, noting that the grumpy, pot-bellied man was no longer present. 'I was hoping to talk with you ladies.'

'Oh, you were, were you? I see,' the woman said, her expression changing from one of belligerence to something approaching cordiality. 'Tell us first which paper you work for? What's your name?'

Emma produced her business card, handed it to the woman. 'My name is Emma Boylan, I'm an investigative journalist with the *Post*. Maybe you'd like to give me your name ... and introduce your companions.'

'Yeah, OK, why not,' the woman said, looking at the card through her thick lenses before passing it to her companions. 'I'm Jane ... Jane Henderson, retired civil servant; you met my husband Sean last time you were here. As you can see he's gone AWOL, shagged off this morning, but he'll be back ... if he knows what's good for him.' Jane introduced her four women companions, adding little titbits of information regarding each of them in turn. 'So, now you know who we are, what did you want to talk to us about?'

'You believe that McDonagh continues to pose a threat to women, don't you?'

The women nodded in unison.

'Well then, Jane, I'm hoping you and your friends here can help me put a stop to him doing it again.'

'We'll do whatever it takes to put him back with the other sex offenders in Arbour Hill,' Jane Henderson replied enthusiastically.

'Good, I'm pleased to hear that,' Emma said, glad to have them on side but surprised at the ease with which the negotiations were proceeding. 'OK, last time I was here you told me you made a note of the times Mr McDonagh leaves and returns to his house?'

'We do, that's right. That'd be Maggie's job, here,' Jane enthused, indicating Maggie Butler, one of the women she'd already introduced. 'Maggie used to be a bookkeeper in Brady's garage before it went belly-up. She keeps tabs on McDonagh's whereabouts from dawn till dusk; if he moves, Maggie records it in her copybook.'

Maggie Butler, older than the other women, was a small sparrow-like creature whose creased and fissured face looked for all the world like a dried prune; not a woman to inspire affection. 'Six pages, I've got,' she said in a strong voice that belied her frail appearance. 'Every time those greyhounds of his are taken for walks or taken to the race track I enter it here.' She opened the copybook and showed the pages to Emma, all of them divided into three columns and written in small neat script. 'I also enter the time he gets back. And when he goes shopping in that ol' jeep of his, I enter that too.'

Emma was impressed. 'Can I see what you've written for St Patrick's Day?' she asked. 'I'd like to know if he left the house between, say, 2 p.m. and 4 p.m.?'

'Ah, ha!' Maggie said, her crimpled smile accentuating the dried prune effect to a scary degree. 'I see where you're coming from. We've all read about that girl who was abducted in O'Connell's Street and we've established that McDonagh wasn't the guilty party on that occasion.'

Not the answer Emma had been expecting. 'You're sure?'

'Yeah, he returned from walking three dogs at,' – Maggie stopped to consult her copybook – 'yeah, here it is, at 2.28 that afternoon and, let me see, remained indoors until 4.35, at which point he took his jeep out of the garage and drove down to the corner shop to get an evening paper. He returned at' – she glanced at the columns again – 'yeah, at precisely 4.53 p.m.'

Emma's heart sank; what she was hearing meant that her gut feeling with regard to Matthew McDonagh was a non-runner. 'When did he last take out the jeep?'

'Yesterday evening. Let me check the time for you. Yeah, here it is: Thursday. He left here with two dogs in the trailer at 6.10 p.m. and he returned at 10.50 p.m. He didn't leave again until this morning to get his paper.'

Emma nodded. 'Is there any other way he can leave the house apart from the front gate?' she asked, knowing she was clutching at straws.

At this point, Jane Henderson intervened. 'He can't leave his house without us knowing, not unless he has one of them transporter affairs from *Star Trek*, you know, the beam-me-up-Scotty chambers that can make a person dissolve and reappear in a different place.'

'What about the back of his house?' Emma pressed. 'Could he cross into some other back yard or garden and get out that way?'

'No chance,' Jane said, peering over her specs. 'Well, it's not impossible, I suppose but he'd have to pole vault to get over them walls.'

'I see,' Emma said, disheartened.

'If you'd like, I'll take you to my house,' said Jane. Sean's down in the pub; he won't bother us – let you look out of my window on the landing. That's my house there,' she said, pointing to the semi next to the high wall separating McDonagh's property from the neighbouring estate. 'Overlooks his backyard; you can see everything the bugger owns. You want a gawk?'

CHAPTER 29

J ANE HENDERSON'S HOUSE, typical of the sterile architecture that became the staple ingredient of the suburban sprawl of the late eighties, was neater than Emma had expected. Why she should have imagined it otherwise was probably down to her first meeting with the protesters. That, plus the impression Jane's husband created when he'd harped on about his drink intake and telly addiction. Something else too: Emma would own up to a trace of latent snobbery, the result of being reared in a large country house, maintained with the kind of care and attention that only someone of her parents' financial and cultural standing could provide. In recent years, she'd tried to remedy this character defect but old prejudices die hard.

'Why don't we have a nice cup of tea?' Jane offered.

'That's kind of you,' Emma said, noting an expression that came close to pleading in the woman's face. It seemed like Jane didn't get the house to herself all that often and seldom had the opportunity to invite a guest, someone she could talk to on an unrestricted basis. Emma, who didn't particularly want to be the one to accommodate Jane in this respect, said, 'I'm under a bit of pressure so, if it's all right, maybe you'd show me the view to the back of McDonagh's house.'

Jane nodded, the fleeting grimace of disappointment replaced by an acceptance that Emma was a journalist on a mission, someone needing to use her house to advance her story, someone who, like most of her acquaintances, had no interest in her specifically. Without a word, she guided Emma up a narrow flight of stairs and stopped on the half landing beside an elongated window that stretched from floor to ceiling. The view it afforded, exactly as Jane had said, allowed Emma an uninterrupted perspective on Matthew McDonagh's back yard and garden.

The first thing to strike Emma was its size – more of a field than a garden. The outbuildings too, were more extensive than she expected.

The place made the back gardens of the neighbouring dwellings on either side look like graveyard plots by comparison. A series of sheds stretched the full length of McDonagh's property from the rear of his house to an end wall that delineated the border dividing his spread from the commercial properties on Rosemount Road. A row of dog kennels, all with wire mesh doors, had been incorporated into what looked like a recently built extension. The high pitched roofs threw a deep shadow over the walled-in area but Emma could see several greyhounds behind the mesh.

The ground area not occupied by buildings was divided into a gravel section and a much larger, slightly raised grass area. The gravel section, a dilapidated weedy stretch running parallel to the outbuilding, was speckled with water-filled potholes, the deposits a result of recent showers. In the shadow of a large chestnut tree, an old-fashioned water pump, its handle missing, leaned off-centre like an old abandoned headstone. The image put Emma in mind of a line from Dylan's *Subterranean Homesick Blues* that went, 'The pump don't work 'Cause the vandals took the handles.'

An algae-encrusted stone trough jutted out from the base of the pump, and there, partially hidden inside the trough was the missing handle. Unlike Dylan's ditty the vandals, it would appear, hadn't bothered to take the handle. A few sad-looking vegetable patches spread haphazardly on the grass area appeared to sprout what Emma thought might be winter cabbage, the kind her father used to grow when she lived at home. Half a dozen mature ash trees lined the wall opposite the outbuildings, their upper branches arching over the wall's crown, the whole setting giving an impression of neglect.

Emma pointed to an old green Land Rover parked behind a wooden gate to one side of the house and asked, 'Is that the only mode of transport he's got?'

'Yeah, that's all. There's a trailer goes with it; it's kept in one of the sheds. It's been adapted into wired-off cage divisions to hold the dogs when he takes them racing.'

'Have you ever seen him drive anything else … like, maybe a Mazda, something like that?'

'Nah! Never seen him in anything 'cept that old jeep of his. There's an old tractor in one of the sheds; been there since the place was a farmyard,' Jane explained. 'All the surrounding land, including this house we're standing in, was once part of a farm. The place was abandoned for ages before McDonagh took it over two years ago. Developers tried to buy it at the height of the Celtic Tiger madness, offered millions, but the estate of the late owner got greedy, wanted ridiculous money. Frightened off the buyers. And then, after the property market crashed, it was sold to McDonagh for a fraction of what the sellers had originally turned down.'

Emma pointed to the commercial properties on Rosemount Road, period buildings with backyards abutting the end wall of McDonagh's spread. 'What sort of business is carried out in those?' she asked.

'Well you might ask,' Jane said, dismissively, 'Rosemount Road is a bit off the beaten track and since the economic downturn most of the retail outlets are boarded up. The building backing directly on to McDonagh's is Rosemount Lodge – a guesthouse. Used to be a pretty classy place a few years ago but lately, well, standards have gone to the Devil … caters for married men and their fancy glamour pusses, a knocking shop if you're to believe the gossip around here. Wouldn't surprise me one little bit. They don't advertise any more and their listing is no longer in any of the tourist board publications, I know 'cause I checked. The chalets you see in the back are supposed to be self-catering accommodation but it's anybody's guess what goes on in them. I see cars pulling in and out at all hours of the day and night. Well, I can tell you this: if I ever catch Sean nosing about over there I'll snip his balls off.'

Emma had little or no interest in Rosemount Road, its properties or the local gossip. Her interest was focused exclusively on McDonagh. 'Did I hear you say that he only moved here in the last two years?' she asked. 'I thought that he … I mean, I assumed that this was his home, where he'd always lived.'

'No, no, not at all. He came here after his release. Of course, we didn't know he'd been *inside* at the time; had we known, we'd have kicked up blue bloody murder. The question we all want to know is, how did someone who'd spent two years in the clink get the wherewithal to buy it? Can you answer me that?'

Emma shrugged her shoulders. 'Search me,' she said, intrigued by what she'd heard. 'Depends on what he owned before going to prison, I suppose, or what line of business he was in.'

'Huh! You mean apart from raping young women. None of us have succeeded in ferreting out what he did before he washed up here. Though from the cut of him I'd say it wasn't anything respectable … I mean, come on, can you picture him sitting at a boardroom table or heading up some big international corporation? Well, can you?'

'Frankly, no,' Emma conceded. 'But he must have had something going for him to buy the property, even if he did get it at a knock-down price.'

'Hey, look, look, there he is,' Jane said excitedly, stabbing the window pane with her index finger. 'He's coming out of his boiler room … that's where he prepares the food for those bloody dogs of his; they're a hell of a lot better fed than some of the people I know.'

As though McDonagh had heard Jane, he stopped mid-stride, put down two buckets he'd been carrying, and looked directly towards Emma.

'Shit!' Emma said, withdrawing a step back from the window. 'He's spotted us. I think he knows we're here, knows I'm here with you.'

'So what! Let the bugger know we're keeping an eye on him.'

Emma watched, surprised to see McDonagh make a gesture in her direction. 'Bloody hell, he *does* knows I'm here,' she said. 'How can he know that?'

'Probably saw you talking to us outside his gate. I think he spends as much time watching us as we spend watching him.'

Emma's body gave an involuntary shudder as McDonagh's eyes locked onto hers, his stare as belligerent as any she'd ever encountered. Blood drained from her face. She wanted to back away from the window but felt trapped there, as though caught in a hypnotic spell. In this state of near paralysis she watched him raise both hands to mime the act of typing, his fingers nimbly tapping keys on an invisible keyboard.

'What the hell's that about?' Jane asked.

Emma didn't answer. McDonagh's silent message couldn't have been clearer had he transmitted it in high frequency sound waves and subtitles: *He's annoyed that I haven't taken up his challenge to dig into his trial transcripts. He's impatient for me to write up my findings in the* Post.

'I should be going,' she said, breaking eye contact with McDonagh, turning to Jane. 'Thank you for allowing me into your house.'

Driving back to the office, Emma tried to rationalize the strong feelings of unease that assailed her when McDonagh had locked eyes with her, a feeling that curled her stomach into a knot. The contradictory nature of what she'd learned from Jane Henderson and her fellow protesters had put her head in a spin. On the one hand, the women had provided evidence that McDonagh could not possibly have been involved with the disappearance of Gemma Moore, not unless he had the gift of bi-location. But another part of her – her instincts, her gut feelings – persuaded her that there was more to McDonagh than met the eye. Emma sensed contradictions in the man. He exuded an air of persecution, a victim complex, while at the same time displaying an overbearing degree of arrogance. She was more determined than ever to discover who exactly McDonagh was and where he'd come from.

To that end, she had instigated some new lines of inquiry before setting out for Rosemount Lane. She'd contacted the greyhound board, told them who she was, not bothering to hide the fact that she was a journalist. She'd been switched from person to person and left on hold on three occasions before eventually being patched through to an individual named Seamus Coleman. She asked him if he could supply her with print-outs of the racing forms for specific periods of time – going back over two years – throughout their various venues. Coleman told her that what she wanted would take a considerable amount of time to put together and that, for that reason, it would help if he knew why she wanted it. It was, Emma thought, a reasonable request but she couldn't tell him the real reason, knowing the greyhound authorities would be less than eager to help if they knew she was checking up on dog owners.

'It's part of a broad-based story I'm putting together,' she told him, hoping it sounded plausible. 'I'm trying to tie in a number of unrelated events in order to create an overall picture of a particular period in time.' To help expedite things and reduce the amount of work involved she gave Coleman specific, narrow time frames for the periods that she'd aligned with the dates of the four disappearances she was concerned with.

'You're not looking for much,' Coleman grumbled sarcastically, 'but at least the narrower time frames you've given me will make the task a bit less painful.' He still sounded sceptical about Emma's bona fides as he continued to belly-ache but finally he promised to get back to her, saying, 'What you're looking for is somewhere on our computer system … I said *somewhere*. Finding it, that's the problem. Won't be easy to find someone here with time to chase it down. But look, I'll see what can be done, have someone search the files and download it to you if we get lucky.'

Emma thanked him, not at all confident that she would get the information she sought. It would have been so much easier if she could have called on Connolly to do the search on her behalf. He would have no trouble in securing such information. But, with things being the way they were between them, well, the waters were in something of a muddied state. Besides, Connolly had taken such a strong opposing stance against her pursuance of McDonagh that asking him would be like waving a red flag at a bull. That situation might have to change if the greyhound people failed to deliver – a switch to plan B. Should that happened she would swallow her pride, lay her cards on the table, tell him about the line of investigation she was following and hope that he agreed to do a little foot work on her behalf.

CHAPTER 30

HE DISCERNED AN altered atmosphere. Straight away. Something peculiar. A seismic shift in attitude. The two commissioners looked at him differently, their body language giving off enigmatic vibes, their auras at odds with what prevailed previously. McDonagh had a talent for sensing karma, a finely tuned perceptiveness, even so, he couldn't be one hundred per cent sure of what exactly accounted for the strangeness on this occasion. Several possibilities occurred, none to his liking.

Hostility. Betrayal. Abhorrence.

Arriving for what he hoped would be their last session, he'd been in a foul mood. The appearance of the journalist Emma Boylan in his next door neighbour's house had set him on edge. He'd made it clear to her: *I want you to investigate the case of my wrongful imprisonment.* She hadn't listened. He'd challenged her to write an article in the *Post* that would clear his name. And what had she done? She'd deliberately gone against his wishes, thumbed her nose at him by conspiring with the busy-body protesters who, given half a chance, would string him up from the nearest tree. He had hoped that this meeting with the commissioners would bring him a measure of what Americans called *closure*, not to mention a much needed deposit in his bank account. But, having laid eyes on the two inquisitors, he got that sinking feeling. Bad karma.

'Mr McDonagh,' Collins said, his practised courtroom munificence in full flow. 'We've got what you might call a fly in the ointment, a spanner in the works, a complicated development to contend with since last we met.'

'What? I thought we were going to sign off today,' McDonagh said, noticing how the obese judge was enjoying his own performance.

Senator Maurice McCann attempted to explain what had happened.

'You are, no doubt, aware of the publicity … the media attention you've received in recent days, Mr McDonagh?'

'Can't be responsible for what the press says.'

'Indeed not, none of us can,' McCann offered, leaning forward on his elbows, his attempt to convey camaraderie as phoney as a clown's contrived merriment. 'But the publicity has prompted certain parties – parties who were involved with you during your time in the Beaumont Industrial School – to contact the authorities. Those authorities have, in turn, got in touch with us. We've been obliged to examine certain factors arising from that period in order to conclude our findings.'

Matthew looked at the two men, a stunned expression on his face. The curveball they'd thrown had taken him by surprise. 'I've told you what I know about the Beaumont,' he said, aware that he sounded defensive, unable for once to check himself. 'What's the problem?'

Judge Collins shifted his bulk, his eyes boring into McDonagh, the unsmiling smile on his face cold enough to freeze hell over. 'It would appear that one of the people you've told us about, one of those you accused of inflicting abuse on your person, met his death under suspicious circumstances.'

'Suspicious circumstances?' McDonagh repeated, a questioning expression on his face. 'I'm sorry, I don't have the remotest idea of what you're talking about. Who exactly are you referring to and how can it possibly have anything to do with me?'

'Brother Bernard, you remember telling us about him?' Collins asked.

'Yes, yes, of course I do,' McDonagh answered, still looking perplexed. 'What about him?'

The judge's fleshy countenance remained impassive. 'We've received information with regard to his death twenty years ago, information that connects your name to a murder inquiry that followed his death.'

'Look, what exactly is going on here? I have volunteered to participate in this commission of inquiry. I've offered willingly to give evidence of the abuse I experienced as a child. I've been open and frank with both of you about the despicable things I've endured. The purpose of all this, I was assured, was to identify the people responsible for the dreadful things that happened and to have them answer for their crimes. But what is happening? All of a sudden I seem to be the one who's on trial. It's not enough that I suffered at the hands of those monsters back when I was an innocent child; now I'm being made to suffer all over again.'

'Nothing could be further from the truth, Matthew. We just need to know what, if anything, you can remember about that case.'

'Yes, yes of course, how could I not remember it,' McDonagh said with weary despondency. 'It happened after I'd left the Beaumont. Big news in all the papers at the time. In common with several other ex-residents of the school, I was brought in to help the police with their inquiries.'

Judge Collins fixed McDonagh with his best courtroom stare. 'You were questioned because, before his death, Brother Bernard brought a complaint against you ... against *you* specifically ... to the gardai, claimed you were harassing him, accused you of making veiled threats.'

'This is stupid,' Matthew said. 'Look, we all hated Berno – that's what we called Brother Bernard – and we all called him names, made no secret of the fact that we'd like to see him struck by lightning or run over by a steamroller. I won't pretend I was sorry to see him die. I wasn't, but the fact remains: I had nothing to do with it. I really don't see any point in discussing this matter any further.'

'That's quite understandable,' Senator McCann said, not bothering, on this occasion, to lean forward on his elbows. 'Nevertheless we are duty bound to ask. Even though this business goes back twenty years, we are obliged to check the records of the inquiry that followed his death, see what part, if any, you played.'

McDonagh exhaled loudly, his frustration all too evident. 'Look, this has nothing whatsoever to do with me ... *nothing*. I was questioned at the time, just like dozens of others who knew the old pervert. I had an alibi for the night of his murder. End of story.'

'Well, that's as may be,' Collins said, stroking his chins. 'And, I'm inclined to believe you but we have no choice; we are imposing a temporary suspension on your application for compensation.'

'What? You can't do that! You can't suspend—'

'I'm afraid we can ... and we must. We can't take this any further until certain parties on a higher level than us resolve the matter beyond question.'

'But that's crazy, look, I've just told you I was questioned at the time. I was able to prove that I had nothing to do—'

Collins held a hand up, stopped him. 'It's like this, Mr McDonagh. Because of the media interest in your story there is a need to get to the bottom of this. No stone must be left unturned. Bottom line: the tax payer is paying for this inquiry and for that reason, if no other, we must travel the extra mile.'

Too stunned to talk, Matthew remained silent. He wanted to scream out at the unfairness of it all. He was still being punished and he felt as he'd felt when he was a child, alone and helpless. But there was a difference now, a glimmer of hope he'd never had when he'd been the subject of abuse; that difference, he believed, was the investigative journalist, Emma Boylan. He needed her to take up the challenge he had given her … and when she did – if she did – she could clear his name with regard to the conviction for the attempted rape of Kathy English. He would prove to the two commissioners sitting in front of him that he was an upright citizen of unblemished character.

CHAPTER 31

MUTUAL AWKWARDNESS MARKED Emma's first visit to her parents since the disastrous St Patrick's Day get-together. Discomfort only partly offset by forced affability all round. No mention of the spat. Emma had deliberately left Connolly behind; he wouldn't have come willingly in any case. His presence would probably have reinforced the sense of unease. She needed time and space to clear the air; straighten things out with her parents before the subject of her impending nuptials came under scrutiny again. Fact was, Emma needed to get her own mind straight on the whole issue of the marriage.

She loved Connolly, no doubts on that score, but – why had there always to be a *but*? – but the formality, the solemnity and ceremonial aspect of marriage – a second marriage in both their cases – gave her pause. The sacred vows, the whole 'till death do us part', the 'for better or worse' and the 'in sickness and in health' bit had never sat comfortably with her. She needed to sort out all that ritualistic mumbo-jumbo in her own head before getting involved in a heavy discussion with her parents again. As for Connolly, well, that was another day's work, the biggest question of all, and one that wasn't going to go away, at least not until she'd got a better handle on things.

But before getting into that she had other fish to fry. She needed her father's assistance regarding the very subject that had prompted the Paddy's Day debacle. She waited until he was on his own before broaching the subject. For the past two days she'd thought a lot about Matthew McDonagh and the gauntlet he'd thrown down. He'd asked to have his trial records held up to scrutiny, not something a guilty person would normally do. Could be a double bluff, of course. She hadn't changed her mind about him being guilty but the hard edge of conviction she'd had originally had been slightly blunted.

Her efforts to date to check out his 'case for the defence' had met with little success. When she'd contacted the office of Trevor Shields, the barrister who'd represented McDonagh, the secretary she'd talked to sounded friendly, efficient, spoke with a warm, honeyed voice, but the message remained clear: 'Sorry, Mr Shields is tied up in court for the next three weeks and unavailable to talk to anybody.' Emma had persisted, as was her wont, but to no avail; the answer remained a polite, but unequivocal no.

Sitting in the sun lounge – a recent addition to the house, built to take advantage of its commanding view of the river – Emma swapped chitchat with her father as he gazed out front, relaxed in his favourite easy chair. With April just two weeks away, the weather had greatly improved and the lawns had shaken off their winter hangover. Through the conservatory's glass frontage, Emma and Arthur watched as Hazel, accompanied by Queeny, her favourite cat, refilled the bird feeders and picked daffodils. Emma was impressed by how her mother moved with such ease and confidence, almost as though gliding, her age no impediment whatsoever. She hoped that those good genes had been passed down to her. She noticed that her father too saw this in Hazel, his love and admiration was undiminished over the years. He had not been as successful in combating the disagreeable traits of age, the lines in his face picked out mercilessly in the bright sunlight streaming through the glass frontage. With some reluctance, she interrupted his thoughts, told him why she'd come to him.

He smiled when he'd heard what she was after, a wry smile that confirmed what he'd already guessed: she *needed* something. 'Why do you wish to meet Trevor Shields?' he asked. Emma began to outline the direction her investigative piece on McDonagh was taking but Arthur interrupted her straight away. 'Same story you and Connolly nearly came to blows over last time you were here, yes?'

'Afraid so,' Emma admitted. 'Connolly thinks I'm wrong-tracked. He says there's no hard evidence to link McDonagh to the missing women – calls what I've got a shaggy dog story – and in a way he's right, I mean, yeah, believe it or not there *are* dogs – greyhounds to be exact – involved at every turn, but he's stating facts when he says I've come up with nothing solid to tie McDonagh directly to the disappearances.'

'I don't understand this, Emma; Connolly's a detective, and a pretty good one if I'm a judge of character so he should know what he's talking about, right? Begs the question, why are you persisting with McDonagh?'

'Because I've met the man. Looking into his eyes, what I saw was like ... Jesus, it was like moonlight glinting on a gravestone.'

'Can't condemn a man for what's in his eyes. What kind of world would it be if we judged everyone on appearance? A beauty contest, that's what we'd have. No, Emma, you need something a little bit more substantial than that.'

'I have more. I've come up with what could be called circumstantial evidence – and this is where the dogs come in. I've established that McDonagh attended Shelbourne greyhound track on the night Siobhan O'Neill disappeared. She'd been walking her terrier close to the track when she went missing.'

'I'd call that pretty slim, not nearly substantial enough. I mean, can you tell me how many others attended Shelbourne Park that night?'

Emma had to concede that her father had a point.

Getting no answer, Arthur prodded a little further. 'Do you have any other – what I'll call – *hard* evidence?'

'Yeah, I have; how about this: Kathy English – she's the woman he went to prison over – fact. She lived a stone's throw away from Shelbourne park. Suspicious, wouldn't you say? All right, I accept it's still not proof but I honestly think it adds up. And yet ... and yet, here's the bit that's doing my head in: I don't think McDonagh's the raping kind.'

'What? You believe he's innocent?'

'That's what he'd like us to believe ... and somehow, in his twisted logic, I think he might be right.'

'You've lost me, Emma.'

'It's possible I'm barking up the wrong tree – sorry, I'm slipping into doggie speak; call in the men in white coats when I start barking – but I think he may be guilty of something worse than rape. Think about this: he was charged with attempted rape because he got caught in the act of attacking a woman. What if his intention wasn't rape *per se*? What if he was trying to abduct her? What if he hadn't been caught? What would have happened? Would he have raped her, or – and this is the bit that's doing my head in – would he have subjected her to something far worse?'

'Pure conjecture,' her father said dismissively, his lifetime's lawyer's training coming to bear.

'You're right, of course,' Emma conceded. 'It is conjecture, I accept that, but logic tells me one thing and my gut tells me something else. I do think, though, that there's something really whacky, something unsettling about McDonagh. That's what bothers me.'

'Moonlight glinting on a gravestone,' Arthur said, a mock quizzical expression on his face as he repeated her earlier observation.

'Funny thing is,' Emma said, 'he's asked me to look into the court's findings; he's under the impression they show conclusively that he should *not* have been put away. That's why I need to talk to Trevor Shields; he defended McDonagh.'

Arthur Boylan looked at his daughter, his face tactful as a diplomat. 'I've known Trevor most of my life and I have to tell you that he's one of the finest advocates in the business ... damned expensive, true, but worth every penny. If he wasn't able to get his defendant off, then I'd say his defendant didn't deserve to get off. I've never known Shields to sell a client short.'

'Well, McDonagh is convinced that Shields got it wrong in his case. That's why I need to talk to him. I want to hear what he has to say. I was hoping that maybe you could arrange an introduction.'

'I could do that, sure, no problem. Wouldn't do you any good, though. Shields would never discuss a case with you.'

Emma crinkled her face as if she'd just bitten down on a slice of lemon. 'Why?' she asked. 'Because I'm a journalist, huh?'

'No! Wouldn't matter if you were the Pope's envoy; he would never discuss it outside the jurisdiction of the courtroom.'

Emma looked, and sounded, despondent. 'I'm snookered, that's what you're saying?'

''Fraid so, Emma, but – and I can't believe I'm saying this – I might be able to help.'

'How? Tell me how.'

'Well, it so happens that I'm meeting Trevor this weekend for a spot of golf in the Royal County course. We know, and trust, each other well enough to discuss subjects that wouldn't normally be aired outside the law libraries. If you brief me on what exactly it is you think he can help with, I'll try to get him to talk to you about it. Can't promise you anything but I can at least try.'

Emma ran through the salient points and had just about concluded when Hazel and Queeny returned. The cat brushed up against Emma's legs and put on an energetic display of curling and uncurling in front of her. Contentment personified. Emma got down on her knees and began to gently stroke the cat, thinking how wonderful it would be to have a cat share her apartment, knowing, at the same time that Connolly would never allow a feline beneath his feet. Thinking about this, she caught the expression on her mother's face, an expression that left her in no doubt about what the next topic for discussion would be: love, marriage, Vinny, Connolly, affairs of the heart and just about everything in between.

CHAPTER 32

THE GARDA TECHNICAL Bureau had settled into their work in Tara, camped out on the rain-soaked land alongside the motorway. With all the professionalism of a full-scale archaeological dig, they'd divided the area into a grid of equally proportioned rectangles. Apart from those digging in the clay they'd brought in a raft of specialized personnel to head up areas like 'finds processing', 'documentation' and 'laboratory techniques'. With the enthusiasm of a team on a mission to find the Holy Grail they surveyed the mucky earth with the kind of precision one might describe as obsessive. It didn't yield the kind of results they'd hoped for. Nothing further in the way of body parts had come to light. The dig would continue for another few days but any hope of getting a result had all but faded.

During the course of the excavation Connolly and his team had set about tracking down those who'd owned the land before the NRA compulsorily acquired it. Not an easy task. Scores of small land parcels, stretching from Dunshaughlin to Navan, had been gobbled up and swallowed by the M3 motorway as a great swathe of Meath's pasture land was raped by bulldozers and lost forever, all done supposedly in the name of progress.

Pressure on Connolly to produce results intensified. Everyone from the chief superintendent to the justice minister, to the media and the self-appointed guardians of the peace, the ones who phoned radio and television chat shows, thought they knew better than him how the investigation should be handled. One caller insisted that the recently laid M3 be dug up, the theory being that body parts had been buried beneath the road's foundation during construction. Apart from giving this option serious consideration, Connolly was doing everything humanly possible to achieve results but the cumulative criticism was getting to him. The outcry in reaction to Gemma Moore's disappearance had reached epic proportions.

Ironically, much of the hysteria had been generated by an article in the *Post* written by Emma. In her exclusive, the paper had reproduced a series of happy smiling photos showing Gemma Moore and her friend from the bank enjoying each other's company. The pictures were accompanied by the interview Emma conducted with Kathleen Morrison.

FOURTH MISSING WOMAN

Garda HQ has confirmed that the case of Gemma Moore is being treated as unlawful abduction, and is linked to the disappearances of Joan Keating, Siobhan O'Neill and Annette Campbell. Twenty-six-year-old Gemma Moore has worked in the HTB bank in Henry Street for the past four years. She has not been seen since St Patrick's Day when it's believed she met a mysterious date in the city centre. Her best friend Kathleen Morrison who worked along-side Gemma is distraught. 'Gemma only met the man for the first time the previous day and told me he was a real charmer; they were supposed to meet in the lobby of the Gresham Hotel,' Kathleen claimed. 'We text each other all the time and she promised to let me know how the date turned out.' That promised text message never arrived. When Kathleen tried Gemma's mobile there was no answer. A smiling picture of the two young women beamed out from the screen of Kathleen's mobile but no new messages from her friend. A tearful Kathleen said, 'Like me, Gemma is a true romantic; we both like boys but neither of us are in any way promiscuous.' Gemma, we learned, likes to read romantic fiction and is a big fan of boy bands.

The garda have examined CCTV footage from the Gresham Hotel's security cameras and have established that Gemma Moore and her intended 'date' did not at any point meet in the hotel. When asked....

The combination of the devastating words and the happy pictures reproduced in the paper had connected with the public, the strong impact creating a groundswell of concern for Gemma Moore's well-being. Readers wanted this young woman found, demanding that the person responsible for the abduction be apprehended. They looked to Connolly to accomplish this feat.

He'd released stills from the CCTV footage that showed the man with the hat and coat crossing in front of the Gresham Hotel. The IT crew had attempted to enhance the image by brightening the part of his face bathed in shadow, but the process had been less than successful. Even so, Connolly hoped someone might recognize the man. RTE, TV3 and TG4 had shown the live CCTV footage on their news bulletins but as yet no one, apart from a misguided prankster, had come forward with information.

Connolly had also released a picture of the man's Mazda and its registration number to the media and issued every uniformed officer in the country with this information, their instructions to stay alert and keep a sharp watch out for the car. No luck so far. Connolly was determined not to allow lack of progress to unnerve him or his team. While waiting for the Mazda to turn up, if indeed it ever did, he had invested time and resources into tracking down whoever had buried the Tara bones. This involved sifting through dozens of Ordnance Survey maps and land registration documents and deeds of ownership – time consuming work. Boring as watching snails copulate. Yet there was no alternative; it had to be done. It was the only way to establish whether or not the bones had any bearing on the current list of missing women.

Once again, Emma figured in the machinations. Her earlier article, the one linking old cases to the current investigation had persuaded the public to take her proposition seriously. This notion was further reinforced when her follow-up article honed in on the case of Matthew McDonagh.

Connolly found it hard to understand Emma's dogged pursuance of the McDonagh case. No proof existed that McDonagh had anything to do with the missing women. On the contrary, the evidence available tended to clear his name. McDonagh had not left his house during the period in which Gemma Moore had been abducted. Furthermore, McDonagh drove a ten-year-old Land Rover and had no record of owning any other road-worthy vehicle. But Connolly was reluctant to dismiss Emma's line of inquiry out of hand because if experience had taught him anything, it taught him that her instincts turned out to be right more often than not.

Sitting at his desk, pondering this dilemma, he was cheered to see that the person approaching him looked as though she might be the bearer of good news. That would make a pleasant change. There'd been a distinct lack of anything approaching good news in recent days. Sergeant McFadden, who managed a smile at the worst of times, her morning grouch persona aside, was positively beaming as she pulled up a chair in front of his desk. She'd been the one charged with identifying those who'd owned the lands where the bones had turned up. 'You wouldn't believe how difficult it is to trace ownership,' she said, placing a pile of legal documents on Connolly's desk. 'The land in and around the motorway switched owners several times in the last seven years.'

'Why's that?' Connolly asked.

'Greed! Naked greed, nothing else. It comes down to money in the end, always does. Ever since the NRA decided to push the motorway through Tara, the former owners, in cahoots with the speculators, county councillors and state officials, traded parcels of land in the expectation of turning a profit when the state, free and easy with taxpayers' money, finally purchased the land.'

'So, what've we got?'

'During the period that the bones were buried, the land in question belonged to the estate of the late Tom and Josephine Quinn.'

'Who took over?'

'After Tom and Josephine Quinn died, the estate was controlled by their two daughters – Olive and Eileen. They held on to the property until two years ago; that means they had it during the period when the bones were deposited. They sold it to the NRA sometime after that.'

'So, why aren't they in here? Why aren't we talking to them?'

'That was the plan but some things are easier said than done.'

'Why so?'

'The two women conducted all the business transactions through a firm of solicitors – Farrell, Reid & deBruen. I've made contact with them but they refused to play ball.'

'Have you tried to contact the sisters directly?'

'Of course we have. Problem is, we can't get a fix on them. We're pretty sure one of them lives in London but the other one could be in Timbuktu for all we know. We've talked to the neighbouring landowners but they say the Quinn sisters never resided in the homestead after their parents' deaths. Apparently, they put a manager in charge. From all accounts, he kept himself to himself … did nothing with the land. Seems like he was more a caretaker than anything else, if we're to believe the locals.'

'Well, I don't have to tell you how important it is to find these women, discover the name of the person they hired. The body parts we found didn't get there by themselves. *We need* answers. *We need* to get hold of these women. *We need* to find out if they can shed light on the mystery. Most of all, we need to establish who the bones belonged to when they supported life. Talk to Detective Brian Goode – he ran the unresolved investigations into the earlier missing women back when that hullabaloo was in full swing.'

'You mean the ones Emma Boylan mentions in her article?' McFadden said, enjoying Connolly's obvious discomfort, a mischievous glint in her eye.

'Yes,' Connolly replied, sounding vaguely irritated. 'We need to collate all those cold case records, see if there really is a tie-in between those bones found in Tara and today's missing women. Give this top priority.'

'I'm on it,' McFadden said, snapping to attention and giving a mock salute, a beaming smile fixed on her face.

CHAPTER 33

THEY'D MET FOR lunch, an all-too-rare midday rendezvous. Venue: the up-market Wicklow Hills restaurant, off Wicklow Street, standing on a site adjacent to where the old and venerable Wicklow Hotel once stood. Back in its glory days the hotel was considered one of the city's most fashionable hostelries. It got its name on account of its connections with the horse and hound fraternity who'd hailed originally from county Wicklow. The new eatery could boast of no such heritage. For them to incorporate the *Wicklow* heritage in the restaurant's name was a misnomer and somewhat disingenuous to boot. In spite of its modern decor, a product of the Celtic Tiger days – all chrome, neon and fibre optics – it had a warm and welcoming feel. The initiative to have lunch together had come from Emma. She wanted to put aside the unpleasant atmosphere that had prevailed in recent days, get things back on an even keel, back to where they were before the areas of disagreement had arisen. Meeting for lunch was her attempt at offering an olive branch.

Shown to a good table by the maître d', Emma began to doubt that her efforts at detente would get them out of the icy strait they'd entered. The clue was in Connolly's face: glum, unsmiling, distracted. She was still going to make an effort, enjoy the meal, cajole him into a better mood by gentle persuasion. She craned her neck, scanning the whole dining area, keen to absorb the ambience. The place was buzzing, immune to the consequences of the soul-sapping financial downturn. Every table occupied, serving staff attentive, like penguins on speed, ready to serve the lunchtime clientele.

'People still have to eat,' Connolly was saying, in reply to a remark she'd made about being surprised to see such a capacity crowd. His mood remained as it had been for the past few days – downbeat. She pretended not to notice, determined to win him over with noncombative talk. Allowances had to be made. He was getting a hard time from his superiors, the media and the general public with regard to the lack of progress in the missing women's investigation, but that kind of pressure was nothing new, went with the job.

There was something else bothering him and Emma had a pretty shrewd idea what that something else was. Last night she'd told him about her latest contemplation on their future together. 'I've been giving some thought to our plans for the wedding and—'

'*Our* plans?' Connolly cut in. 'Didn't think they were ever *our* plans. Far as I can tell that area is strictly in your hands ... and your parents' of course.'

'Well yes, you might have a point there,' Emma said, wanting to jump down his throat but managing to retain her conciliatory tone. 'I'm sorry about that. I know it's my fault that the question of procedures was allowed to overshadow what's really important ... our feelings for each other. So, on mature reflection, as the politicians like to say, I think we should put the wedding on hold for the moment.'

Connolly glanced at her, brow furrowed as though in disbelief. 'Not go through with the wedding ... scrap it?'

'*Postponement*,' Emma said with emphasis. 'A temporary postponement of the ceremonial part of things – ease the more immediate pressure we're under, give us more time, more space, to get the arrangements right, keep all parties happy. What do you think?'

'What do *I* think?' he said after a short silence. 'I think ... I think you must do what you feel is best.'

He'd lapsed into an ominous silence after that. This for Emma was unexpected. She hadn't known what to expect but this response, this bout of sullen calm, had not been among the many reactions she'd considered. She decided not to intrude on whatever was going through his head, opting instead to allow herself to contemplate the ramifications of the decision she'd made. Coming on the heels of the long, soul-searching discourse she'd endured with her parents, she felt that the decision to postpone the wedding represented the most sensible choice on offer.

The parental/daughter session had brought things to a head. Mother and father had sat her down, determined to discuss every aspect of the subject thoroughly, all the while insisting they'd got her best interests at heart. 'Things went awry first time round,' Hazel had stressed, 'let's make sure we do things right on this occasion.' Arthur's counsel had been more measured, more subtle; he'd employed the debating skills honed to perfection in his law practice to get his point of view across while also cunningly letting her know he was willing to help her get the information she required on her current case. The old man may have retired but he'd lost none of his mental dexterity. Emma saw it for what it was: his idea of *quid pro quo*, with a little emotional blackmail thrown in for good measure. Together, her parents had convinced her to hold off on the registry office marriage, a decision that had, in any event, been playing on her mind in recent days.

Telling Connolly was something she'd had to think carefully about. She was well aware of the trials and tribulations he'd endured, and survived, in his previous exposure to the matrimonial condition. Because his first marriage had been such a disaster he was as anxious as she was to get it right second time round. Iseult, the woman he'd wed rashly in a fool-headed haze of lustful infatuation, had played free and easy with her sexual favours from day one. Must have been humiliating for him – not something he could sweep under the carpet very easily.

These days he avoided all mention of that experience, the memories too painful, too bitter, too humiliating, to revisit. Conscious of this, Emma dreaded to think how he'd react when she told him of her decision. She'd waited till they'd gone to bed before bringing up the subject. To her great relief he'd listened without engaging in histrionics. The ensuing silence had been a bit disconcerting but she'd taken it for what she hoped it was: his contemplation of the decision and acceptance of the sensible logic behind it.

But now, facing him across the lunch table, seeing him look as irritated as she'd ever seen him, she felt less confident. *Did I get it wrong?* Perhaps he hadn't accepted the news as readily as she'd believed after all. As soon as the waiter had taken their order she gently probed, wanting him to talk, open up about what was bothering him. 'I was determined to get you away from work for an hour, away from all that pressure. I know it might seem like I've been difficult lately and I'm sorry about that, Jim; I don't set out to upset you.'

'Really?'

'Yes, Jim, *really*. What we have is ... well, it's special. I would hate to see anything spoil that. So, let's just enjoy this lunch, put the troubles of the world to one side, enjoy each other's company for a change.'

Connolly made no reply for what seemed like an age. When he did speak his words seemed cold and distant. 'Some days I feel like throwing in the towel,' he said, not looking at Emma. 'It would be so easy to walk away from the whole damn mess.'

Efforts at detente were going to be more difficult than Emma had first envisaged. 'Please, Jim, please talk to me ... tell me what's wrong,' she said, thinking, *He's more annoyed with my flip-flopping on the wedding than I thought.*

Connolly grimaced. 'I've just come from viewing something I wish I didn't have to see,' he said with an almost imperceptible shake of the head. 'The drug squad wouldn't normally involve me but, on this occasion, they thought I should know.'

'They thought you should know what?' Emma asked, relieved that the marriage postponement wasn't to blame, glad now that he wanted to talk shop, hoping that by doing so he would shake off whatever was causing all this pent-up anxiety.'

'You haven't heard?'

'Sorry, Jim; I don't know what you're talking about.'

'Stephen Murray's been murdered; I've just come from identifying the body.'

'Oh my god! Murray – you mean Annette Campbell's partner? When? Where? How did it happen?'

Connolly waited, allowing the waiter to serve their food before answering. 'His body was found in a pub outside Finglas village – The Wheel Barrow – a vile dump owned by one of our more notorious drug barons. They found him in the gents' bathroom, naked, his head wedged down a toilet bowl. He'd been subjected to the most horrendous assault.'

'Jesus! What, they beat him to death?'

'No, wasn't the beating that killed him. Forensics will need to carry out tests but I talked to the pathologist and she's of the opinion that he died from a drugs overdose – an enforced overdose. They found a syringe on the floor beside him; looks like it contained a mixture of household bleach and a cocktail of drug substances. Not pretty!'

'That's terrible, Jeesus! They called you? That means his death is connected to ... to the missing women?'

'Don't think so; we did suspect him initially, thought he was looking good for Annette Campbell's disappearance. We brought him in, questioned him, decided he had no direct involvement. Have to confess, though, I didn't like him or his attitude, his silly bravado and arrogance, but damn it all, no one deserves to end up like that.'

'Was he involved with the drug trade?'

'As a user, yes, we knew he was an addict. We questioned the young woman he hooked up with after Annette vanished. She told us about his dependence on E, hash, speed, heroin, Christ knows what else. Seems like he was in serious hock to his suppliers.'

'That's why they killed him?'

'About the size of it. The enforcers don't take kindly to users who fail to meet the payments. Murray's death represents just another ugly statistic in the upsurge of drug-related murders in the city.'

Emma and Connolly were silent as they tucked into their food – sea bass for her; beef, peas and gravy for him – both of them retreating, at least temporarily, to their own private thoughts, Emma taking sideward glances at the other patrons in the restaurant every so often.

'You expecting someone?' Connolly asked, dabbing his mouth with the starched, white linen serviette.

'No no, not at all. What makes you say that?'

'Ever since we came in, you've been looking around, glancing over your shoulder as though expecting—'

'I'm sorry,' Emma cut in, sneaking another covert glance to her left. 'Didn't realize I'd been doing it.'

'You're still doing it. What's the hell's the matter?'

'I don't know … it's just that, you're going to think I'm losing it, but I keep imagining that someone's watching me. The oddest damn thing. I've had the feeling for the past few days. It's as though someone's following me around. Did you ever have that feeling?'

'Persecution complex,' Connolly said, dismissively. 'Could be Vinny, of course. Maybe he's planning to spring another surprise on you.'

'No, wouldn't be him; he's had his pound of flesh.'

Connolly took a discreet peek around the other tables, saw nothing out of the ordinary, just lunchtime diners enjoying their food, some happily chatting, some quaffing wine, others reading the dessert menus or checking their watches, concerned, perhaps, about getting back to work. 'They look a decent enough bunch to me,' he said. 'Your imagination's working overtime.'

'Yeah, you're probably right. It's this damn case … it's got to me; it's got to you too. It's got the two of us arguing, something we never do, something we shouldn't allow to happen now. But for whatever reason, it's doing my head in … those poor women. Every time I think about what might have happened to them, I get a sinking feeling.'

'Know what you mean,' Connolly admitted. 'And you're right, we're letting it get on top of us. Trouble is, in my case, it's my job to sort out the problem ... but for some reason it feels as though everyone wants to get their kicks in, that I'm somehow responsible for what's going down.'

'And you're not exactly overjoyed by what I've been writing. I know it might look as if I'm one of those getting their kicks in, but that's not how it is. I'm only trying to do my job, the best way I know how ... same way you do yours. That's what I was trying to say that time when we rowed in front of my parents. What I said then came out all wrong and I'm sorry for that, I really am.'

'Look, Emma,' Connolly said, 'I know you mean well but – how do I put this – you have this weird ability, a talent really, to get right up my nose at times, and when that happens I tend to get pig-headed.'

'I have noticed.'

'So, let's not discuss it any further, not here, not now, let's just park it for the moment.'

'Yeah, that's what I want, too,' Emma said, not sure she believed her own words. 'But at the risk of breaking the rule already, can you tell me if you're any nearer to resolving...?'

Connolly shrugged. 'We've got a few irons in the fire, but, well, truth is, we've got little enough to go on. As you know, we've issued pictures of the man who abducted Gemma Moore; we've given out a description of his car and its registration plate. Not a peep from the public.'

'Someone must know him, know where he's hanging out. And the car, it can't be invisible.'

'Ain't that the truth,' Connolly said, his words accompanied by a defeated smile. He signalled for the bill, saying, 'Time I got back to the shop.'

'Me too,' Emma added.

Watching Emma and Connolly leave the restaurant, the obese woman who'd been dining at a table close by, put her knife and fork down. 'So, that's Emma Boylan,' she said. 'She looks ... younger than I expected, smarter too.'

'She is smart, a bit too smart for her own good,' Richard J. Bradbury said, removing his dark Dolce & Gabbana glasses. 'She's on the ball, the only person to seriously connect the old cases to the current ones.'

'Could you hear what they were saying?'

'Not really! Had my back to them but the noise level's too loud, I couldn't catch a word. Could see her, though, caught her reflection on the inside edges of my shades.'

'Have you thought about how we're going to get her?'

'Going to need more planning. Got to find a new set of wheels, search the ads, find someone who'll sell for cash.'

The woman frowned. 'Just remember my supply of cash is not endless.'

'Yeah, sure,' Bradbury said, drumming his fingers on the tablecloth. 'And you might bear in mind that I'm doing this for you. There's nothing in it for me.'

'Nothing ... except your continued survival, that is,' the woman snapped.

CHAPTER 34

THE JUDGE'S SUMMING-UP was interesting. It didn't provide the kind of answers Emma sought but she had to admit it *was* interesting. It was the first time she'd used the internet to dig up information of a legal nature. Surprised her. Courtroom proceedings were there for anybody who bothered to Google them. Made her wonder if Matthew McDonagh was aware of the great leaps technology had taken. Did he know his trial was online? Voyeurs could pick through it like vultures dissecting the entrails of an abandoned animal carcass. Double click, and hey presto, there it is. Though Emma would never admit to voyeurism – perish the thought – she was not averse to taking advantage of the miracle of modern science. She printed off Judge Rory McCall's three-year-old summing-up in the state versus McDonagh case.

The judge directed his attention initially to the case the prosecution had presented. He reminded the jury that Ms Kathy English (*the victim*) was a young unmarried mother of one child (*a boy, aged three years*) who lived at the time with her partner (*a porter in the Palace Hotel, Ballsbridge, Dublin 4*) in a flat in Beggar's Bush. The crime occurred on a warm summer's night, 14 July at 11.15 p.m. Ms English had accompanied her partner to the bus stop on Northumberland Road, from where he'd boarded a no. 7A bus that took him to the hotel for his night shift roster. Walking back to the flat Ms English noticed a man sitting behind the wheel of a stationary car. It caught her eye because it was parked within sight of the entrance to her block of flats. She'd just passed the car when she sensed someone approaching from behind. In an instant she felt an arm grab her by the neck while, simultaneously, a knee rammed into the small of her back. The force used would've floored most women but Kathy English was not like most women. She'd attended self-defence classes and knew how to react. She employed her survival instincts and her defence reflexes as she'd been instructed. A struggle ensued. Her knee connected with the attacker's privates. She scraped his face with her nails, pulled his hair out by the roots. Her quick reaction wrong-footed him at first but his strength and aggression proved way too powerful. She continued to fight, taking a beating as he punched, slapped, kicked and grabbed at her hair and clothes. Her face was a mess of bloody cuts and bruises, her light summer top ripped to shreds, her bra torn and practically pulled off.

As her strength and mental reserves failed, she felt herself being hauled bodily towards the open door of a car. Fortuitously, her bellowing had been heard by several residents living in the area. People came out of their homes to see what was causing the racket. Seeing a woman they knew in distress had them running to help her. The attacker, knowing the game was up, abandoned his prey, dashed back to his car and sped away, almost colliding with two of the rescuers in his haste. The number of the car had been noted and twenty-four hours later Matthew McDonagh was apprehended and lodged in custody. In a hastily arranged line-up McDonagh was identified. The garda forensics unit examined the hairs and skin fragments that Kathy had gouged from her attacker. The samples provided proof that McDonagh was the guilty party.

Emma paused to consider the report, many of the facts already known to her. The area where Kathy English had been attacked was within walking distance of where Siobhan O'Neill had been abducted, both locations less than half a mile apart. This was as near as dammit to confirmation, at least in her mind, that Matthew McDonagh was involved in Siobhan O'Neill's disappearance. And, if he was responsible for her disappearance it followed surely as day follows night that he was also ... but she was jumping way ahead of herself.

Emma went back to the report.

The judge went on to outline the essence of what had been McDonagh's defence. As a child, the accused had been subjected to extraordinary, terrifying and confusing circumstances. These emotional scars were, according to his defence, permanently engrained in his mind; they could be suppressed but never fully erased. McDonagh's psychiatrist argued that his patient sometimes, in a state of suspended reality 'quit' his body without having the mental capacity to dissuade the invading 'other self' from taking over. Afterwards, McDonagh would regain his true consciousness, find himself in an unexpected location, with no memory of what had transpired during the period he'd vacated his body.

Judge Rory McCall invited the jury to pay special attention to this aspect of McDonagh's case. He reminded them of the prosecuting lawyer's description of it as pseudo science, suggesting it represented an unsafe and unproved submission. 'We're dealing with a vicious attack on a young woman here,' he'd pointed out to the jury. 'A terrified woman ... beaten, clothes ripped, dragged by the accused to his car, actions motivated by a depraved desire for sexual gratification ... perhaps something worse.'

The psychiatric assessment presented to the court was according to the state prosecutor, an insult to the intelligence and, for the victim, an additional insult to injury. 'This court,' the prosecutor went on to say, 'rejects the theory put forward as having no basis or credibility in legal or scientific terms. This is a court of law. We require hard facts that will stand up in court.' (*Laughter in court.*) Emma couldn't tell from reading the report if the prosecutor's statement had been deliberately facetious or had by accident created the inherent innuendo. Whatever the intentions, it hadn't affected the outcome. McDonagh got three years; served two before being released.

Emma put the report aside, a tingle of excitement running through her. What she'd read gave her an idea for her next piece in the *Post*. Her previous article on McDonagh had not gone down well. It wasn't just Connolly who felt she'd overstepped the mark. Other commentators too, claimed it had encouraged 'vigilantes' to victimize McDonagh – a man who'd served his time for his crime. Rival newspapers accused the *Post* of indulging in 'low standards' in journalism. The words 'pot' and 'kettle black' came to mind.

When she'd confronted Matthew McDonagh on his doorstep, he'd told her that her article amounted to lazy, sloppy journalism. And now, after reading what the judge had had to say on the subject she was forced to acknowledge that McDonagh might have a point. Yes, she should have read the court report before rushing into print. Well, she wasn't going to make the same mistake a second time.

Crosby was greatly exercised by what Emma had told him – not in a bad way. Emma couldn't remember the last time she'd seen him so worked up about an idea that she'd brought to the table. He'd given the go-ahead on the initial article with regard to McDonagh's criminal record. The backlash generated by that article was viewed by him as an attack on his integrity and professionalism. Being summoned to the paper's chairman to discuss the repercussions and justify its publication had hurt. What Emma had brought to him now would, he hoped, justify his initial stance on the subject and answer his critics. He had to be careful, though, had to get the balance right. Getting it wrong could bring about his retirement a little sooner than he wished.

With Crosby's help and the cooperation of the newsroom team, Emma amassed enough material to run with an in-depth feature on the McDonagh case. To augment the judge's summing-up, she'd availed herself of the Freedom of Information Act and got full transcripts. The *Post*'s art department produced a diagrammatic graphic of the Dublin 4 area showing the location where McDonagh's victim, Kathy English, had been attacked. It highlighted the spot where Siobhan O'Neill had disappeared and picked out Glynn's Inn, the pub where Annette Campbell was seen by barmen and customers alike on the night she'd gone missing. The triangular-shaped area stretched from the Shelbourne greyhound stadium to the Lansdowne rugby grounds, extending as far as Glynn's Inn at the third apex. Overlapping red circles indicated how close the locations were to each other.

Emma worked with the head of graphics, a bright, young, red-haired artist named Joan O'Hara, to create a design that would inform her readers in stark visual terms. She'd used inserts on the periphery of the map to show the different elements she'd brought together, inserts that included pictures of Annette Campbell, Siobhan O'Neill, Kathy English, Matthew McDonagh (walking his greyhounds), Glynn's Inn and a print of the man with the hat and coat, lifted from CCTV footage. A second, less elaborate, diagrammatic illustration featured the Ledwidge Apartments where Joan Keating resided before her disappearance and where Mary Shaw had been attacked and, less than two miles away, the spot where the Tara Bones had been uncovered.

The greyhound authorities had produced the details Emma requested on all race meetings that had taken place back at the time when the four earlier women had disappeared. The organization, it turned out, had seventeen tracks in the Republic of Ireland and three affiliated tracks in Northern Ireland. Four of the locations in particular caught her eye: Harold's Cross, Newbridge, Longford, and Mullingar. These locations had all featured in her recent article on the earlier missing women, the same piece that had caused such friction between her and Connolly. In the course of the article she'd given descriptions of four women: Shannon Hughes had lived with her parents in Harold's Cross before she'd gone missing. Melanie Sweeney shared a flat in the town of Newbridge before her disappearance. Rachel Fagan, a student nurse, who shared an apartment with three other nurses in Longford, had vanished never to be seen again. The fourth woman, Alison Hogan, a single mother, had worked in the planning department in Mullingar's county building. She'd failed to turn up at the crèche where her baby son was being cared for. All four women had lived in locations boasting a greyhound stadium.

The greyhound board, Emma had established, had no racetrack in Navan, a factor that puzzled her at first. On further investigation she discovered that the Navan track was not part of the official organization. It was what was known as a flapper track – a privately run operation where approved rules and regulations didn't apply. It allowed owners to test their dogs in trials that weren't recorded in form books. This allowed owners to get better gambling odds when their dogs competed in legitimate stadiums because the bookies remained ignorant of the dog's 'real' form.

Crosby decided not to use the material regarding the four greyhound track locations or the one in Navan, fearing it would complicate their message. This reservation apart, he was receptive to everything else Emma had dug up. He wanted to know if Matthew McDonagh and the man with the hat might not be one and the same person. Both men, he argued, looked roughly the same age and had similar builds and height. 'Don't forget,' he warned, 'no one has got a decent picture of our friend with the hat, as yet.'

'I thought they might be one and the same at first,' Emma admitted. 'That's why I checked with the protesters outside McDonagh's house. They keep tabs on his comings and goings. They place him inside his house at the time the CCTV cameras captured the man with the hat in the company of Gemma Moore. The gardai also had him under surveillance. They have evidence that he remained at home during this period. So, unless McDonagh has the power of bi-location he can't have taken Gemma Moore.'

Crosby looked perplexed. 'So, riddle me this,' he said. 'Circumstantial evidence places McDonagh in these locations. Could it be we're looking at two men working in tandem?'

'I don't know about that,' Emma said dismissively. 'But here's the bit

I can't figure: it was McDonagh who invited me to look at the trial transcripts; told me I wasn't doing my job properly. Well, now I've accepted his challenge and it's done nothing to prove his innocence; what I've discovered, has in fact, confirmed – at least in my mind – that he was guilty as accused.'

Crosby shook his head and pointed to the article and the graphics. 'When this hits the streets there'll be skin and hair flying. The liberal contingent will be up in arms as usual, accusing us of conducting trial by media.' He looked Emma straight in the eye, his hands splayed as though appealing to a higher power. 'Are you sure ... I mean, one hundred per cent sure, we can stand over every last word in this article?'

'Yes, we can. I've double-checked. Everything I've used is taken verbatim from existing documentation and the location maps speak for themselves. Anyway, we don't *actually* accuse McDonagh ... not in so many words. We just set out the circumstances as we see them – let the readers judge for themselves. We can handle any backlash if there is one.'

'Oh, there'll be a backlash all right,' Crosby said knowingly. 'You can bet your bottom dollar there'll be wigs on the green. I just hope you have a strong rebuttal all ready to hit back with.'

Emma beamed. 'Oh, ye of little faith; of course I have.'

CHAPTER 35

DEEP IN DISCUSSION, Connolly and DS Bridie McFadden stopped short all of a sudden when Chief Superintendent Smith approached. He placed his copy of the *Post* on top of the one already sitting on Connolly's desktop. Connolly had expected this. Emma's front page article was bound to have repercussions.

'Perceptive insight, don't you think?' Smith said, addressing the two detectives. 'If I didn't know better I'd say Ms Boylan's perspective on the case holds up.'

Connolly hid his surprise; Smith had a habit of berating Emma's articles, especially when they strayed into current policing policies or offered opinions on ongoing cases. His criticisms never failed to imply that Emma might be the beneficiary of insider information coming from someone close to home. Smith's hint of praise for this, her latest article, represented a new departure. Connolly found himself in the unusual position of being the one to pick holes in what she'd written. 'Tells us nothing we don't already know,' he suggested, feeling disloyal but determined at the same time to push his own agenda. 'McDonagh has been in our sights from day one; we know he's been seen in places associated with a number of the missing women. We've visited his house and interviewed him after each of the women were reported missing – did it before his name found its way into the papers. We discovered nothing to put him in the frame.'

'Even so,' Smith said, leaning his back against the room's partition wall, 'there's something mighty peculiar going on, wouldn't you say? I know we've got similar diagrams on the boards in the incident room but these maps, or graphics, or whatever the hell we want to call them, that the *Post* have pulled together, well, they're compelling. Very compelling. Can't dismiss them out of hand, can we? I mean, when you consider the size of this city, population just over a million, and yet, here we have, in the case of the Lansdowne map, a postage stamp-sized Bermuda triangle where *people*, not aeroplanes, have vanished into thin air. It's like something from the *X Files*. And this McDonagh fellow that the article concentrates on is linked, to some degree, with all of the incidents. A common denominator, if you will. Coincidence? What do we think? I can accept coincidence; such things happen, no doubt, but surely what we have here has got to be more than just happenstance.'

'I agree, sir,' McFadden said, retrieving the *Post* from the desk. 'I think there's something very off-beam about McDonagh. Our inquiries tell us he's not the one picking up the women but, given all this circumstantial stuff, he has to be involved. I suggest we bring him in and, while he's here, take the opportunity to search his house.'

'Bring him in – on what charge?' Connolly asked, an edge to his voice, not liking the way the conversation was going. Not for the first time, he felt decidedly wrong-footed by Emma's article, even more so by the apparent support it was getting from the chief super and McFadden.

'Wouldn't be prudent to bring him in,' Smith answered. 'Not until we've got something solid to charge him with. No point arresting him, then letting him go; we'd end up with egg on our faces.'

'Could get a search warrant, turn his place over?' McFadden offered.

'Yes, we could do that,' Smith agreed, 'but that amounts to the same thing, plus we'd have the press crucify us if we came out empty handed. No, I don't want that. Best we can do is to follow him every time he goes out ... round the clock surveillance.'

'Already in train,' Connolly said, trying to regain the initiative.

'What else are we doing?' the chief super asked.

'Still looking for the Mazda. We get that, we get the driver. We get the driver, we find Gemma Moore. We find her, we hit pay-dirt; find the others ... solve the mystery.'

Smith smiled disingenuously and rolled his eyes heavenward. 'Simple as clockwork, eh! That's the strategy?'

McFadden decided to put her oar in. 'I'm chasing down the Tara bones. I've discovered that the place where the bones were found belonged to people called Quinn, a few years before the NRA took it over.'

'I see! So, you're going along with Ms Boylan's contention that there's a connection between those old bones and today's missing women?'

'Needs checking,' McFadden said with a shrug, 'In the absence of anything else, it's worth pursuing. Trouble is, I'm having difficulty getting hold of the two remaining members of the Quinn family.'

'Why would that be?' Smith asked.

'When the NRA purchased the Quinn land, the deal was conducted through solicitors on both sides. Obviously, the two Quinn sisters – Olive and Eileen – had to have been involved in the sale but tracking them down is turning out to be a real bugger. We've gone through the telephone directory but you just wouldn't believe how many Quinns there are out there. We're now concentrating on official records, documents, online directories both here and in the UK, examining everything there is ... a real slog.

'What solicitors do the sisters use?' Smith asked.

'A firm called Farrell, Reid & deBruen. We've spoken to them but they're being rather sniffy, refusing to part with any information. I told them how serious it was, impressed on them that what we're investigating is a murder case. They refused to budge so I've applied for a court order. Trouble is, that's going to delay things a few days.'

Smith stroked his chin between thumb and index finger. 'Hmmm,' he said at length, 'I should be able to work something on that score. I'll get back to you on it presently.'

Smith was about to leave when Detective Sergeant Dorsett pushed through the opening into Connolly's cubicle. Not expecting to see the chief superintendent, he decided to execute a quick heel turn, come back later, but the move was too late; Smith had seen him.

'Sorry,' Dorsett said, holding a hand up in mock surrender, 'didn't mean to interrupt.'

'Just leaving,' Smith said, moving past him. 'Any developments I should know about?'

Dorsett gave Connolly a quick look before answering. 'I hear there's a spot of bother outside McDonagh's house. The story in the *Post* today has the natives baying for blood – worse than last time. Media's there in droves. The uniforms have their work cut out ... it's getting ugly.'

'Situation's already ugly,' Smith said, looked directly at Connolly. 'We need this sorted, Jim.'

E MMA DIDN'T PLAY golf. Didn't *get* the game. The idea of spending a day chasing a small white ball over the undulating grounds of the Royal County golf course didn't appeal to her. Not one little bit. However, enjoying a drink or a bite in the clubhouse was a different matter entirely. Over the years her father, a one-time captain who played off scratch back in his prime, liked to treat her to lunch or dinner there. Today it was lunch. Emma had taken care to dress appropriately: a mid-grey tailored trouser suit, white silk blouse and minimal make-up. The weather had picked up nicely and, for late March, the place was as busy as ever she'd ever seen it. Mostly men. Grey business types. Quite a respectable showing of women too; wives, girlfriends, singles. None afraid to sport lively colours and fake tans. A few casually clad younger men, with an eye to moving up the social pecking order, ignored the sneers from the older alpha males, while welcoming the admiring glances from the opposite sex.

Overlooking the eighteenth green, Emma sat at a table with her father and his friend Trevor Shields. They'd had a light drink at the counter before moving to the dining area next to the viewing window. Arthur Boylan had introduced his daughter to the off-duty barrister and the flow of chitchat had been pleasant, the two men, curators of gossip, swapping salacious tales from the law library's rich pageant. Emma felt excluded but still found herself warming to Shields. She was aware of his reputation, knew that his work at the bar was distinguished by his success rate and his preference for keeping a low profile. Of average build, fifty-five-ish, he had a smiling, agreeable face, nothing remarkable in the looks department except for an impeccably barbered head of silver hair.

They were well into their meal before Arthur, whose repository of superfluous information which had provided great merriment, ceased.

With consummate ease he introduced the subject responsible for bringing Emma and Shields together. It was clear to Emma that the two men had already aired the topic privately before today's get-together. This was fine as far as she was concerned; meant they could get to the meat of the matter without too much preamble. Arthur nodded to his daughter, a signal for her to get the ball rolling. Prompt taken, Emma went for it. 'Mr Shields, I'm hoping you can give me the benefit of your thoughts on Matthew McDonagh.'

'Yes, your father has filled me in,' Shields said, eyeing Emma. 'I've read your pieces; wanted to see what you said about my one-time client.'

'What was he like to deal with?'

'Impossible! I tried to walk away at one point.'

'Why was that?'

'McDonagh made it impossible to mount a proper defence.'

'But you didn't ... walk, I mean.'

Shield's face cracked into an amiable grin. 'True, I didn't. We barristers may, as the saying goes, fart in silk but nevertheless we still have a living to make. The people behind McDonagh paid over the odds to retain me.'

'You're saying someone else picked up the tab?'

'Certainly! I doubt if he had the kind of juice to defend such a case.'

'In what way did he prevent you from mounting a defence?'

'Well, his position was pretty much cut and dried. Forensics had taken fingerprints, blood traces, fibres and hairs from the crime scene. McDonagh was identified by no less than three witnesses – one of them the victim – in a line-up. In a situation like that we usually go for the obvious defence, you know, discuss traumatic amnesia, introduce a list of extenuating circumstances, establish human frailty, elicit sympathy from the jury – appeal to their compassionate nature.'

'And what, you're saying McDonagh didn't cooperate?'

'Wouldn't play ball. For that kind of strategy to work, it would've been imperative to have everyone, including the defendant, sing from the same hymn sheet, as they say nowadays. Didn't happen. He fought me all the way, contested every point, refused to take advice. Insisted he was innocent – they all say that, of course – but he went a stage further, claimed he wasn't even there.'

Emma put her knife and fork down, enthralled by what Shields was saying. 'How did he explain away the DNA ... the physical evidence ... the blood ... the finger prints?

'Said his blood had been stolen,' Shields said. 'Claimed another person had borrowed his fingerprints.'

'And being recognized in the line-up?' Emma asked.

'Unbelievable,' Shields said, rolling his eyes heavenward. 'The trial took on surreal dimensions, like something from science fiction. He informed the judge that someone else had invaded his body, I kid you not.'

'That's why the case was lost?'

'Well, yes, the prosecutor laughed us out of court, made supercilious remarks about some old movie called *The Invasion of the Body Snatchers*, but, on a more serious level, they cited a raft of case histories where such a defence had been blown out of the water as having no basis in law.'

Arthur Boylan, who'd been contentedly getting on with his meal, allowing his daughter to pose the questions, decided to throw in a few questions of his own. 'Would you say McDonagh was psychologically disturbed?'

'Absolutely, yes. There was evidence of psychiatric disturbance, paranoia; anyone could see that the man was pathologically unwell, on the brink of psychosis.'

'Well, bearing that in mind, I imagine the jury would have gone for a plea of temporary insanity. You didn't go down that line, did you?'

Shields' voice dropped to an ominous whisper. 'Wasn't allowed to. His psychiatrist objected, insisted on taking the stand himself.'

'Who was the psychiatrist?' Arthur asked.

'An old guy into his seventies. His name was – let me think, yes, I remember. Dr Belcher. Very eminent in his field, or so *he* informed the jury. I was being paid to do the job but McDonagh insisted that Belcher, more or less, conduct the defence; he brushed my objections aside, wouldn't listen to anyone else, swore by everything the old codger said.'

'Belcher?' Emma queried. 'You don't mean Dr *Tim* Belcher?'

Shields didn't answer. Like her father, his attention had been diverted to the window, watching three golfers putt out on the eighteenth green. Emma hid her irritation, thinking, *Men and their balls*. She watched patiently as the three players took their time, hunkered down, stepped up and back to the hole, observing the slopes and dips on the carpet-like surface before, eventually, each putted out in turn.

'Sorry,' Shields said. 'Got caught up in the action there for a sec. Golf, it's addictive. Where were we? Oh, yes – the psychiatrist. You're right, his name *was* Tim, Dr Tim Belcher. You're not going to tell me you're in need of…?'

'No, no, God no, nothing like that. I got to know him about eight or nine years ago. He was involved in a very distressing assignment I was working on at the time.'

'In his capacity as a psychiatrist?' Shields asked.

'Yes! Actually, now I come to think of it, it involved a person who was afflicted by a personality disorder not all that dissimilar to the sort of thing McDonagh claims to be afflicted by.'

Shields nodded, drained his glass and paused to consider what Emma had said. 'May I offer a suggestion?'

'Certainly. Feel free.'

'According to what I read, Emma, McDonagh's house has come under siege again, protesters and media watching his every move.'

'Yeah! And guess who they're blaming for that? Me.'

'Well, that's as maybe but the fact that he hasn't appeared outside his door for hours is a cause for concern. I'm sure none of us wants this to end in tragedy. Seeing as how you're already acquainted with Dr Tim Belcher, I think you should contact him. Through him, you might get a better understanding of what's supposed to be wrong with McDonagh, find a way of communicating with him, bring this saga to some kind of conclusion before something bad happens. If nothing else, Belcher might offer some sort of explanation to you that might throw some light on the bizarre defence presented at the trial.'

'I might just do that,' Emma said, but neither her father nor Shields was paying attention; they were caught up again in watching two young female golfers making their way from the clubhouse to the first tee.

Back at her desk, Emma searched through old files until she found the contact number for Dr Tim Belcher. Got through on the first attempt, told him who she was, reminding him that they'd met some years earlier. He surprised her by saying he remembered her. When she asked if she could meet with him, his voice became guarded. 'Why?' he asked.

'I've been talking to Trevor Shields about Matthew McDonagh,' Emma replied. 'Shields suggested I talk to you.'

His reaction was immediate. 'I think it is totally unethical of Shields to have talked to anyone about a former client. I never breach confidentiality with clients and that goes for you too; I have no wish to speak further on the matter.'

Emma tried to persuade him that what she had in mind might be to McDonagh's advantage but at some point, without knowing exactly when, she realized that the psychiatrist had hung up.

She sat at her desk fuming, her fingers unconsciously tapping out a tattoo that sounded not unlike the intro to the *William Tell Overture*. Talking to Trevor Shields had given her an interesting angle for the article she intended to write but having a statement from Dr Tim Belcher would give it depth, an edge to transform ordinary reportage into something more substantial. Still drumming *William Tell* with her fingers, she glanced at the two trophies on her shelf – both 'Journalist of the Year' awards. On days like this, looking at the awards helped remind her that she was good at her job.

The first trophy, a hand-cut crystal ink jar and silver pen, had come at an early point in her career. Happy days. The *Post* had been a noisy place back then with the constant rumble of an in-house printing press to contend with; that plus a clutch of word processors, larger-than-life characters, boozy lunches, laughter, gossip and glamour. Different atmosphere today. The *Post* had become similar to every other office: no presses, no characters worth talking about, noiseless keyboards, sobriety, timesheets and conformity the order of the day.

Change had already begun by the time she won her second award – a framed lithographic plate from a newspaper front page, dated June 1996. It featured the murder of crime correspondent Veronica Guerin with a picture of her red Opel Calibra. Guerin had stopped for traffic lights at Newlands Cross on the Naas Road when a drug dealer, riding pillion on a motorbike, shot her dead with a .357 Magnum. Caused outrage in the country, brought about the creation of the Criminal Assets Bureau (CAB) a body with powers to seize criminals' assets. The trophy's subject (the death of Guerin) had no direct connection with Emma except that the judging panel had picked the seminal event to highlight the serious nature of work done by journalists. It was also supposed to improve the public's perceived notion of what a journalist's job entailed. This was an ideal that Emma subscribed to, something she aspired to but not, she hoped, at the expense of her life.

There was space on her shelf for a third trophy but if progress on the present assignment was anything to go by, then she might be waiting some considerable time to fill it.

She was about to ring her father, thank him for the lunch at the golf club when a call came through. It was Dr Tim Belcher. 'Been thinking about our conversation,' he said, sounding awkward, apologetic. 'On reflection, I think it could be useful for my client to have the media hear his side of the story. So, Ms Boylan, if you still wish to talk, I'd be pleased to arrange such a meeting.'

'Thanks for getting back,' Emma said, trying not to sound as pleased as she felt. 'Very kind of you. When can you see me?'

'Not today, I'm afraid. Let me see; how would' – he made a clucking sound with his tongue – 'how would tomorrow suit? Say 4.30 p.m.?'

'No problem; that'll suit me fine.'

'Good! You know where I live?'

'Yes, I do. I'll see you then. Thanks … thanks very much.'

CHAPTER 37

IT TOOK LONGER for the train to get from Stansted railway station to Liverpool Street than the Ryanair flight had taken to cross the Irish Sea from Dublin. Didn't bother Bridie McFadden though. Not a bit of it. She was just glad to get away from the squad room in Pearse Street, if only for forty-eight hours. That Connolly had picked her, not DS Dorsett, to go to London gave her a sense of pride. Connecting the Quinn sisters to the Tara Bones had, after all, been down to her. She was the one who'd traced the siblings back to the firm of solicitors who acted for them. Trouble was, the firm jealously protected the sisters' anonymity. She'd hit a brick wall. But her boss of bosses, Chief Superintendent Smith, knew Kenneth deBruen, one of the principals in the solicitor's firm, (both men were Opus Dei members and shared the same alma mater). Smith had managed to get an address for one of the sisters; Eileen Quinn lived in London. She'd married, and divorced, a wealthy business man. Retained his name. She was now Mrs Alex Jones.

Unfamiliar with the tube system McFadden hailed a taxi at Liverpool Street, instructing the driver to take her to the Montague Hotel on Russell Square. It was late evening and she wanted to see some of the great city before dark. Her driver, a convivial cockney, after establishing that she was 'Oirish' trotted out his full complement of knowledge on his perceived take of Irish culture: Terry Wogan, Graham Norton, Bono & U2, Bob Geldof, Guinness and Riverdance, all the usual suspects. Bridie attempted to introduce a measure of balance by mentioning Irish icons that, in her opinion, better represented the country, names like Synge, Shaw, Beckett, Wilde, Joyce, O'Casey and Heaney. The driver, unimpressed, said, 'You're forgetting Maeve Binchy, the wife's favourite; she has all Maeve's books, saw some of the flicks, too.' The taxi man continued to talk about everything and anything, unaware that Bridie had tuned out for the most part. She was determined to enjoy the sights and noises and smells all around her. At one point, delayed at a cross-roads, she spotted the towering Centre Point building as the dying sun glowed furiously on its glass frontage. *Wonderful*, she thought, *God, I love this city.* The hotel turned out to be plusher than she'd expected – huge room, great bed, nice view of the gardens, everything top notch. Her appointment with Mrs Alex Jones was set for 11 a.m. the following morning but she was determined to see a bit of the city in the little time she had.

Getting out of bed early the following morning, gave her plenty of time to make the appointment, and she enjoyed the sights along the way, strolling past Sotheby's and down the busy Tottenham Court Road, feeling carefree. The sun beamed brightly and there was that end of March crispness in the air that she loved, meant she didn't have to bother with an overcoat or hat. To kill time she did a little shopping, bought the latest iPhone from a handsome shop assistant who was only too willing to show her how to operate it. While demonstrating the intricacies of the technology the assistant – his name badge said Nigel – had managed with some degree of subtlety to give her his best chat-up lines. McFadden, who'd been dumped by her long-time boyfriend a month earlier felt reassured to know that, at thirty-two, she still retained pulling power. She was never going to challenge the likes of Angelina Jolie in the beauty stakes but she was happy in her skin. She prided herself on her good taste in fashion. She knew how to accentuate the few precious assets she possessed and she could hold her own with the best of them when she took the trouble to 'put on a face' like she'd done that morning. Before leaving the shop Nigel had got her to agree to meet him if he visited Dublin for a long weekend (for *long*, she read *dirty*). It would probably never happen but the exchange had cheered her up and boosted her confidence.

With three minutes to spare, and an extra spring in her step, she located Grove Row, the address she sought. It turned out to be a tree-lined avenue off Goodge Street, flanked on either side by well-maintained Georgian houses.

A young oriental woman opened the door and, after establishing that she had an appointment, asked McFadden to follow her inside. Stepping out of the bright sunlight into a cool, spacious entrance hall, McFadden squinted to adjust her eyes to the change of light. She followed the woman through a sumptuous hallway, its polished checkerboard floor of black and white marble reflective as a mirror, its walls lined with discreetly illuminated oil paintings, into an equally sumptuous drawing room. The oriental woman – McFadden thought she looked exotic, beautiful – asked her if she cared for something to drink. She declined the offer, not bothering to add the rider, 'not while on duty'. She understood now why Connolly had sent her, not Dorsett. He'd obviously been tipped off by the chief super with regard to the Jones residence, and knowing how DS Dorsett could be mistaken for a down-and-out, thought better of it. The room, like something McFadden had only ever seen in magazines like *Home & Garden*, made her contrast her surroundings with her parents' small farmhouse in Tipperary, a dwelling whose totality could fit in this one room.

Minutes after the oriental woman had left the room, a more mature woman entered. She extended a tapered, discreetly manicured hand to McFadden and after introductions were exchanged, sat down. Mrs Alex Jones, an impressive woman in her forties who could have passed for thirty-something, was dressed in top-end designer casual, her face rich in character and intelligence. 'I'm told you wish to speak to me about the business in Tara,' she said, only a hint of her Irish brogue evident. 'How can I help you?'

McFadden, on instructions from Connolly, told her everything she knew about the discovery that had been unearthed in the property Mrs Jones once owned. 'We need to establish who the bones belong to ... and to do that we need to know who buried them.'

'Goodness gracious!' Mrs Jones exclaimed, eyes widening. 'How very extraordinary.' She shook her head as though unable to comprehend what she had heard. 'I'm truly shocked, I really am, but I can't see that I can help you. From what you've told me, the bones were buried after my parents died, during the period when my sister and I were trustees. I never set foot on the property during that time and, to my knowledge, neither did my sister.'

'I talked to other land owners in Tara, and they said they saw a man there during the period we're discussing. They seemed to think he might have been some sort of caretaker; would you know anything about that?'

'Yes, I do. My sister Olive – she still lives across the water – looked after that end of things. It was easier for her to find someone to keep an eye on the place.'

'Don't suppose you know the name of the man?'

'I do as a matter of fact. You see, until we sold it, I had to shell out my share for the upkeep of the place … and that meant paying half the fellow's wages.'

'His name?' McFadden prompted.

'McDonagh, yes, that was it; I remember writing his name on the cheques: Matthew McDonagh. Name mean anything to you?'

Before McFadden could answer, the oriental woman entered, and informed Mrs Jones that she was wanted on the private line.

'Will you excuse me, please?' she said to McFadden. 'I have to take this call. I won't be more than four or five minutes.'

Left alone, McFadden decided to call Connolly on her newly acquired iPhone. She knew he'd want to know that she'd established a connection between the Tara Bones and McDonagh. That would give Connolly reason enough to bring McDonagh in, search his property. If she got through to him without delay, she'd be finished by the time Mrs Jones got back to the room. She wanted to find out more from the woman, like, for instance, how to get in touch with her sister.

Within twenty minutes of getting the call from DS McFadden, Connolly and Dorsett were banging on the door of Matthew McDonagh's house. The two detectives had run the gauntlet of protesters and media at the gate. Connolly took it in his stride, welcomed it in fact; it helped to be seen to be actively pursuing the case. With so much negative press in recent days and being told by one government minister to 'get off their arses', the publicity would do no harm at all. Yet he still couldn't figure how Emma had managed to hone in on McDonagh at such an early stage, at a time when he'd poured scorn on her intuition. He might have to do some serious grovelling, he acknowledged, admit to her that she'd been right all along and he'd been wrong. But it hadn't come to that yet. He remained sceptical about McDonagh's involvement in the crimes, knowing as he did that they had CCTV footage showing a different person in the act of abducting Gemma Moore.

They waited outside McDonagh's door for over five minutes, banging the knocker at fifteen second intervals. The door remained closed, no sounds from within. Connolly knew from the protesters that McDonagh was inside. He double-checked with the plainclothes officer who'd been planted in a neighbouring house for the past forty-eight hours, tasked with the job of monitoring any comings and goings. The plant confirmed that McDonagh had not left the house since he'd last entered it.

Connolly called Chief Superintendent Smith to see if the search warrant he'd requested earlier had been granted. He was told it would be ready within the hour. Heading back to their car, Connolly and Dorsett were set upon by the protesters and the gathered media. Through the cat-calls and jeers, a statement was called for. The two detectives remained tight-lipped, looking, and feeling, somewhat foolish as they retreated from the scene empty handed. A potbellied drunk slurred his way through the nursery rhyme that had the Grand old Duke of York marching his troops to the top of the hill and marching them down again. Connolly was tempted to give the protesters the old Arnold Schwarzenegger line – 'I'll be back' – but the detective inspector didn't do humour.

CHAPTER 38

W HILE Bridie McFadden sat amid luxurious surroundings in London, Emma Boylan diced with congested traffic on Rock Road, heading towards Blackrock on her way to meet Dr Tim Belcher. She remembered his house from the last time she'd been there, part of a gated enclave catering for well-to-do residents and private businesses. It was impossible not to be wowed by the view from the granite steps that led to the front entrance. There was a slight nip in the air, but not a cloud in the sky. A picture-postcard vista of Dublin Bay stretched in front of her, a whiff of brine in the air, the lighthouse on Howth Head clearly visible in the distance. The discreet, matte-grey nameplate spelled out the psychiatrist's name, his qualifications and the clinic hours.

The last time she'd called, a middle-aged receptionist had met her; this time the doctor himself let her in. He offered a limp hand to shake as he ushered her inside. It was plain to see that Belcher had succumbed to the ravages of time. He was thinner than she remembered, his face a sickly grey pallor, deeply lined and mottled. A scattering of fine white hair had been strategically combed over his bald crown. Emma sat in his consulting room on one of the two leather upholstered mahogany chairs; he sat behind an old-fashioned desk on a high-backed chair. 'I'd better start by telling the truth,' he said. 'And the truth is, I didn't want to meet you at all, Ms Boylan.' His voice struggled for definition through phlegm-ridden lungs, each word underscored with withering scorn. His expression remained venomous. 'I've read your reports in the *Post* and I'm appalled by the ill-informed content being peddled to the readers. What you've done to my patient, Mr McDonagh, is reprehensible. Without understanding any of the complexities at play in his case you've set yourself up as judge, jury and lynch party. You have deprived a good man, a troubled man, of his rights to live a normal life.'

'So, why have you asked me here?' Emma asked, taken aback by his hostility, but conscious at the same time of an underlying anguished sincerity in his voice.

'That's a very good question,' he said, nodding gravely. 'After you called me I contacted Mr McDonagh. I informed him that you'd phoned and told him that I'd refused to see you. He suggested I call you back, avail of the opportunity to put his side of the story to you, let you hear what the court refused to listen to. Reluctantly, I agreed to comply with his wishes. The *real* question, Ms Boylan, is, are you willing to listen.'

'It's why I'm here,' Emma replied, feeling decidedly uneasy, knowing that McDonagh himself was involved. 'All right if I record this?'

'Wouldn't have it any other way, Ms Boylan. Your readers deserve a fair and accurate account of the lack of justice meted out to my patient.'

Emma placed her microcassette recorder on the edge of his desk and sat back as Belcher went into a long, winding discourse that sought to explain the infinite complexities of the brain. He talked about the hundreds of patients he had treated, dealing with everything from drug and alcohol abuse to a wider variety of phobias and neuroses, taking in a plethora of sexual perplexities along the way. He took pains to explain the symptoms associated with a patient who is suffering from what used to be called Multiple Personality Disorder, what has since come to be recognized as Dissociative Identity Disorder – or DID.

Emma knew a little about DID. The subject had, in recent years, become particularly relevant in crime detection and the wider field of forensics. She'd come up against it on a few previous cases and decided to let Belcher know. 'Far as I can tell,' she offered, 'DID syndrome is viewed by most respectable psychiatric practitioners as nothing more than a con-job that allows so-called patients an excuse for the crimes they've committed.'

'Yes, that's been the situation in a few well publicized instances but that does *not* mean it doesn't exist ... because I can assure you it does. What I'm telling you is indisputable fact. Leading psychiatrists have found increasing incidents of DID in the aftermath of severe or prolonged bullying or sexual abuse, the kind highlighted in the recent revelations of what was going on in many of the state institutions for children. So, I ask the question again: Do you wish to hear what I have to say or do you want to argue with me?'

'Sorry! Go ahead, I'm all ears.'

Belcher didn't like her glib reply but let it slide. 'In McDonagh's court case, I tried, but failed, to make his defence counsel understand that it's possible for two or more personalities to lead independent lives within one body. In the case of the woman who claimed my patient attempted to abduct her, McDonagh had unknowingly – I repeat, *unknowingly* – provided the host-body for the entity who'd actually attacked her. Because of the childhood abuse he suffered, he has developed an ability to take himself outside his body, see himself as others see him, but what I'm talking about now is something of a different order, a different magnitude, something way more serious.'

'May I ask a question?' Emma said, putting her hand up like a school girl. 'While the crime – the one he was imprisoned for – was in progress, what was the *real* McDonagh doing … I mean while the other person inhabited his body?'

Belcher heard the scepticism in Emma's voice but decided to ignore it. 'McDonagh experienced a period of blankness during that period,' he said. 'For all intents and purposes, he ceased to exist … except in a void. You see, the invading entity creates a separate and distinct personality from that of McDonagh. This entity has its own pattern of perceiving and thinking, its own emotions, attitudes, tastes, talents, behaviour, speech, body language and dress code.'

Hearing this, Emma's thoughts flashed back to the recent meeting she'd had with Shields, remembering him tell her how the prosecution team in McDonagh's trial had mentioned in jest, *The Invasion of the Body Snatchers*. Listening to Belcher now, she could understand their scepticism. However she refrained from making comment to the psychiatrist on this point, listening instead as he became more and more exercised with every word.

'So, Ms Boylan, blaming Matthew McDonagh for actions beyond his control, actions that his conscious "self" has no knowledge of, is wrong and unjust. He – that is, his true self – was *not* present when that woman was attacked.'

Emma, not convinced by the argument, was about to cut in again when the door behind her burst open. She jumped with fright. The look of horror on Belcher's face was akin to Munch's painting, *The Scream*. A man strode into the room and pushed up to Belcher's desk. 'Please allow me to introduce myself,' he said, glancing between the psychiatrist and Emma. 'I'm Richard J. Bradbury and I'm here to see you, Ms Emma Boylan.'

Dr Belcher leaped from his chair and began remonstrating but Emma was momentarily struck dumb, immobilized on her chair. As though in a trance, she watched the man remove his hat and beam a smile at her, a malevolent smirk that held her in a hypnotic state of fear. She was looking at the face, the eyes, of Matthew McDonagh.

Mrs Alex Jones apologized for leaving McFadden on her own while she'd gone to take the telephone call, insisting the detective have tea and biscuits with her by way of amends. McFadden obliged, glad that her host seemed in no particular hurry to be rid of her. 'You were telling me about your sister Olive,' she said, attempting to restart their interrupted conversation. 'You said she looked after the arrangements regarding the disposal of the property in Tara. Is that right?'

'Yes, but I insisted that she ran all transactions by me first.'

'And it was Olive who hired this man, Matthew McDonagh?'

'Right! Apparently she'd known him for years, going all the way back to a time when she was a nun.'

'Olive was a nun?'

'Yes, you wouldn't believe it if you knew her. Wild as a March hare when we were kids. Still mad as a hatter today, if you ask me. Always in trouble, very demanding, spoiled rotten ... broke Mum and Dad's hearts, a right little brat. But when her best friend at school, an angelic girl named Rosie, decided to join the Sisters of the Holy Rosary, nothing would do but our Olive should join as well. She signed up on the same day. They were both fourteen. Olive wasn't cut out for the religious life but, fair play to her, she stuck it out for eighteen years before they....'

'What? She left the nuns?'

Mrs Jones laughed. 'Goodness, I can see why you joined the police force. It's questions all the way with you. But I don't mind. Tell you the truth, Olive and I never really did see eye to eye. Anyway, she didn't leave the nuns of her own volition. There was a bit of a scandal – something to do with an overly intimate liaison she'd had with one of her own kind – so they threw her out, excommunicated her or whatever it is they do to someone they disapprove of.'

'Where is she now? What does she do for a living?'

'Goodness, but you're a devil for the questions. Well, as you already know, we sold the land in Tara, got an obscene amount of money for it – it being at the tail end of that mad period when the Celtic Tiger was still roaring – so, after we divided the spoils, Olive went into business, something to do with the hospitality trade, I think. What a laugh! Not her scene at all but I suppose she had to do something.'

'I'd like to meet Olive,' McFadden said, 'just to clear up the business of hiring Matthew McDonagh. Do you have an address for her?'

'Yes, I have her business card. I can let you have it.'

Emma's mind grappled with what was happening, her panic intensified by the eyes holding her captive.

'Been watching you, you know,' the Richard J. Bradbury/Matthew McDonagh person said with something of a canine grin. 'Watched you dine in that fancy restaurant the other day with your detective friend.'

'What's this about?' Emma said, finding her voice, knowing how frightened she sounded, but trying to regain a measure of control.

'The time has come for you and I to get to know each other a little better. I have a friend who is just *dying* to meet you ... up close and personal.'

Emma rose from her chair, ready to confront him but before she'd made a single step, he sprang forward and slammed her back in the chair. 'Hey, that's good, I like the ones who show a little fighting spirit,' he said circling her chair, stopping behind her. In a move that took her by surprise, he pulled the chair up by the back legs and pushed it forward, sending her sprawling, face downwards, onto the floor. Blood gushed from her nose but she quickly turned her head, saw him approaching with a hypodermic syringe. She scrambled, crab-like, away from him, catching sight of Belcher as he attempted to grab the assailant. For an old man, he put up a hell of a fight. Through a fit of coughing and wheezing he yelled, 'Matthew, you're ruining everything, what are you doing? Matthew!'

McDonagh shot back, 'Who the fuck's *Matthew*, you shrivelled up old fossil. There's no one here by that name.'

While the two men went at each other, Emma spotted her mobile; it had been thrown free from her pocket when she'd fallen. She retrieved it, hit the speed dial for Connolly, got through to his answering service. 'Help,' she said, 'I'm in trouble. I'm in—'

But that's all she said.

Bradbury's foot connected with the mobile, kicked it from her hand, sent it flying across the room. 'Bitch,' he shouted, kicking and pressing her back to the floor. Through the pain, she felt the prick of a needle in the back of her neck. Almost immediately she felt herself being rocketed through a portal, the whole world spinning, spinning, spinning into infinity.

CHAPTER 39

ONE HOUR AND fifteen minutes after it had been sent, Connolly got Emma's 'Help' message. He cursed, then called his friend Crosby. In what seemed like hours but was in fact only fifteen minutes, Crosby was back on the line, said he'd talked to someone who claimed Emma had gone to see McDonagh's psychiatrist, a Dr Belcher, at his home in Blackrock. Minutes later, Connolly, alongside Dorsett, was speeding through Ballsbridge, on the way to Rock Road, sirens blaring, yelling at other motorists to get the hell out of the way.

Emma's car stood outside Belcher's house. 'Oh, thank Christ,' Connolly said. 'At least we know she's still here.'

'Sss-something's wrong,' Dorset stammered. 'Look, the door, the door is off the hatch, it's—'

Connolly pushed the door open, stepped into the hallway. 'Hello?' he shouted. No reply. Together the two men, swapping nervous glances, pushed into the house. They banged on doors, looked into several empty rooms until they found one that stopped them in their tracks. A man's body lay sprawled on the floor, head and shoulders propped against the side of a desk. 'Oh, sweet Jesus Christ,' Connolly said. 'What the fuck ... where's Emma?'

Dorsett knelt beside the body, felt for a pulse, shook his head. 'Dead,' he said. 'Looks like he was thrown against the corner of the desk; back of his head's cracked like an egg.'

Examining the crime scene, Connolly spotted the Olympus recorder peeking out from beneath the body, recognizing it straight away as Emma's. 'Can't disturb the scene,' he said to Dorsett, 'but nobody has to know.'

Dorsett, a stickler for by-the-book procedures, said, 'OK, I haven't seen you touch it.'

Connolly rewound the tape, listened to it as Dorsett contacted the personnel required to process the crime scene. Connolly, impatient with the tape, fast-forwarded it every few seconds, listening to bits that interested him. The name Richard J. Bradbury ... he'd heard that name before. That was the name of the man who'd bought the Mazda from the woman on the Navan Road, the man who'd abducted Gemma Moore. Connolly fast forwarded the tape again. He stopped it at the part where Emma is told she'd been observed with him in the restaurant. Further on, she is told about a *friend who is just dying to meet you ... up close and personal.* But it wasn't until he heard the psychiatrist call out, *Matthew, what are you doing?* that all the pieces fell into place. 'Oh, sweet Jesus, McDonagh's got Emma,' he said, almost disbelieving his own words. 'We need to get over to his place fast. He must have taken her there.' Connolly glanced at his watch. 'Bollocks! It's now two hours since Emma made that call – that's what scares me most.'

'I'll stay here until the crew arrive,' Dorsett offered.

'No, I want you with me – the body isn't going anywhere.'

Dorsett shrugged, uncomfortable at leaving the crime scene unattended but duty-bound to do as instructed. Something else bothered him: he was aware that Matthew McDonagh's house was under round-the-clock observation; that meant that if McDonagh had gone there, with or without Emma, reports of such an occurrence would have been received by now.

That hadn't happened.

Emma knows she's not dreaming; what's happening is real, part of the living world. She's been taken on a journey, a passage through a dense smoky fog, or at least that's what her drugged brain is telling her. The man with the evil eyes carries her in his arms before tossing her into some kind of moving vehicle. After an indeterminate time, the journey ends and she is taken out again. He speaks, the sounds indecipherable, coming from an otherworld dimension. She feels insubstantial, feather-light, buoyant enough to blow away.

She is in a room, an unpleasant-smelling room. She is on a bed, or a mattress perhaps, she can't be sure. There's another presence in the room. A woman? Red lips opening, closing, protruding tongue, burrowing into her mouth. Her clothes are gone, evaporated, no longer there. The other presence, obese, naked like her, is groping her, all over, speaking, calling to her. Yes, she can hear her own name: Emma, Emma, Emma. It is repeated over and over again, a woman's voice, deep, guttural, echoing down some endless funnel. She smells sweat, a foul musky stench. Another name is spoken, what is it? Olive? No, more like Oliver. Kissing, sucking, biting, she is being abused; she knows she is being abused but she is powerless to prevent it. She desperately wants to push away the presence, the thing, the bloated pale-skinned creature, the rapist called Olive – or Oliver – from her, stop the hurting, but her defence mechanisms refuse to respond.

And now, a greater violation, the ultimate degradation is visited upon her defenceless body. Some deep recess in her brain tries, unsuccessfully, to blank the invasive action. The focus of pain slithers, crawls, paws, sucks, kisses and bites all the way down, inexorably, down, down to the core of her very soul. She is conscious of the horror, the debauched encroachment, the tearing penetration when, mercifully, her brain, unable to cope with the assault, finally allows her to escape, allows her to retreat to a state of unconsciousness.

There was no hanging about this time. Connolly gave the order for the battering ram to be employed to break down McDonagh's door. A few good shoulder pushes or well-aimed kicks would probably have done the job just as effectively but Connolly's blood was up; he needed this show of strength to quell his frustration, satisfy the anger within him. The door disintegrated on first impact, the old timber crumbling like so many matchsticks. 'Search every room, every nook and cranny,' Connolly barked at the officers entering the house. The interior looked as dilapidated and forlorn as the exterior, smelled of old age and cabbage.

It was soon evident that neither McDonagh nor Emma were in the house. 'We need to look out the back,' he instructed Dorsett. 'Get the gang on it. Have them search the outbuildings, one by one; take the place apart, they've got to be here.' Only as this exercise swung into action did an obvious truth dawn on Connolly, a truth that Dorsett had been aware of for some time. In his haste to charge after McDonagh he'd allowed anger to blind his judgement. Rational thinking would have told him that had McDonagh, with Emma as his captive, come back to this house, they would have been seen by the protesters and the media gathered at the entrance. His garda observer would also have witnessed their arrival. To confuse matters further, all these witnesses insisted that McDonagh had not left the house during the past four hours. It didn't add up.

While his team systematically combed the property, searching each outhouse in turn, even removing the greyhounds from their lock-ups, Connolly decided to play the microcassette again. This time he would listen to it more carefully, making no skips.

McDonagh loved the smells. Putrid meat. Fear. Blood. Wearing his multi-stained white boiler suit and wellingtons he organized his butchering knives, one by one, in a neat row on the timber bench. 'Bet you never thought this was how you'd leave the world,' he said, checking to make sure he'd secured the chains properly to the pulley. 'But think of it this way: at least my greyhounds will be happy when I feed you to them, portion by succulent portion.' He could see the mouth working, opening and closing as though gasping for air, see the shape of words that wouldn't come, the eyes so full of terror. What was it he saw there – pleading? yes, Lord but he loved that. Smiling, he attached the ankle hooks to the chains. He began to turn the handle that raised the body, feet first, into an upright position, the head dangling above the ground. 'No fight left in you?' he asked, feigning an expression of surprise. 'They usually jerk about like crazy at this stage,' he said, now feigning disappointment. 'But of course you're different; you're the wise one, the dispassionate bitch who likes to play high and fast with other people's lives.'

McDonagh took a boning knife from the bench, hunkered down, pulled back the head of his victim and let the knife's blade slice into the throat, right through to the jugular vein. Blood gushed from the opening wound, splashing onto the tiled floor beneath. 'Good riddance and goodbye,' McDonagh said, straightening up, wiping the blade of his knife on his apron.

CHAPTER 40

THE SEARCH WAS now well into its second hour. No sign of McDonagh. No sign of Emma. Every inch of the place had come under scrutiny. The warren of outbuildings dated back to a time when they'd been part of an extensive farmyard, a once busy hub that functioned at the heart of surrounding pasture lands capable of sustaining herds of cattle. It had all been swept away in favour of tar and cement, new housing estates and commercial buildings. Were it not for McDonagh's shabby dwelling house and the buildings at the rear, this centre of agricultural activity may well have never existed. Connolly was reluctant to call off the search, feeling frustrated, knowing he should be doing something else, but not knowing what that something else should be. Looking at his watch, he realized that almost four hours had now elapsed since Emma's SOS. Christ, he could still hear the panic in her voice. He didn't want to dwell on what might have happened to her since that call.

He was about to ask Dorsett to halt activities when a call came through on his mobile from Bridie McFadden. 'I left a second message for you back at base,' she said. 'You didn't get it?'

Connolly thought for a second, then remembered. Yes, there'd been another message waiting on his answering service when he'd listened to Emma's call. He'd been so exercised by what she'd said, he had neglected to run it. 'Sorry, Bridie, I didn't get a chance to listen. What've you got?'

'I talked to Eileen Quinn – who is now Mrs Alex Jones – and she confirms that the man who looked after their land in Tara was none other than Matthew McDonagh.'

'Figures!' Connolly said. 'Pity we didn't know that a bit sooner, might have saved ourselves a hell of a lot of grief. Turns out that McDonagh also goes by the name Richard J. Bradbury. The bastard's got Emma!'

'Oh my God! Oh my God, no, not Emma! I don't believe this. Do you know … have you got … can you…?'

'I can't talk to you now, except to say I have a recording of Emma's visit to a psychiatrist. That's how I know that Bradbury – he's the guy who bought the Mazda from Mrs Gribben – is Matthew McDonagh.'

'What? The man with the hat, the Peacock; he's been McDonagh all along?'

'Yes, and he's got Emma. Problem is we don't know where he's gone with her.'

'Oh my God, I can't believe what I'm hearing. But wait a sec, listen, I think I might know where he's taken her.'

'What? Where? Tell me?'

'Mrs Jones gave me her sister Olive's business card. She runs a guesthouse. The address on the card struck me as being familiar. Rosemount Road, number nine Rosemount Road. So, while waiting for my flight in Stansted I searched the internet; brought up the Ordnance Survey map for that area and discovered that the guesthouse backs onto McDonagh's property.'

Connolly gasped. 'Bloody hell! All the time the answer's been staring us in the face, just over the damn wall.'

In Connolly's excitement, he'd cut the connection without thanking McFadden. There was no time to hang about. He needed to organize a strategy for getting in next door. He felt sure Emma had to be there, her life probably in danger. He needed to act quickly. No time to wait for search warrants, no time to bother with regulatory procedures.

McDonagh lowered the body, began to unshackle the ankles. 'Should have done that years ago,' he said, pulling the body to one side. He turned to look at Emma who'd just witnessed the slaughter. 'Thought it might interest you to see what I've planned for you. I hope you took some satisfaction in seeing your rapist get her just deserts.' He looked for a reaction from Emma. Got none. Incapable of speaking, she sat propped up against the white tiled wall, naked, her body still bloodied from the ordeal she'd suffered at the hands of her rapist. The horror of what McDonagh had done to the woman reflected in Emma's eyes. She remained traumatized; couldn't speak. The drugs had short-circuited her primary motor cortex, impairing her control and ability to move her limbs.

'No more Olive Quinn to bother you; no more Olive Quinn to bother me,' McDonagh said with a snort of dark laughter. 'Knew her first when she was a nun – Sister Marie-Theresa ... she taught me the Kyrie, the Gloria, the Sanctus and the Agnus Dei. Can you believe that? The dead slut. Can you fucking believe it? She taught me a lot of other things besides ... protected me from Father Troy and Brother Bernard, two of the most depraved monsters ever allowed to stalk the dorms of the Beaumont unhindered ... *Jesus*. But, in her own way, she was even more debauched than either of them. I was a child and the wrong gender for the kind of shit she got off on. Didn't stop her, though, did it. The real shit began the day she witnessed Brother Bernard lashing me with his fan belt. Through my screams she saw a new sensation take over my body. With each stroke I began to feel an alien sense of gratification. I'd begun to channel the pain into pleasure, experience a feeling of sexual release ... a stirring down deep, my arousal on display for all the fucking world to see – Brother Bernard, Father Troy and this bitch here. Of course we called her Sister Marie-Theresa back then. For some reason the sight of my boyhood erection turned her on. Probably why she decided to save me from them, although the word *save* might be somewhat of a misnomer.

'As soon as I entered her domain I knew that my rescue was no escape at all. "Those brutes really did a number on you," she said after she lowered my trousers to inspect the cuts and bruises. She held up a mirror, got me to crane my head around to look at the damage they'd done. Every stroke had left a different impression, streaks of blue, purple, black and ugly reds where blood had lodged on welts where the belt had cut into the soft flesh.'

McDonagh pointed to the dead body on the floor. '"Satan's Rainbow", that's what she called the stripes on my arse, said they were a sign that the devil had been driven out through the back door, exorcised because I had grievously sinned. I think she might even have believed it; I should have asked her before I finished her. Anyway, to get back to what I was saying. She set about cleansing the inflamed area with a sponge and water before spreading dollops of thick white cream in a circular motion with her fingers. The bitch was loving it. The circumference of the arcs gradually began to inch away from the affected area until ... well, I need hardly tell you what it led to.

'What a cunt. Went from bad to worse in the weeks and months after that. Dressed me up in girly clothes, ribbons, knickers, the lot. Lipstick, make-up, perfume. Called me her walking, talking living doll, like the old song she liked to hum. Should have killed her then, almost did a few times. I hated her, hated that big mass of white flesh, hated my need for her to inflict the masochistic pleasure and pain I'd come to crave, hated our mutual depraved demands for what passed as carnal delights.'

McDonagh pushed Olive Quinn's body into a long storage basket affair made of plastic and removed it from the room, leaving a trail of blood. He returned minutes later and began to mop up the pool of blood on the floor, glancing at Emma every so often, his words pouring out with what sounded like relief at finally being able to offload all that oppressed him.

'Father Troy and Brother Bernard – Sister Marie-Theresa's great nemeses – found out what she'd been up to and reported her to her superior. She lost her job at the Beaumont, got kicked out of the nuns. But she held on to me, kept me close, decided to look after me. Through me, she orchestrated her revenge on the two men. Father Troy was first on her list. The old bastard was ill and within just one year of retirement when I helped hasten his demise – this was six months before I left Beaumont. Simple plan really.

'I applied to be assigned to kitchen duties, something most boys hated. I started off as a general dog's body, scrubbing pots, pans, burners, worktops, floors, you know the sort of thing, but I stuck with it until eventually I was allowed to help with the preparation of food. It gave me an opportunity to work on the food being served to the table of the brutes in charge – and that included Father Troy. I was patient, held back on my plan of action till the time was right. I needed to gain the trust of the kitchen staff and the monsters I served.

'Discovering that Father Troy was partial to mushrooms gave me the leverage I needed. Father Troy, you see, fancied himself as a bit of botanist. He liked taking us on conducted tours of the school's grounds spouting on about lichens, mosses, leaves, conifers, pines, spruces, bark beetles and how much water a grown apple tree could take in on any given day, stuff like that. Most of us poor buggers couldn't tell an ash tree from an oak or a sycamore from a beech. Once, he told us about the properties of the deathcap mushroom, pointing out how similar they appeared to ordinary field mushrooms, warning us of the deadly consequences that would follow if any of us were dumb enough to eat one.

'That's what gave me the idea. I found a cluster of deathcap mushrooms growing around the roots of an oak tree in the grounds. I waited until mushrooms were on the menu and sneaked a portion of the poisonous fungi onto his plate. It took the bastard five days to die. I watched with delight as he struggled to breathe. They called a doctor, of course, but he hadn't a clue … he was powerless to ease the old fart's stomach pains. They all watched as he vomited and shit out blood-laden diarrhoea until he was totally dehydrated. There was a half-arsed inquiry, of course. The rest of the food was examined. The others who'd eaten mushrooms displayed no ill effects. I would like to have poisoned the lot of them but, in an act of self-preservation, I'd spared them. I made bloody sure to leave none of the deathcaps lying around. In the end, they put his death down to old age and an aggravation of the multiple ailments already diagnosed. I never came under suspicion; matter of fact they never even questioned me.

'That all happened because of her. I was under her control all the time, dependent on her. She made use of me and I … or at least part of me … needed her. She used me to get even with Brother Bernard too. She was the one who arranged to have the old queen topped in a city gym. Me, I was happy to go along with the scheme. I'd already left the Beaumont when that sweet little escapade went down. My job was to keep tabs on him, report to her on a daily basis. I found out about his visits to gay-friendly establishments like Bartley Dunnes, The Viking, the back room in Rice's and a couple of gyms. He was forever sniffing out the best places to find young men sympathetic to his particular inclinations. I was following orders, doing what was demanded of me by the one person who hated Brother Bernard as much as I did, maybe more. I must admit, though, I would have happily done this one on my own behalf in any case Still, it was nice to be rewarded for my services. By tracking his movements in the back streets and alleyways in the city I helped her plot the basis of a plan that brought his dirty little game to such an appropriate and sullied end. That said, I was not the one who left his mutilated body lying in a pool of blood in the hallway of the Gym Zone. Made all the papers at the time … the media had a field day: gay sex, religion and dark places; they put it down to homophobia.

Our relationship changed after that. I was growing older. I'd lost my angelic looks, lost my golden locks, began to shave. She just put on weight, used sex toys to play with herself and became obese. Oh, she still used, abused and serviced me from time to time – acts of desperation on both our behalves – but for her, well, I no longer provided the kind of kicks she sought. She still controlled me, of course, allowed me a living … if you can call the functions I provided for her a living.

'She was the one who made me apply to the state's inquiry into abuse in Irish institutions. Hilarious isn't it? The person who, more than anyone else, had fucked with my mind and body since I was a child wanted the state to pick up the tab, compensate me. She said I should have more independence ... but at a price. I would be retained as her pimp, her supplier of young female flesh. I would continue to fetch her trinkets from the sex shop, that kind of thing. What I did with the women afterwards, after she'd done her number on them, well, that never seemed to trouble her too much, and besides, disposing of the bodies served a purpose – recycling, you might call it – nourishment for my dogs. The bones, of course, were a different matter. I would never like to repeat the mistake I made when I buried the bones in Tara. I mean, how was I to know a great bloody motorway would be built where I'd hidden them, and the land sold.

'I've got a spectacular idea for your disposal.

'Cremation.

'That's the plan. A master stroke. Came to me when I was being interrogated by the commissioners on the reparation board. They were asking about the fire that destroyed my first experience of state institutions, a hell hole named St Joan's Orphanage. This happened before your time but let me tell you it created quite a stir at the time. Seven children and two supervisors went woooosh! Up in flames. Did I feel sorry for them? Not a bit of it. Two of the dead lads, Jacky Clancy and Studs Moran, had made my life a hell on earth. I was nine and they were two or three years older than me. I was the smallest boy there and I have a photograph, taken at the time, that shows me with the most angelic face you ever did see. The two bigger lads made me their slave – that sort of thing went on a lot in St Joan's. They forced me to steal cigarettes and matches and beat the crap out of me if I failed to deliver. They hit on me every day, got me to give them hand jobs, stubbed out their fag ends on my arms and legs. I had to put a stop to it. Took all my ingenuity to think up a way to do it. The matches I stole provided the answer. I set the whole damn place on fire, got rid of the problem. No questions asked.

'And that's what is going to happen here. I intend to torch the place and then move into Olive Quinn's place and collect the insurance on this dump. All evidence of our little venture will turn to ashes, blow away on the wind.

'But you want to hear the best bit? The supreme irony that tops everything else? This morning the reparation board contacted me, let me know they've awarded me full monetary compensation for what was done to me. Don't you just love it?'

He stopped what he was doing, stood and stared at Emma. 'As a journalist, an *investigative* journalist, I thought you'd like to hear all that, satisfy your natural curiosity, fill in the blanks on those half-arsed articles you like to churn out, never quite getting the facts quite right. Such a pity you'll never be able to write this one. What a scoop that would be for you, eh? Get you another Journalist of the Year award. Hey! Maybe they'll give it to you posthumously! But enough of this frivolity. It's time to get the show on the road.'

C ONNOLLY WANTED TO go next door, demand to be let in, break the door down if necessary. He'd told Superintendent Smith to arrange a warrant asap but advised that he had to go in straight away without the warrant on the basis that there was probable cause that lives – he didn't name Emma specifically – could be at risk. Smith, always one to cover his arse, intimated, without actually saying yes, that Connolly could do whatever he deemed necessary.

Straight away Connolly ordered his team to gather round. He told them they were going to go into the guesthouse on the far side of McDonagh's end wall. He had begun to brief them on what he expected to find there when, suddenly, he halted mid-sentence. Ever since he'd come into McDonagh's back yard and supervised the search something nagged at the back of his mind – a piece of logic, a simple inescapable fact: McDonagh had to have found a way of coming and going from his house unobserved. In an instant he felt he'd resolved the puzzle.

'Hold everything,' he said, moving to where the greyhounds had been housed. The kennels were built with modern materials, nothing like the ramshackle condition of the older buildings or the walls that formed the boundaries of McDonagh's property. 'There's something damned odd here. Look at the wall behind the kennels; now look at the wall on either side of the new construction. Notice anything peculiar?'

Everyone examined the dogs' quarters, then stood back, looked to the left exterior, looked to the right exterior, observing the back flanking wall behind the kennels.

'What are we supposed to be looking for?' Dorsett asked.

'The wall forming the rear of the kennels doesn't line up with the boundary wall,' Connolly said. 'The alignment is out; there has to be a space behind it.'

Dorsett's eyebrows shot up. 'You're right,' he said. 'Something's wonky about the alignment.'

'Give me a leg up,' Connolly said, moving towards the end boundary wall to the left of the kennels. 'I want to see what's on the other side.'

Two uniforms hoisted Connolly up, pushing his head above the crown of the eight foot high wall. On the far side he could see a lean-to shed that looked to him like an old building, probably one dating back to when it formed part of the original farm yard. 'Let me down, quickly, quickly. Let's take a closer look at how the kennels have been constructed.'

'Seems solid enough to me,' Dorset said, kicking the stone structure with his Doc Martens. To one corner of the rear wall, several dogs' leads hung on hooks that had been affixed to a wooden panel. A selection of muzzles, dog jackets and collars, racing cards and betting slips, were stacked on a shelf. 'It's got to be this,' Connolly said, pushing his shoulder against the wooden panel. It felt hollow. He pushed harder. It sprung open like a door. Connolly, followed by Dorsett and his team, stepped into a passageway, not more than eighteen inches in width. A large, steel-plated door had been inserted into the properties' dividing wall. It had a wheel-like device to one side, similar to an old fashioned safe handle. It looked as though the door had been erected in recent years. The surrounding plasterwork was at variance with the older, time-worn structure.

'Shhhhh!' Connolly said as he gingerly turned the handle. There was a slight creaking sound as the heavy door opened inwards. He knew that this opening had to lead to the next door property. Aware of this, he proceeded forward, cautiously entering a rustic chamber, a small space crammed with garden implements, sacks of coal, an old bicycle and cans of paint. Here and there, red bricks were visible on the wall where patches of plaster had fallen away. What looked like a large deep freezer chest took up the base of one full wall. On the opposite wall to the one Connolly had entered from, a second steel-plated door, similar to the first one, stood.

Connolly moved stealthily towards it, then stopped, holding a hand up for silence. 'Listen! What's that?' he asked in a whisper. Like those behind him, he could hear a noise.

Clack, clack, clack.

It came from behind the door.

Clack, clack, clack.

He could not identify the sound but instinct told him it wasn't good. Taking a deep breath, he reached for the door handle, swung it back in one swift movement. He gasped. Shocked. McDonagh, in a dirty white coat, was turning a wheel with a chain attached to it. A naked woman, manacled by the ankles, was being winched up on a set of chains to a steel animal carcass frame.

'EMMA!' he screamed.

McDonagh turned to see who had entered. He stopped what he was doing, his face twisting into an ugly snarl. In one bound, he leaped towards a bench and grabbed a cleaver. He lifted it, aimed, and let it fly. Connolly ducked. The missile missed him by centimetres, crashing into the wall instead. Dorsett rushed McDonagh, brought him to the floor in a bone crunching rugby tackle. McDonagh fought back, struggled to push the detective off, his arms and legs flaying about wildly as he screamed, grunted and groaned. One of the officers came to Dorsett's assistance, jammed his boot down on McDonagh's neck, pinning him to the floor. This provided Dorsett with the break he needed. He grabbed McDonagh's arms, jerked them behind his back and cuffed him.

While this tug of war was in progress Connolly rushed to Emma. He hunkered down beside her, saw the life in her eyes. 'She's alive,' he yelled. 'Thank God, she's alive. Someone, quick, get me a blanket, I need to cover her, she's ... just hurry! Get me a towel. I need to get her down off this damn contraption. Call an ambulance, somebody – quickly!'

CHAPTER 42

THE BIGGEST STORY of the year – as big as the time Fred and Rosemary West were convicted of the abuse, murder and disposal of nine young women in their Gloucester home back in 1994 – and Emma hadn't written it. She'd become part of the story. For three whole days she'd been confined to a hospital bed, reading of the developments, reading about her own involvement in the horror. A mixture of emotions had her; glad to be alive on the one hand, thankful for her last minute rescue, but the dominant feeling coursing her mind was one of abject disappointment. It had been her story, her scoop, and she'd missed the payoff. In the report that appeared in the *Post*, her name appeared in the byline. A nice gesture from Crosby. The piece was well written but it failed to provide the kind of satisfaction she would have got had she written it herself.

Bob Crosby felt the byline credit was no less than she deserved. He knew exactly how she felt. He appreciated that it was down to Emma that McDonagh's name had made it into the media in the first place. Crosby was able to supply the results of Emma's inquiry with the greyhound authority to the investigation team. The records showed that McDonagh and his dogs had attended races in the four relevant venues on the dates that Shannon Hughes, Melanie Sweeny, Rachel Fagan and Alison Hogan had gone missing. This left no doubt that McDonagh had been responsible for the four earlier disappearances. It was news that would provide little comfort for their loved ones but at least now, thanks to Emma's persistence, they knew what had happened. Crosby couldn't heap enough praise on her. She'd gone out on a limb, followed her instincts, her contribution crucial in alerting the gardai. Knowing how much it hurt her to miss out on writing the concluding chapter, he sought a way to show his appreciation for her investigative talents and for the spectacular results she'd achieved. Wearing his editor's hat, he was also conscious of the fact that it wouldn't hurt circulation to let his readers know that one of the *Post*'s very own reporters had played such a pivotal role in bringing a mass murderer to justice.

With that in mind he'd called his golfing buddy, Chief Superintendent Smith, begging a big favour. Smith, not knowing what the favour was, needed to know the nature of the request before agreeing.

'Would you allow me visit the crime scene?' Crosby asked.

'Well, now, Bob, that's a big ask. The place has been cordoned off – no media. Think of the families; we're conducting a very sensitive operation.'

'I'm aware of that,' Crosby said. 'I know the place is being taken apart and that the families of the bereaved are being kept in the loop, but I wouldn't ask if it wasn't important.'

'OK, Bob, I'll have to personally accompany you on the site, otherwise there'd be hell to pay.'

'I appreciate that. I will have one person with me, is that OK?'

'You're asking a lot, but OK, I'll see you there in half an hour.'

Crosby went to see Emma in the hospital as he had done on the two previous days. At first he'd been shocked by her appearance. But the improvements since then had been nothing short of remarkable. She still looked worse for wear but the smile was back on her face and the cuts and bruises didn't look as awful as they had done. He sat by her bedside and brought her up to date with all that was happening. 'I want to get the hell out of here,' she told him, 'I want to get back on the job.'

Crosby told her he might be able to arrange that. 'I've talked to the doctors and nurses here and they've been very helpful. How would you feel about taking a visit to the crime scene … if I were to take you there?'

'I'd love that,' she said. 'Can't wait to write my personalized account of what happened.' But even as she agreed, she knew she wasn't being honest with Crosby or, for that matter, with herself. More than anything else she wanted to be with Connolly. Connolly didn't know about Crosby's plan to bring her to McDonagh's house. He'd been told not to expect her home from hospital until the following day. As the person in charge of the investigation he was under enormous pressure and, she suspected, could do without the distraction of having her appear in the midst of all the activity.

It had been three days since her near-death experience. She still felt the effects of what had happened, still felt battered and bruised. She knew it was too soon to go back to the hell she'd escaped from – the ghostly echoes still fresh in her mind. But facing such a horror had made her look at the world with a new perspective, made her question her priorities. She thought about silly things, like the row she'd had with Connolly and her subsequent decision to postpone the marriage. She regretted that decision – she'd been too easily swayed by her parents; should never have treated Connolly in such a cavalier way. She vowed that when all this ugly business was over and the dust had settled down, she would make it up to him.

Emma received a round of applause from the group gathered outside McDonagh's gate. Jane Henderson and her band of protesters had found a bouquet of flowers from somewhere and pushed through the garda cordon to present it to her. Henderson's husband, Sean, belly bigger than ever, looked the worse for drink, shouted something at her, his words lost in the hubbub.

Chief Superintendent Smith was waiting for her and Crosby at the back of the house. It surprised her that the chief super should be so warm, his unexpected amiability in stark contrast to his more usual frosty attitude towards her. He praised her contribution to the successful conclusion of the case. The term 'successful conclusion' struck Emma as peculiar. How could finding that the missing women were dead, be termed a success? They'd been butchered, stuffed in a boiler, cooked and fed to animals, the bones removed and buried. Success? She held back from voicing this thought, not wishing, or indeed having the energy, to break this new mood of benevolence.

Her head retained a buzzing sensation and her eyes remained slightly blurred, something she'd neglected to tell her doctors in order to be allowed to leave the hospital. The scars on her body would heal in time, she knew, but they were nothing compared to the scars inflicted on her psyche, they would leave a lasting footprint.

Last time she'd seen the back of McDonagh's place had been from the landing inside the Henderson house. It looked so different now. A small army of white-suited personnel were busy combing every inch of the place. The dogs had been removed and the passageway that led next door pulled apart. The boiler room – the spot where McDonagh had stared at her – had been demolished, the huge boiler in which he cooked for his dogs in the process of being removed. A shudder ran through her.

She'd learned from press reports – the ones she wished she'd written – that Olive Quinn's body along with parts of Gemma Moore had been recovered from the slaughter house. This room of unspeakable horror where she'd come so perilously close to death dated back to a time when the farm butchered its own livestock and supplied local shops and restaurants. It was now being subjected to a most meticulous examination.

The Mazda that McDonagh had used – under the guise of Richard J. Bradbury – had been found in the garage of the guesthouse. One of the guestrooms there had, it transpired, been used by McDonagh on an ongoing basis; in it they discovered a fake garda uniform and a variety of costumes that included a hat and overcoat, items that had been so much a part of the investigation. A quantity of small personal items linked to Joan Keating, Siobhan O'Neill, Annette Campbell and the four earlier victims, had also been uncovered.

The technical experts had brought in machinery to dig up the gardens on both sides of the dividing wall. Nothing had been found so far. A search in the well beneath the pump had proved negative on first inspection. This was mainly due to the fact that McDonagh had placed a large circular water tank at the base of the well – a relic from the time it was used to water cattle. He'd filled it with water so that if inspected from the top, looking down, everything would appear normal. Only after a more thorough examination did the ingenious ruse come to light. Beneath the container they found bones and human remains and belongings. It would take the technical crew, making full use of the latest DNA techniques, months to establish what identifications were possible.

'How could McDonagh have done this?' Crosby asked, sickened by what confronted him. 'Do you think, I mean, is it possible a person can be born evil ... or is it something that's beaten into them?'

'Hard to say,' Smith said. 'Lots of people have suffered at the hands of state institutions. Doesn't mean they all go on to kill people.'

'What about his so-called Dissociative Identity Disorder,' Emma asked, 'Does anybody believe that's an issue here?'

Smith shrugged. 'DID has been discredited in the States and elsewhere. There's no doubt that McDonagh is mentally disturbed, susceptible to delusional behaviour ... but do I believe this Jekyll and Hyde stuff? Do I believe he involuntarily changed into this other person – Richard J. Bradbury – and didn't know what the other manifestation was doing? That's horseshit and we all know it.'

'You're right,' Crosby agreed. 'Take the elaborate lengths he took to get in and out of his house unobserved, all that *Alice Through the Looking Glass* stuff with the boundary wall ... planned down to the last detail. I mean, come on, who was he supposed to be when that little engineering operation was under construction – Matthew McDonagh or Richard J. Bradbury?'

'Suited him to go along with the mumbo-jumbo Dr Belcher put to him,' the chief super suggested. 'He used it to further his psychotic urges.'

'You could be right,' Emma agreed, 'but I don't think it's as cut and dried as you both seem to imagine.'

'Why do you say that?' Crosby asked.

'I can only go by what I saw, what I witnessed firsthand.'

Both men looked at her with raised eyebrows.

'When McDonagh barged into Belcher's room, he appeared to truly believe he was Richard J. Bradbury. I mean his whole demeanour, his voice, his speech patterns, the way he moved, none of it was in any way like what I'd seen when I visited his house and spoke to him. I wouldn't have recognized him except for the eyes ... those eyes ... Jesus!'

'So what are you saying?' Crosby asked.

'I think he adopted this personality as a device to distance himself from the actions he undertook when pimping for Olive Quinn. I'd say he found that aspect of their relationship too distasteful to handle, so he invented the Richard J. Bradbury personality. In the end, I think he genuinely got confused by the two personalities ... couldn't distinguish between what was real and what wasn't. Dr Belcher, the poor deluded man – he did his best to protect me from McDonagh – tried to explain to me about the fickle nature of the human mind and how pliable it is when it comes to accepting false beliefs and denying reality. And yet, his theory comes nowhere near explaining this: when Olive Quinn finished with the victims, he had no difficulty, as *himself* – as Matthew McDonagh – butchering them and feeding them to his greyhounds. I'd like to hear the good doctor, were he still alive, explain that one away.'

'Well, maybe we'll get a better handle on all this when it comes to trial,' Crosby suggested.

'I doubt very much it will ever get that far,' Smith said.

'Why do you say that?' Crosby asked.

'McDonagh will be judged unfit to stand trial on mental grounds – diminished responsibility or some such psychological assessment.'

'Surely not. How could they—?'

'Just you wait and see. We'll be handed down some smart-arsed Freudian psycho-babble that'll show justification for what he's done. We'll be expected to feel sorry for him – see him as a victim. I don't believe he will ever stand trial.'

'That can't be right,' Crosby said. 'That would mean the families of the bereaved will be deprived of their day in court, denied justice, denied the satisfaction of seeing someone pay for what's been taken from them.'

Emma listened as Crosby and the chief super discussed the case, her mind flitting back to the ordeal she'd suffered within yards of where she now stood, the *clack, clack, clack* sound echoing in her head. She shook her head to dismiss the vision and was about to say something when she caught sight of Connolly. Through the passage that led to the abattoir, she saw him and the state pathologist Dr Mary McElree in deep conversation, both wearing white overalls. She wanted to rush over to him, throw her arms around him, tell him how much she loved him but some second sense stopped her.

There was something about their body language that struck an ominous chord with her. She watched Connolly and McElree finish their conversation and move away from each other but, before they'd gone more than a few yards, both turned their heads to glance back at the other. The smile on Connolly's face said all Emma needed to know about what was happening; she'd been the recipient of that smile so many times.

Crosby, who hadn't spotted Connolly, glanced at Emma. He saw a tear roll down her cheek. 'I'm so sorry,' he said, sounding truly apologetic. 'I should never have brought you here; the memory of what happened to you is too fresh. Come on, I'll take you home.'

'Yes, please do,' Emma said. 'I've seen quite enough.'